D1255144

SCOTTISH SHORT STORIES

SCOTTISH
SHORT STORIES

edited by
FRED URQUHART

FABER AND FABER
24 Russell Square
London

First published in mcmxxxii
by Faber and Faber Limited
24 Russell Square, London W.C.1
Second edition mcmxlii
Reprinted mcmxlvii
Third (revised) edition mcmlvii
Printed in Great Britain
by Ebenezer Baylis and Son, Limited,
Worcester and London

CONTENTS

INTRODUCTION

by

FRED URQUHART

Anthologies are always fair game for critics. I'm aware that I have laid myself open to accusations of having ignored this or that author or of not having included such-and-such a story. And so I must take the war into the enemy's camp by saying that in compiling it I set myself three rules: 1. All stories should be by writers of Scottish birth and should be about Scottish characters and Scottish scenes; 2. They should have been published roughly within the past fifty years; 3. They should be stories which I personally enjoyed.

As the older generation of Scots story-tellers like Stevenson, Barrie, S. R. Crockett and Neil Munro are so well known, it seemed unfair that a proportion of the limited space of a 90,000 words book should be devoted to them and not to living writers. Yet, I rejected them with reluctance, for although not in complete sympathy with many of their sentiments, I would have liked to have included "Thrawn Janet", one of the *Auld Licht Idylls* and one of the *Para Handy* stories so that the reader could have compared them with more modern stories. In the same way, it would have pleased me to print "The Little Tinker" by Jane H. Findlater, a lesser-known writer of that period. For even if "The Little Tinker" does not hold water as a short story in the accepted modern sense, being discursive and too long, it gives a colourful picture of a Scotland that has disappeared: a pre-Welfare State Scotland in which not only could a rich, eccentric woman plan to adopt and educate a tinker-woman's baby but the tinker could have the freedom to decide that she was for none of it and go back with her child to the wild, wandering life she had always known, without having officialdom on her track.

Space also has prevented me from printing two or more stories by some of the authors I have selected. A single story, I always feel, is never sufficient to show an author's scope and capabilities. For instance, Ronald Macdonald Douglas' "A Woman of the Roads" should be read in conjunction with his utterly dissimilar "A Hike to Balerno". And "The Head", brilliant though it is, and the story which won Dorothy K. Haynes the Tom-Gallon Trust Award for 1947-48, shows only one facet of the vivid and at times macabre imagination of this author, who was born in 1918 and is the youngest represented here. To appreciate it more fully, one should also read "The Bean Nighe" or "Windfall"; indeed, any of the stories in her volume *Thou Shalt Not Suffer A Witch*. Similarly, although "Beattock for Moffat" and "In The Family" are first-class stories, neither is completely representative of R. B. Cunninghame-Graham (1852-1936) and Naomi Mitchison. Because of my first ruling, however, they are printed in preference to any of Don Roberto's South American sketches or Mrs. Mitchison's better-known stories of Ancient Greece and Rome from *Black Sparta* and *When The Bough Breaks*.

Readers will probably have their own favourite stories by Eric Linklater, Neil M. Gunn, Winifred Duke and John Buchan, but these chosen are the ones which appeal most to me. There are many amusing samples of Eric Linklater's wit and rumbustiousness in his collections *God Likes Them Plain* and *Sealskin Trousers*. Neil M. Gunn's compassion and his wide knowledge of the crofter and fisher folk of the Highlands can be seen in almost any of the stories in *The White Hour*, especially in one, "The Old Man", which I wish I could have printed alongside "The Tax-Gatherer". Grimmer examples of Winifred Duke's art are to be found in *Tales of Hate*, but "The Hallowe'en Party" is a delightful story in her lighter vein, its East Coast dialect being pithy and authentic.

Introduction

Some of the authors represented are not known primarily as short story writers. A. J. Cronin (b. 1896) has gained an international reputation with his novels, *Hatter's Castle*, *The Citadel* and *The Spanish Gardener*. His talents require the wider field of the novel-form, but "The Provost's Tale", although it is somewhat melodramatic and the inevitability of its ending is too pointed, is worthy of attention as one of his excursions into the short story *genre* since it gives a good picture of Scottish small-town life at the turn of the century. Moray McLaren (b. 1901) is well known for books like *The Highland Jaunt*, a description of a journey in the tracks of Boswell and Johnson, but he is interested in the short story as an art-form and there are some charming studies of Edinburgh life and character in *A Dinner For The Dead*. Alexander Reid (b. 1914) and Robert MacLellan are best known as playwrights. Reid has had considerable success with *The Lass Wi' The Muckle Mou'* and *The Warld's Wonder*, and MacLellan with *Toom Byres* and *Jamie the Saxt*, all notable for their handling of Braid Scots; but each has also written stories, and "The Kitten" and "The Mennans" can stand comparison with most written by their English, Irish or Welsh contemporaries. Robin Jenkins (b. 1912) has made a name for himself with several novels, including *Happy For The Child*, *The Thistle and The Grail* and *Guests of War*, a sympathetic and often amusing account of the havoc created in a country town by the onslaught of a contingent of war-time evacuees from the slums of Glasgow. Ruthven Todd (b. 1914), an Edinburgh man who now lives in America, is a successful poet and writer of children's books. He writes short stories occasionally, however, and "The Big Wheel" is a welcome antidote to the sickly, sentimental stories of the Kail Yard school.

There is no echo either of the Kail Yard in the stories about Glasgow by Margaret Hamilton, Edward Gaitens, George Friel and J. F. Hendry. It is not the Glasgow of J. J. Bell, whose pawky *Wee Macgreegor* stories gave such a distorted picture of the Second City of Empire not only to fellow-Scots, who should have known better than lap them up, but to overseas readers. There may have been, and there may still be, little boys like Macgreegor—though I doubt it—but they no more "belong to Glasgow" in the words of the late Will Fyffe, whose music-hall sketch, although slightly exaggerated, was the epitome of Glasgow working-class life, than the razor-slashers of sensational novels like *No Mean City*. A much more authentic and vital picture of the "poor old working man" is to be found in *Growing Up* by Edward Gaitens (b. 1897). His stories of the perjinketty, bawdy, life-loving dwellers in the Gorbals are not for those with rose-coloured glasses, but their virility is real and honest and will stand the test of time. Equally full-blooded are the characters of Margaret Hamilton's "Jenny Stairy's Hat", a story which our grandmothers would have considered "not nice", but which is a remarkable portrait of an embittered woman. Miss Hamilton (b. 1915) has not yet collected her stories in a volume, but she has published *Bull's Penny*, a powerful novel spanning eighty years of a man's life from his childhood on the Isle of Arran to his death in the poorhouse. George Friel (b. 1910) published a number of stories in the days of the *Modern Scot* and *Outlook*, periodicals which did much to encourage Scots writers in the 1930s, but he has not written much in recent years. J. F. Hendry (b. 1912) is a poet and critic who has published a volume of stories about Jugoslavia as well as several about his native Glasgow.

I have tried to choose stories of varied lights and shades, stories showing different aspects of Scottish life, whether Highland or Lowland, city or country, contrasting them as much as possible by the order in which they are printed. Indeed, *Something Different*, the title of the story by Orgill Mackenzie, is a guide to the book's scheme, if one can say that a collection of stories by twenty-two authors, so divided in time, outlook and temperament, can have a scheme. It is a book of contrasts, and those who do not appreciate the robust earthy gusto of Lewis Grassic Gibbon's "Smeddum" and Edward Scouller's "Murdoch's Bull" can always turn to the sardonic humour of Linklater's parched "Kind Kitty", searching for solace in Heaven or the witch-laden atmosphere of John Buchan's "The Outgoing of the Tide", the oldest story in the book.

The selection will show, I hope, that the art of the short story is still alive in Scotland. Though it is an art which is having to struggle hard to maintain its existence, it can and will struggle as long as authors have stories to write, places where they can be published, and readers who have the apti- tude, intelligence and leisure to read them. But how long can this unequal struggle go on? Twenty years ago, ten years ago, the author who did not want to write popular romantic trash could be reasonably sure of having his or her work published somewhere. But today, even for a small country, Scotland has too few first-class literary periodicals. The sentimental clutch of the Kail Yard was not as strangling as the even more corny hand of television and the popular press. Today, to gain an audience for his work—and this does not apply only to Scottish writers—the writer has to have a "gimmick". And as good writers do not have gimmicks (a horrible word so typical of the tasteless and arbitrary editors who use it) the future looks bleak. It is true that the B.B.C. does help by broadcasting short stories (two of these in this volume were first heard on the air) but because of the varied states of mentality, intelligence, age and prejudices of its listeners, the B.B.C's selection must of necessity be limited.

In *Understanding The Scots*, Moray McLaren writes: "If only one-tenth of the money spent annually in whisky, haggises, and the hire of rooms to celebrate the birthday of a great but dead poet were to be given to the foundation of a magazine which could regularly display the latest Scottish verse, it would make all the difference to the living inheritors of the Burns tradition."

Mr. McLaren might have added that another tenth of this misspent money could found a magazine for the living in- heritors of the tradition of Scott, Stevenson, Violet Jacob,

Introduction

Lewis Grassic Gibbon and R. B. Cunninghame-Graham. Scottish authors who do not wish to write slick, popular, emasculated stories need a platform as much as the young poets who write in "Lallans".

January 1957.   FRED URQUHART.

Eric Linklater

KIND KITTY

" Thay threpit that scho deit of thrist, and maid a gud end.
Efter hir dede, scho dredit nought in hevin for to duell,
And sa to hevin the hieway dreidles scho wend."

DUNBAR

Nine out of every ten people in Edinburgh never look at
anything but the pavements and the shallow shop-windows
and the figuration of neighbours as belittled as themselves.
This is for safety, and to keep their wits from wandering,
because whoever will raise his head suddenly to the Castle
may see Asgard looming in the mist, and the hills above
Holyroodhouse, that one day are no more than slopes for
children to play on, the next are mountains that thrust huge
shoulders through the clouds and bare their monstrous brows
in the heights of the sky. So also if you look down at the
houses that press numerously against the outer walls of
Holyrood you may see nothing but a multitude of mean roofs.
But you may as easily surprise a coven of witches dancing
in the smoke, and warlocks leaping on the chimney-pots.

This was a sight that Kind Kitty saw whenever she came
up out of the Canongate to sit on a seat in the gardens under
the Calton Hill, with a flat little bottle of whisky in her
pocket, and a bonnet with a broken feather precariously
pinned to her dirty grey hair.

Kind Kitty was never afraid to look at the hills and the
air-drawn heights of the town, for though they might steal
her wits away she had no wealth or position that needed her
wits' attention and nothing to lose, though her thoughts took

holiday for days on end, but a dozen hens and the wire-netting that confined them. It was the odour of hens that strangers first noticed, and most urgently disliked, when Kitty sat down beside them in the Gardens. It overcame the other smells that accompanied her, of smoke, of clothes incredibly old, of a body long unwashed, of yesterday's beer and the morning's dram. It was a violent unexpected smell, and Kitty's casual neighbours would soon rise and leave her. Then she would grumble through her old blue lips, and peer after them malevolently with her red and rheumy eyes, and unwrapping a piece of newspaper from the little bottle she would take a quick mouthful of whisky. "Tae hell with you, then, for a high-minded upstart," she would mutter, and wipe her mouth, and a water-drop from the end of her nose, with the back of her bony hand. But in a minute or two she would forget the insult, when her bleary eyes were captured by witches and warlocks dancing in the smoke, or by a flank of the Pamirs that pushed its stony ribs against the firmament. Then she would think of life and death, of the burnside in Appin where she had been born, of the great soldier, Sir Hector McOstrich, and the lovely wicked Lady Lavinia. The weave of life, like gun-metal silk shot with bright yellow, shone for her, at such an angle, with the remote and golden-lovely frailty of sunset after a rainy day. Misery in the morning was forgotten, and squalor after noon, beneath that aureate sky, returned like rain to the deeps of the earth.

But sooner or later the sunset would fade from her thoughts, the hills diminish, the warlocks dissolve into bitter vapour, and her belly protest its emptiness with loud exclamatory repetition. Then, with a twitch of her bonnet, a hitch to her dusty skirt, and a pull at her broken stays, she would rise in a sudden temper, and muttering furious complaints against the littleness of small whisky bottles, she would hobble back to the Canongate and stop to stare balefully at The Hole in the Wall, whose doors were not yet open. "The mealy-mouthed thowless thieves," she would mutter. "The bletherin' kirk-gaun puggies!" And she would spit on the

16

pavement to show her contempt for the law, and those who made it, that public-houses should be closed while thirst still grew unchecked.

It was drink, not food, that her empty stomach clamoured for. She ate little, and took no pleasure in such tasteless stuff as bread and potatoes and tinned beef. But for beer and black stout and whisky she had so great a love that her desire for them was unceasing, and her relish for their several flavours more constant than any carnal love. Except for a shilling or two that she was sometimes compelled to pay for rent, and a few coppers that went on corn for her hens, she spent all her money on drink and still was dry-mouthed for three or four days out of seven. She had the Old Age pension, and ten shillings a week was paid her, though unwillingly, by Sir Hector's grandson, who was not a soldier but a stockbroker, and bitterly resented such a burden on his estate. This income might have been sufficient to preserve her from the most painful and extreme varieties of thirst had she been content to drink draught ale, and that in solitude. But Kitty was both extravagant and generous, she liked whisky and good company, friendship and bottled beer, and twenty shillings a week was sadly insufficient for such rich amusement. Many of her friends were poorer than herself, and none was more wealthy, so their return for Kitty's entertainment was always inadequate. They would sometimes treat her to half a pint of beer, more rarely to a nip of whisky, but usually they repaid her with cups of tea, or half a herring, which gave her no pleasure whatever. She never calculated the profit and loss of good-fellowship, however, and so long as her neighbours had lively conversation and a cheerful spirit she would share her last shilling with them.

But a friend of hers, an old cast whore called Mima Bird, found a ten-shilling note one Christmas, and buying a dozen bottles of Bass, invited Kitty to come and drink six of them. The nobility of this entertainment inspired Kitty with a great desire to emulate it, not in vulgar competition, not for the ostentation of surpassing it, but simply to give again, and enjoy again, the delights of strong liquor and warm fellow-ship, so after much thought, and with high excitement. She formed a plan and made arrangements for a Hogmanay party that would put the Old Year to bed with joy and splendour.

New Year's Eve fell on a Saturday, and on Friday Kitty drew her Old Age pension and cashed the ten-shilling order that came from young Mr. McOstrich. But a pound was not nearly enough to furnish such a party as she intended. She went to see James Campbell, the landlord of The Hole in the Wall, and after long discussion came to an agreement with him, and pledged her whole income for the first two weeks in January in return for thirty-three shillings in ready money and the loan of five tumblers. These were the best terms she could get, for Campbell was a hard man.

But Kitty did not waste much time in bemoaning so heavy a rate of interest. She had no reverence for money, as respectable people have, nor concern for the future; and her mind was occupied with entrancing preparations for the party. She bought two bottles of whisky, two dozen bottles of beer, and a dozen of stout. Nothing like so huge and extravagant an array had ever been seen in her dirty little kitchen in Baxter's Close, and the spectacle filled her with excitement that yielded presently to a kind of devotion, and then became pure childlike joy. She set the beer, orderly in rank, on the table, with the two whisky bottles on the mantel-piece, and the porter like a round fender before the empty fire. Then she stood here and there to admire the picture, and presently rearranged the bottles and marshalled the beer, like a fence, in front of the wire-netting that closed her dozen hens in a small extension of the kitchen that might, with a more orthodox tenant, have been the scullery. The hens clapped their wings, and encouraged her with their clucking. Then she made patterns and plans on the floor, now a cross, before which she signed herself with the Cross, and now a rough plan of Tearlach's Hall, in Appin, where Sir Hector and Lady Lavinia had lived in pride and many varieties of sin.

Her old hands took delicately the smooth necks of the bottles, she patted into place a label that was half-unstuck, she made a shape like a rose, the bottles standing shoulder to shoulder in the middle, and the tears ran down her cheek to see the loveliness of that pattern. Weary at last, replete with happiness, she fell asleep with a bottle of whisky in her arms.

When morning came she woke in pride to be confronted with such riches, and her demeanour, that only her hens observed, was uncommonly dignified. Setting the bottles on the table, according to their kind and now without fantasy, she carefully considered her arrangements and debated their sufficiency for the imminent party. Was her house properly furnished for entertainment? There were five tumblers that she had borrowed, one that she possessed, a bed where four might sit, a chair, a stool, and more drink than had ever been seen in one room in all her memory of Baxter's Close. What else could be needed for the pleasure of her guests?

A thought entered her mind that she first repelled and then suffered to return. Some of her visitors might like something to eat. If that were so, it would be a great nuisance, and for a little while Kitty thought impatiently about the frailties of humankind and the monstrous demands that people made for their contentment. But presently she counted her money and found she had still four shillings left. So she put on her bonnet and went out shopping.

The wind blew coldly down the Canongate, with a flourish of rain on its ragged edge, but Kitty, with money in her purse and in her heart the intention of spending it, was too important to notice such small discomfort, and going first to a baker's she bought for two shillings a Scotch bun. With that fierily sweet and bitter-black dainty under her arm she turned and walked slowly, over greasy pavements, to a corn chandler's in the High Street, where for ninepence she obtained a large bag of Indian corn for her hens. Then she returned to the Canongate, and having purchased three-pennyworth of cheese she entered The Hole in the Wall at the very moment when its doors opened, and made a satis-

fying meal off a shilling's worth of draught beer and the
bright wedge of American cheddar.

The afternoon was slow in passing, but Kitty amused herself with ingenious new arrangements of the bottles, and with
feeding her hens, and soon after six o'clock her first guest
arrived, who was Mima Bird, the old whore. Then came
Mrs. Smiley, who made a small living by selling bootlaces;
Mrs. Hogg, who should have been well-off, her husband
having had both his legs shot off while serving in the Black
Watch, but he spent all his pension on threepenny bets and
twopenny trebles; old Rebecca Macafee, who had been a
tinker till she married a trawler's cook, who deserted her,
and varicose veins kept her from the country roads; and Mrs.
Crumb, who had a good job as a lavatory attendant, but had
to support a half-witted husband and three useless sons.
These were Kind Kitty's oldest and favourite friends, and
when she saw them all sitting in her kitchen, each with a
dram inside her to warm her stomach and loosen her tongue
and flush her cheeks, each with a glass of beer or stout in her
hand and another bottle beside her, then she was so happy
that all of a sudden she cackled with laughter, and rocked to
and fro on her stool, and began to sing an old song in a loud
hoarse voice:

> *"O Sandy, dinna ye mind," quo' she,*
> *"When ye gart me drink the brandy,*
> *When ye yerkit me ower among the broom,*
> *And played me houghmagandy!"*

"It's better among the broom than in the meadows on a
cauld winter night, or up against the wall of Greyfriars Kirk
with a drunken Aussie seven foot high," cried Mima Bird.

"Ay, but they'd money to spend, had the Aussies," said
old Rebecca, "and faith, they spent it."

"It was a fine war while it lasted," sighed Mrs. Hogg,
whose husband, for three good years, had been more use to
the Black Watch than he had ever been to her.

"The boys did well enough," said Kitty, "but the generals

and the high heid yins were a pack of jordan-heidit losingers."
And she thought, sadly and lovingly, of Sir Hector McOstrich,
who would have shown them how to win battles had not
shame, not war, untimely killed him. But far-off thoughts
could not long endure the loud immediacy of her cummers,
whose laughter grew more frequent, whose tales and jolly
memory became with every passing minute more rich and
lively and delectable. Now and again their laughter would
wake even the corn-fed hens to responsive clucking and
scratching; and in the smoky light of a dingy lamp the coarse
and weather-beaten cheeks of the six old women, their
wrinkled eyes and creasy necks, were lovely with a life invin-
cible. The air was full of the rich odours of beer and stout,
and ever and anon its heavy layers would lift and waver before
the genial shock of a great crackling belch. Kitty gave them
another dram, and thick slices of black bun.

> *If whisky was a river, and I was a duck,*
> *O whisky! Johnny!*
> *I'd dive to the bottom and I never would come up,*
> *O whisky for my Johnny!*

sang old Rebecca. "When that man I was married on, and
a hog-eyed lurdan he was," she said, "would come home
from sea, he was so thick with salt it would fill you with thirst
to smell him half-way up the stairs."

"You must have robbed a bank to give us a party like
this," said Mrs. Crumb. "It beats the High Commissioner's
garden-party at Holyrood just hollow. Why, we've drink
to every hand, and the very best of drink at that, but there,
so they tell me, the ministers' wives are fair tumbling over
each other, and tearing each other's eyes out, to get to the
eatables and the drinkables, and them nothing but lemonade
and ha'penny cakes."

"It's the very best party I ever was at," said Mrs. Hogg.

"It's the only one I've ever been to," said Mrs. Smiley,
and that was a lie, but she thought it was true and began to
cry, and got another dram to stop her.

So the evening wore on, and by half-past eleven there was nothing left in the glasses but dry feathers of froth, nothing in the bottles but a remembering air. By then, however, it was time to go out and join the multitude, coming from all directions, that was crowding the pavement before St. Giles and filling the night with a valedictory noise. These were the common people of Scotland, come to tread underfoot, as bitter ashes, their lost hopes of the Old Year, its miseries they had survived, and to welcome the New Year with hope inexpungable and confidence that none could warrant and none defeat. The procession of the months would give them neither riches nor wisdom, beauty nor holiness, but under every moon were many days of life, and life was their first love and their last. So the bells rang loudly as they might, the little black bottles were offered to friend and stranger—for all were brothers out of the same unwearying and shameless womb, and many were drunk enough to admit the relationship—hands were held in a circle by unknown hands, songs were sung, and a boisterous dance was trodden. The New Year was made welcome like a stranger in the old days of hospitality, though none knew whether he was whole or sick or loyal or lying.

Now when the old women, who had spent such a fine evening with Kitty, came out into the night, the cold air beat on their foreheads and made worse confusion of their befuddled minds, so that four of them lost control of their legs and nearly all cognizance of the world about them. Mrs. Smiley lay in the gutter and slept, and Mrs. Hogg, lying curiously across a barrel, slept also. Mrs. Crumb, walking in a dwaum, clung to the arm of a kind policeman, and old Rebecca, having bitten the hand of an officer of the Salvation Army, vanished in the darkness of a near-by close. But Kitty and Mima Bird staggered valiantly along and came near enough to St. Giles to be caught in the crowd and to join their cracked voices in song, to lurch bravely in the dancing, and to crow their welcome to the infant year.

It was late the next morning when Kitty woke on her

dirty and disordered bed. Her boots had made it muddy, her broken bonnet lay on the pillow beside her. How she had reached home she could not remember, nor did she worry her aching head to try. Her mouth was parched and sour, her eyes smarting, her stomach queasy. She lay for a long time before she had the strength or courage to move, and then agonizingly sat up, her head splitting beneath a great jolt of pain, and wretchedly set her feet to the floor. She groped among the debris of the feast, holding bottle after bottle with shaking hands to the dim grey square of window to see if any sup remained. But they were all as empty as though a hot wind of the desert had dried them, till at last, hidden by the greasy valance of the bed, she found one that held—O bliss beyond words!—a gill of flat beer. This she drank slowly and with infinite gratitude, and then, taking off her boots and putting her bonnet in a place of safety, she returned to bed. "What a nicht with Burns!" she murmured, and fell asleep.

In the middle of the night she woke with a raging thirst. Headache and nausea had gone, but her whole body, like a rusty hinge, cried for moisture. Yet water was no good to her. She filled her rumbling belly with it, and it lay cold and heavy in her stomach and never penetrated the thirsty tissues. Her tongue was like the bark of a dead tree, her mouth was a chalk-pit, her vitals were like old dry sacks. Never before had she known such thirst. It seemed as though drought had emptied her veins, as rivulets go dry in the high noon of summer, and her bowels resembled the bleached and arid canvas of a boat that has drifted many days beneath the parching pitiless sun of Capricorn. In this agony, in this inward and ever-increasing Sahara, she lay till morning, while her very thoughts changed their direction with a creak and a groan.

But when the time came for it to open, she went to The Hole in the Wall and pleaded with James Campbell for a little credit, that she might save her life with a quart or two of beer. He, however, refused to let her have a single drop, not a sparrow's beakful, till she had paid into his hands, on the following Friday, her Old Age pension and her ten shillings from young Mr. McOstrich. Then, he said, out of pure Christian kindliness he would let her drink a pint or so on consideration of her pledging to him another week's income. Nor could he be moved from this cruel and tyrannous decision.

It seemed to Kitty, as she walked home, that her body at any moment might crumble into dust and be blown away. She opened her mouth to suck in the wind and the rain, but the wind changed in her throat to a hot simoom, and choked her with a sandstorm of desire for the slaking gold and cool foam of bitter beer. She sat in her dark room gasping for assuagement, and tormented by the vision and the gurgling noise of ale cascading into glass. The marrow dried in her bones.

But despite the unceasing torture she would not yield to the temptation to beg sixpence or a dram, supposing they had it, from her friends. To sorn like a tinker on those whom she had so lately entertained like a queen was utterly impossible. Her spirit was too proud to stoop so low for comfort. Her torment must continue. She had nothing to sell, nothing that anyone would conceivably buy, not even her hens, for they were long past laying and too thin to be worth the plucking. She was shipwrecked, and she must endure till time should rescue her.

But she had not so long to wait for relief as she feared, for about six o'clock in the evening, when The Hole in the Wall was open again for those who had money, her hens began clacking and chacking as though they were mad, and anyone who had been there might have seen Kitty's head fall to one side, and one hand slide stiffly from the arm of her chair. She was dead, and it was thirst that had killed her. Thirst had sucked out the vital essence of her life, and left nothing but dry tubes and a parched frame behind. Her body was dead and as dry as a powdery sponge in a chemist's shop.

Some time later her soul felt better, though not yet at ease, when she found herself walking along Death's Road to the worlds beyond this world. She was still thirsty, but

not agonized with thirst. She was worried by the flies and
the midges on the lower part of the road, and she was angry
to find herself dead; for she had enjoyed being alive. But
she kept bravely on her way, knowing the proper thing to do,
and she felt exceedingly scornful of the innumerable travellers
who grumbled at stones in the way—for it was not a motor
road—and complained about the lack of signposts, and
sulkily lay down in the shadow of a hedge to wait for a bus
that would never come.

The road climbed slowly round the side of a hill whose
top was lost in a luminous mist. After a few hours Kitty
became reconciled to death, and trudged on with growing
curiosity. The farther she went the lonelier the road became,
till for a mile or two she saw no one at all. Then, at a fork
in the road, she found a group of some twenty people, very
well dressed for the most part, who were discussing which
way they should go. For on the left hand the road led downhill to a valley shining in the sun, but on the right it climbed
steeply and narrowed in a few hundred yards to a mountain
track. The majority of the disputing travellers favoured
clearly the low road, but a dubious minority furrowed their
brows and looked without relish at the upward path. The
debate came to an end as Kitty drew near to them. A well-
bred female voice, like a ship's bell in the night, exclaimed:
"The idea is absurd. As though such a wretched little path
could lead to anything or anywhere!" "Unless to a preci-
pice," added a tired young man. And the party, with
scarcely a glance at Kitty, turned downhill with resolute steps
or a shrug of the shoulders.

"Tyach!" said Kitty, and went the other way.

The path she took was not unlike the little road that leads
to Arthur's Seat. The resemblance comforted her, and so
did the mist, which was like a Scots haar with the sun coming
through it. The track bent and twisted and crossed a depression between three hills. It rose into the mist. She walked
for a long time in a sunny vapour, and lost her breath, and
grew thirsty again.

Then the view cleared, and on the forefront of a great plateau she came to a high wall, with a tall white gate in it, and beside the gate a house with an open door, two bow-fronted lower windows, and three upper ones, from the centre of which jutted a green holly bush. So Kitty knew it was a tavern, and taking no notice of the ivory gate in the wall she walked gladly in and rapped on the bar. But when she saw who came to answer the summons, she was so astounded and so abashed that she could not speak, though a moment before she had known very well what she meant to say.

It was a lady with high-piled golden hair who came to serve her—but the gold was dim, the colours of her dress were faded (it had been fashionable when King Edward VII was crowned), her mouth had forgotten laughter—and Kitty, seeing not only all that had changed but that which was unchanged, knew her at once.

"Well," said the lady, "and what can I give you?"

"Oh, your ladyship!" stammered Kitty, and twisted her dirty old hands in joy and embarrassment.

Then, before either could speak again, a tall thin man came in through the outer door with a basket on his arm. He had a nose like a hawk's beak, a pair of fine moustaches like the wings of a hawk, he wore a deer-stalker's cap and an old Norfolk jacket, and the basket on his arm held a loaf of bread, a beef-bone, and some vegetables. He put the basket on a table and murmured to the lady with the dimmed golden hair, "A customer, my dear? Things are looking up, aren't they?"

"Sir Hector!" said Kitty in a trembling voice.

But though she recognized them, they did not remember her, for she had lived longer than they had, and life had used her inconsiderately. It was only after long explanation, after much exclamation, that they knew her, and saw faintly in her dissipated features the sweet young lines of Kitty of the Burnside. Sir Hector was visibly distressed. But Kitty, giving him no time to speak his pity, indignantly asked, "And what are you doing here, in a pub at Heaven's gate, who never soiled your hands with work of any kind on earth below? Is there no respect in Heaven? Or has someone been telling lies about you, and dirty slander, as they did in Appin, and London, and Edinburgh too?"

"We have been treated with understanding and forgiveness," said Lady Lavinia; and Sir Hector loudly cleared his throat and added, "It was a situation of great difficulty, a very delicate situation indeed, and we have no complaints to make. None whatever," he said, and took his message basket into the kitchen.

But Kitty was sorely displeased by the indignity of their condition, for in her youth they had been great and splendid figures—though shameless in their many sins, dissolute in all ways, and faithful only to their mutual love—and in her loyalty she vilified the judgment of Heaven that kept them beyond its gate. She swore that if they were not good enough for God's company, then He could do without hers also. She wouldn't go to Heaven. Not she, she said. Not though God and all His holy angels came out to plead with her. "Be damned if I'll consort with you," she would say, and that would teach them what other people thought of their treatment of a great gentleman like Sir Hector and a lady like Lady Lavinia.

So for a few days Kitty stayed in the inn by Heaven's gate, and the beer there was as good as she had ever tasted, and her heart was glad to be in such grand company. But she could not restrain her curiosity to see what Heaven was like, and one morning she knocked on the ivory door, and when St. Peter opened it she did her best to slip inside. But St. Peter pushed her back and asked her who she was. Nor did he seem much impressed when she told him.

"And how did you get here?" he asked.

"Well," said Kitty, "it all began with a Hogmanay party in Baxter's Close in the Canongate."

"That's enough," said St. Peter. "We want none of your kind here." And he shut the door in her face.

Now having been refused admission, Kitty's curiosity

became overwhelming, and she made up her mind to enter Heaven by hook or crook. So she walked up and down muttering angrily, till she thought of a trick that might beat St. Peter's vigilance, and the following morning she knocked again on the ivory door.

St. Peter frowned angrily when he saw who it was, but before he could speak, Kitty exclaimed, "There's an auld friend of yours in the pub ootbye that's speiring for you, and would like you to go and have a crack with him."

"What's his name?" asked St. Peter.

"I just canna mind on't" Kitty answered, "but he's a weel-put-on man with whiskers like your own."

"It's not like any friend of mine to be spending his time in a public-house," said St. Peter.

"You wouldna deny an auld friend because he likes his glass, would you?"

Now at that moment Kitty had a stroke of luck, for beyond the wall a cock crew loud and piercingly, and Kitty said quickly, "You'll remember that once before you cried out you didna ken a man you kent full well. You'll not be wanting to make the same mistake again, I'm thinking?"

At that St. Peter's face grew dark red with rage and shame. But he tucked up his gown and went swiftly out and over to the inn, leaving the gate of Heaven open. And Kitty, as soon as his back was turned, scuttled inside.

It seemed to her that Heaven had a rather deserted look. She had expected to see well-dressed crowds and a fine air of prosperity and well-being. She had hoped to associate with lords and ladies, or at least with wealthy people of the kind that lived in Heriot Row and did their expensive shopping in Princes Street. But the only people she saw were almost as shabbily dressed as she was, and even they were few in number.

She stopped and spoke to a mild little man who sat on a green chair beneath a white-flowering tree. "The others will have gone for a picnic?" she said. "Or they'll be busy with their choir practice?"

"There are no others," he answered. "At least, not here. Some of the farther regions, that people of an older birth have chosen, are well enough populated, but here we are very few in number. So many on earth today have lost their faith. . . ."

"The glaikit sumphs!" said Kitty, and continued her walk, but without much enjoyment. She was saved from boredom, indeed, only by discovering, in the shelter of a little wood, a henhouse with a run attached, in which a score of finely feathered Rhode Island Reds were gravely scratching, their ruddy plumage a very pretty contrast to the green leaves and white sand. While Kitty stood watching them with interest and admiration, she was surprised, and somewhat perturbed, by the approach of Our Lady and a young woman in a khaki shirt and cotton breeches.

Kitty most reverently curtsied, Our Lady as graciously smiled, and the young woman in the breeches went into the hen run. Presently she reappeared with a dejected look on her face and two small eggs in her hand.

"Now really," said Our Lady, "that's *most* disappointing. Two eggs today, three yesterday, and four the day before. They're getting worse and worse. I do think you might persuade them to do better than that, Miss Ramsbottom."

"I'm giving them the very same feeds that were recommended by the Government College of Dairying and Poultry Management," said Miss Ramsbottom unhappily.

"Well, if that doesn't suit them, why not try something else?"

"But I don't know anything else. We weren't taught anything else in the Government College. It took us so long to learn. . . ."

"You let me look after them, Your Ladyship," said Kitty. "I kept a dozen hens in a back kitchen in Baxter's Close, in the Canongate in Edinburgh, and fed them on anything I could find, or on nothing at all, and they laid like herring-roe for eight or nine years, some of them, till the poor creatures were fairly toom, and nothing could be done with them at

29   c

all. But with bonny birds like these we'll have eggs dropping all day, like pennies in the plate at a revival meeting."

"All right," said Our Lady, "I'll give you a trial and see how you get on. And if there's a choice—though there hasn't been for a long time past—it's the brown eggs that I prefer, especially for breakfast, though the white ones are good enough for omelettes, of course. Now come along, Miss Ramsbottom, and I'll find something else for you to do."

So Kitty was given work in Heaven, and for several weeks she was happy enough to be looking after such handsome and well-disposed fowls, for under her care they became not merely prolific but regular in their habits. Two circumstances, however, kept her from settling down in whole contentment, one being the lack of congenial company, the other the fact that in Heaven there was nothing to drink but light wines and beer, and the beer was poor in quality.

She took to wandering far afield, and found that regions more remote from the gate were fairly thickly populated. But many of the inhabitants, to her disgust, were foreigners, and even among those of Scottish or English origin she found few with whom she had much in common. Yet she continued to explore the upper reaches of Heaven, for having met Our Lady she was seized with ambition to encounter God the Father and the Son of Man.

It was after a very long walk that by chance she saw God. He was sitting in a pleached arbour drinking wine with a bald man in doublet and hose, his head the shape of an egg, and another in sombre garments, with a broad bony forehead, untidy thick hair, and a wild mouth. Their voices were loud and magnificent, and a pleasant lightning played about the forehead of God the Father.

"I wrote your true morality," said the bald man, "when I made Parolles say 'Simply the thing I am shall make me live.'"

"And I," said the man with the bony forehead, "I wrote your pure wisdom in the third movement of my Emperor concerto, when I put the Hero—the Conqueror, the Fool—

in the middle of a ring, and fenced him round with dancing countryfolk and laughter that would not stop."

"So you're my Moralist, and you're my Philosopher?" said God the Father. "And what was I when I said 'Let there be light'? Simply the Artist for art's sake?"

"A pity you hadn't also said 'Let there be understanding,' " said the man with the bony forehead.

"Then would you have robbed poor dramatists of their trade," said the bald man.

Now this kind of conversation, though it appeared to please its participants, had no interest for Kitty, and without waiting to hear more she went on past the pleached arbour, and came presently to a little rocky foreland in the cliff of Heaven, and looking over the edge she saw something of the world below.

She had never known till then what evil there was upon the earth. But looking down, through the clear light of Heaven, she saw lies and tyranny and greed, misery like a dying donkey in the sand and greed like a vulture tearing its vitals. She saw hunger and heard weeping. She saw a fool in black uniform who had made his people drunk with lying words and threatened all Europe with war. She saw bestial stupidity consume the horde of humanity like vermin on a beggar's skin. And then she found that she was not alone on the little foreland, for in a cleft of the rock was the Son of Man, weeping.

So Kitty, in a great hurry to escape unseen, came quickly away from there, and without waiting to look at anything else, returned to her henhouse and the comforting plumpness of her Rhode Island Reds. She was hot and leg-weary after her long walk, and very depressed by what she had seen of the farther parts of Heaven. She wanted to sit down in a comfortable chair, and take off her boots, and drink a quart or two of good strong ale. She needed ale, and plenty of it, to soothe and reassure her. But as luck would have it, the beer that night was thin as a postcard, sour as vinegar, and there was very little of it. Kitty lost her temper completely, and let anyone who cared to listen know just what she thought of Heaven and the only brewer—since men brewed their own —who had ever succeeded in swindling his way into it. At dinner-time the next day she repeated the whole story, for again the beer was small in quantity and less in quality, a cupful, no more, and little better than swipes.

She rose from the table in fury, and went straight to the gate, which was unattended. She threw it open, and without any feeling of regret heard it slam behind her.

But in the tavern below the wall, with a tankard of their own brewing before her, she soon found good temper again, and told Sir Hector and Lady Lavinia a fine story of the hardships she had had to endure.

"Not that I wasn't real pleased to be working for Our Lady," she said, "and a fine time *she* had while I was there, with two good brown eggs to her breakfast every morning, but apart from her the company was poor—no gentry at all— and there were sights there that I wouldna care to see again, and talk that made no sense, and the beer was just a disgrace. It's maybe all right for them that like it, and God knows I wouldna say a word against the place, but I think I'll be better suited here, if you'll keep me. I can peel the tatties and scrub the floor and clean your boots, and if you won't grudge me a nip and a pint when my work's done, I'll be far happier here than in ahint that wall of theirs. And I wouldna find it easy to get by yon birkie with the keys again," she added.

There, then, in the inn at Heaven's gate, Kind Kitty found her proper place. There she is still, doing a little work and drinking a good deal, and whomsoever Death takes from this world, whose legs and faith are strong enough for the hill-ward path, will do well to stop there and drink a pint or two for the good of the house and his own comfort. For Kitty's presence is sure proof that the ale is still good. Had its quality failed she would have gone elsewhere long before now.

Orgill Mackenzie

SOMETHING DIFFERENT

Nancy had never seen such a tiny station. And the train they had just got out of—two coaches, an engine and a van—was just the length of the platform, as neat as anything. She stood holding Mrs. Spence's hand while just one porter all by himself made the noise that a station simply must have. He rolled and dumped and banged empty milk-cans from the van to the platform, slowly, with a very satisfactory noise indeed.

Mrs. Spence had handed him their tickets, had waved and shouted to a man—a surprisingly red man—who waited with a horse and cart at the crossing gate on the other side of the railway. The porter had finished. The guard, standing at the station pump, rolled his eyes at Nancy over the brim of the iron cup from which he was drinking. They were bulging eyes that looked as if they might fall out any minute. Nancy thought that if they did fall out he'd catch them in the cup easily—but would he see to catch them? Then he had finished, too, and his eyelids came down over his eyes so that there was no longer any danger of their falling out. He jerked one hand to the engine-driver: "Right you are, Jim," he shouted, and as he waited for his van to come to him he wiped his mouth comfortably in a way that had long been forbidden to Nancy. The train puffed, grunted, rattled, squeaked, moved! Would the guard catch it? Along came his van with its gaping door. Nancy held her breath. The heavy guard swung gracefully aboard. Nancy clapped her hands appreciatively, and "Hoots, child," said Mrs. Spence.

Mrs. Spence was like that. If you did or said anything at

all, Mrs. Spence was sure to say something about it. Nancy felt, somehow, that nothing she did was wasted when Mrs. Spence was there.

They crossed the railway-line. Nancy shivered as she put her foot on the shining metal, and she gave a hurried little skip.

"There, what's your hurry now? If you're not the impatient piece!" said Mrs. Spence. There are plenty of people who would never notice a little girl's shiver and skip, far less say anything about it. Nancy could count on this friend.

"I thought a train," she said vividly. "It went over us with a squash and a crunch."

"Well, if that wasn't a silly thing to go and think, and not another train coming through this day. Hullo, Ned!" she hailed the red man.

"I think I'd rather call you 'Red'," said Nancy gravely, taking in the redness of his hair, moustache and face, and the ruddy brown of his suit, and the fire-bright red of his cart.

"Nancy!" said Mrs. Spence severely.

"Red?" said the man who had eyes like little blue dishes, and he laughed so loudly that Nancy blinked. "Red! Why so A im. Did ever! An' here's me never thocht on't. Red a' ower A im."

"No, not your eyes, nor your boots," she corrected.

"Did ever!" he said again admiringly, and swung her up into his brilliant cart that Mrs. Spence entered, more dolorously, by climbing in puffily from the hub, and Ned by the shaft. Off they set down a strange road. There was a wild white sunset and a fat black cloud that looked as if it were just at the end of the road, ready to fall smack. The puddles were white and the grasses beneath the hedge were bleached and queer-looking, and the unpruned thorn hedge straggled tall and naked and purple-black. Nancy had never seen anything like it. It wasn't like the garden-lined streets of home; it wasn't like holidays where there was always seaside. And to ride through this in a cart with Mrs. Spence and "Red" was one of the most different things that ever happened.

"Had ye tae ask if they'd let her come?" Ned nodded

towards Nancy, who was leaning over the side watching with much absorption the broad wheels splash through the puddles, breaking up their whiteness.

"Ask! Who should I ask? And not a soul but our two selves in that forbidding black house! It's my opinion if the blessed lamb died there'd be no questions asked."

"What blessed lamb, Spencie? Am I a blessed lamb?" Nancy's absorption had been less than they had thought.

"That you're not!" said Mrs. Spence emphatically. "Not a lamb, neither blessed nor otherwise."

"Well, I wonder who is. Is it anybody I know?"

"No, that it isn't."

"Well then you don't know her either," said Nancy triumphantly, " 'cos you've told me about everybody—about Ned and his Sarah that he's going to marry, and her fat white mother that just sits in a chair and eats tea-leaves—she doesn't sound very nice, Mr. Red; but then if she stays in one place it's not quite so bad as if you kept meeting her, is it? But p'raps you've got used to her."

Mrs. Spence hushed her charge urgently; but Nancy was excited, and nothing would silence her. Ned just grinned. "You're a caution," he said.

"I'm sorry I haven't got a new frock for your wedding. But Mummy and Daddy have been away ever so long. And Spencie says they're too busy to think about a blue frock. It wouldn't really take more'n about a minute. If they just said, sort of quick, to a lady in a tight black dress: 'A blue frock for Nancy, about so long,' and gave her some money, she'd be nearly sure to send one next day, don't you think?"

Ned took off his cap and scratched his head.

"She might, to be sure; or again she mightn't," he managed to say.

Nancy weighed his remark in silence for a moment, and then said scornfully: "That sounds just silly to me. I don't believe it means a thing."

"There's Clachan Knowe. D'ye see, Nancy lass, wi' blue reek abune it's lum?"

35

"Lum, lum, lum!" sang Nancy with sudden cheerfulness, dancing on the floor of the cart. "I like lum. What is a lum? Just a chimney!" she exclaimed disappointedly. "It sounds fatter. I'd like to hug a lum."

"Nancy, don't be silly," said Mrs. Spence, and then, as a figure appeared in the low doorway of the cottage, she waved wildly. "There's Sarah. Hullo, Sarah!"

Nancy liked Sarah the moment she saw her. Her black hair was in curling pins all round her forehead and in tiny tight plaits down her back. She had white shining teeth and a big red mouth and a laughing sort of voice.

"Well, if this is no' fine, Annie! A'm that pleased to see you—and Miss Nancy."

"Spencie always just says 'Nancy': it doesn't sound so cross, don't you think?"

"Bless her heart! 'Nancy' it is, to be sure!"

"Mother! Here's Annie come and the wee lass she's carin' fur." Sarah's big voice rose to shrill heights. Nancy, peering round Sarah's skirt, saw Sarah's mother in her rocking chair in a dark corner, whiter and fatter even than she had hoped for—and deafer besides.

"What's that ye're sayin'?"

Sarah pushed Mrs. Spence and Nancy forward towards the white face and the great black body. Fat white hands came out towards Nancy. She shuddered and wriggled out of reach.

"She's shy," neighed the old woman—her voice was wheezy and surprisingly thin. Sarah, setting a stool for Nancy by the fire, felt her hand convulsively seized. "There, there," she said soothingly, "she'll no hurt you. She likes wee lassies."

Ned stood sheepishly at the door. "A'll be gettin' ower-bye, Sarah. A maun get my claes shiftit. The time's gettin' on."

" 'Deed is't," said Sarah comfortably. "Noo, min' ye, Ned, seven o'clock, an' if ye're late ye'll ne'er hear the last o't."

"A'll no be late," said he stoutly. "Sae lang iverybudy."

The door was shut. The lamp was lit—oily-smelling and dim. The peats were stirred and the big black kettle sang lustily as the flame licked about it.

"I think this is the loveliest room I ever saw," said Nancy with conviction. There was a huge bed in a dim alcove gleaming white with starched curtains and stiff new bedspread. There was a big yellow dresser with blue and white dishes and a row of meat-covers shining on the wall; a meal chest of battered oak. There was a funny chair like a sentry box, and a white scrubbed table with high piles of floury soda scones on it, and golden-brown pancakes, and thin potato scones spotted like a fox terrier. There was a black and white collie stretched out on a grey rag rug. There was a wee window all filled with frilly white muslin. Nancy's eye took in every detail, and though she sat still she was like a dog that noses out every corner of a strange room before he will make himself at home.

She sighed contentedly. Sarah gave her a glass of milk and a warm scone, split and buttered. She was so intent on licking carefully round her scone to save the melting butter before it fell that Sarah and Mrs. Spence left the room unnoticed by her. They had gone into the tiny room off the kitchen where Sarah's wedding finery was displayed—a bright blue frock of jap silk, bright blue stockings and high-heeled patent leather shoes with great diamond buckles. All these lay on the bed ready to put on: the shoes at the foot of the bed and a stiff little wreath of artificial orange blossom on the pillow, and the frock between, so that it looked as if a body had been in them and had melted away.

"I'll get the tea, Sarah, and you dress yourself quietly so's not to hurry yourself."

"Hoots, A'll get the tea. It'll no tak' me lang tae doll masell."

"Is the supper set?" Mrs. Spence asked anxiously.

"Aye, a wheen o' lassies lent a haun. Fine it looks. A maun say. In the barn, ye ken. Holly an' ivy an' the guid kens what forbye. The cake got a bit dunted in the cairt. Ned brocht it back whan he cam' frae Market on Friday. But, fegs, it looks fine. Jeck's comin' wi' his fiddle. An' deed, A don't ken what mair we can dae."

"Ye've got some nice things, Sarah." Mrs. Spence looked at the table littered with the strangest assortment of cushions and tea-cosies and cruets.

"Aye, they're weel eneugh," said Sarah complacently.

"Well, my dear, it's glad I am to see you this length on the road to matrimony."

There was heavy virtue in the voice. Sarah's eyes twinkled.

" 'Deed, it's gled A im masell. Ned was ower quick, an' then he was ower slow," she said cryptically. Her voice dropped to a whisper: "It's feared for the minister he is. There's Ned sittin' in the choir—for fine he likes a bit music —the minister roarin' damnation abune his heid—'careless lads an' lassies forgettin' that the kirk is the ae road tae parentheid, an' stottin' doon the primrose path tae everlastin' flames wi' their bit bairnies at their heels.' A canna credit it masell; but Ned ettles tae be on the safe side, an', dod, that suits me fine. No but what he's geyan fond o' me in his wey," she added thoughtfully.

"I think you were taking a grave risk, Sarah."

"Hoots, wumman! Ned wad niver hae merrit me else. An' here's the croft wastin' for a man aboot it since ma brither Tam deed. An' whan ma mither dees 'twad be a lanesome place eneugh. An' Ned's a fine upstandin' lad, an' biddable forbye."

"Well, well, Sarah, we must hope for the best," said Mrs. Spence despondently. And then Nancy found them and exclaimed delightedly over the blueness of the wedding dress, the shininess of the wedding shoes, the yellowness of the tea-cosy and the plenty of bright shining things.

Then back they trooped into the warm kitchen, and Nancy saw for herself how Sarah's mother ate pinches of tea from a little tin box which she kept behind the cushion of her chair: crunch, crunch, she went after she had taken a pinch, and then, though her jaws still moved, she made no more sound. Mrs. Spence shook her head.

"Sarah, 'tis mortal bad for her, I'll be bound."

"Weel, weel," said Sarah, "she has et tea-leafs this mony a lang day. A'll no say but she's failin'; but losh bless us, she's mair nor eichty. Gin she dees it'll no' be wi' chowin' tea."

They had tea, Sarah and Mrs. Spence standing each with a teacup and a deftly managed teaspoon in one hand and a floury scone in the other. After that, all was commotion. Nancy and Sarah's mother had their faces and hands washed with a warm hairy flannel and scratched dry with a hard brown towel. Nancy's white frock was slipped on in front of the big peat fire. Sarah's mother just kept in the same frock; Nancy saw no way of getting her out of it. Such a hurry and bustle getting Spencie into her red frock and Sarah into her blue one, getting all the little plaits combed out and fluffing out the hair from the tight curling pins. And the minute it was done, Sarah said, "There's somebody chappin' at the door," and she laughed and ran away into the little cold room.

All the people seemed to come at once: laughing and talking they were, girls in blue and pink and green and white, and everybody's face was red and shining except the minister's. He came last in his smooth black coat and his dazzling white collar that looked to Nancy as impossible to get into as Sarah's mother's frock was to get out of. Everybody came quiet at once except Sarah's mother. She talked and talked, and nobody paid any attention. Ned stood beside the bedroom door and his face was redder than ever, but his suit wasn't so red. And the door of the little room opened and out came Sarah. Everybody looked at her as if Sarah was new and not just her clothes. But her mother didn't look. Her neck was too fat to turn: anyhow Sarah couldn't have looked very new to her. She just sat and talked and put little lots of tea into her white face. But Sarah's face wasn't white; neither was Spencie's, neither was anybody's—except the thin minister's and Sarah's fat mother's.

When Nancy looked at the minister again he was shaking hands with people, and somebody was getting him his hat and coat from the white bed.

"But I thought Ned and Sarah were going to get married," said Nancy.

"Well isn't that just what they've gone and been?" asked Mrs. Spence delightedly.

"Well, if that's married, I don't think much of it." Nancy felt cheated.

"Hoots, child," said Mrs. Spence, and then pushed forward to kiss Sarah.

The minister went away. No, he wouldn't wait for his supper.

"He looks dour-like," whispered Mrs. Spence.

"Wha cares!" said Sarah.

The minister stood at the garden gate in the darkness trying to light his bicycle lamp. It was a fine wintry night, a full moon waded gamely in a cloudy sky; there was a wild sough to the wind that swept the weather-twisted trees to the northeast. While he struggled with his matches the door of the croft opened. The light from the kitchen lamp struck bravely out into the dark, and out tumbled, with noisy fun, burly farm-hands in their thick Sunday suits, and their girls, whose thin frocks blew close against their sturdy legs and dragged across their high bosoms. The wind snatched at their frizzed hair. They grouped about the door. Sarah and Ned came out; a volley of rice, hard-flung by muscular arms, greeted them. Sarah half-turned as if to retreat. Her tell-tale figure in her thin silk frock stood out boldly against the lamplight.

"Disgusting!" said the minister and, his lamp lighted, he pedalled off hurriedly into the dark towards his big empty manse and the respectable company of his books.

The kitchen door was closed. Rover crept out from his refuge beneath the bed and settled down on his rag rug. Sarah's mother sat alone by the peat fire mouthing fresh tea leaves.

The little company entered the barn to the sound of a violin being tuned, to the rattle of cups and saucers and spoons, to the smell of hay and of the tea urn.

Sarah's heart sang, "I have got my man." Ned thought contentedly of the little house, the dim wintry fields, this watertight barn: "Mine," he thought.

And Nancy, standing on the threshold of the barn, forgot all her disappointment over the marriage ceremony at the sight of the long board on trestles piled high with things to eat—a ham and chicken and scones—at the sight of the fiddler perched high on the hay and already beginning a rattling tune.

Nancy ate and she danced and she hooched wildly at the reels, and then she was put up beside the fiddler on the hay where she watched for a while, clapping her hands and shouting.

It was after midnight before she dropped to sleep on the hay. Mrs. Spence covered her with a coat, and the fiddling and dancing shot dreams through her sleep. It was six in the morning before the dancing ended, and not till then was Nancy put to bed. It was Ned who carried her through the yard to the house. Roused by the hubbub and the cold night air, she opened her eyes and asked very clearly, "Have you any wee chickens in your bag?"

"Did ever!" said Ned. But she had forgotten all about the chickens when she awakened in a queer lumpy bed in a dusky room. She heard voices, and then she remembered this was the wedding-present room and the voices came from the kitchen. The moment she realized this she was out of bed and had the door open. There before her were an ordinary Sarah, not a blue silk one, and an ordinary Ned in a dirty coat; but that made no difference to their glory, for Nancy remembered last night. Getting married was very beautiful indeed.

That was in December. In April Nancy and Mrs. Spence were back at Clachan Knowe. In the bleak fields were wobbly-legged lambs with tails like old-fashioned bell-ropes. In the sheltered hollows there were primroses. In the garden there was a tatterdemalion old hen; her comb was nearly white, her feathers tousled, but she had a flock of beautiful clean little chicks—like Easter-egg chicks, like big dandelion-seed puffs mounted on thin shanks, and with surprising beaks and surprising eyes.

In the kitchen there was a cradle of dark brown wood that Sarah's mother kept rocking with her foot most of the day as she sat crunching tea. Under the dark hood of the cradle there was a fat baby—fat to make you wonder and as monstrously pale as Sarah's mother.

There was the old scurry of people dressing. Not Nancy nor Mrs. Spence this time. But Sarah shed her blue print frock for a blue silk blouse and a brown skirt: Ned washed outside at the pump with his braces hanging down his back, and the water went whoosh, wallop, about him till Nancy gasped to hear it; and now there was the baby to dress in a long white robe with ribbons on it, and as soon as he was dressed, if he wasn't sick on it! But Sarah tied a bib over the wet place and she tossed her head and she said, "What odds?" And as the baby didn't mind, there really didn't seem to be any.

Mrs. Spence looked at the baby gravely. "Two months he is, you say? Big for that, Sarah. A very big child; but a thought pale, wouldn't you say?"

"Mebbe that," said Sarah complacently.

"Do you get him out enough, do you think?"

"Oot!" said Sarah. "Na fegs! There's time eneugh for that gin the summer comes. A dinna haud wi' thae newfangled notions. The wean's fine."

And then the minister came—whiter than ever. And Ned came in, redder than ever. And Sarah stood up, a lot thinner. And her mother sat, every bit as fat. And there they were all again, even some of the wedding guests. And the minister put water out of a white bowl on the baby's face and called him "Joseph". The baby didn't seem to like being called Joseph, and screamed; but nobody paid any heed.

The minister wouldn't have any wine and cake and he went

away home. He didn't need any light for his bicycle this time, and his face was as unfriendly as ever as he hurried off. Then there was whisky for the men and port wine for the women and ginger wine for Nancy. The wedding cake was passed round.

"It's no' that lang since we tasted this cake afore, A'm thinkin'," said a big burly man, who laughed uproariously at his little joke as he dug his elbow into Ned's stomach. The company roared in chorus; Ned choked on his whisky, and Sarah said complacently, "Weel, weel, it micht be waur." Everybody laughed—even Nancy, though she found this a good deal less fun than the wedding. Still, she did enjoy herself afterwards christening the eleven chicks in the yard out of the very same bowl as the minister had used. She decided that the white chicks should be girls and the creamy ones boys, and she drove the bedraggled hen to a fury by following her chicks doggedly till each had got a drop of water on his fluff and had been given a highly ornamental name that worried him a good deal less.

"It was heavenly," sighed Nancy, as they travelled home.

That was in April. Back they came in September.

"You must keep very quiet this time," Mrs. Spence had told her.

"Why?" she had asked—but had not been told.

The kitchen was very queer looking. Nancy soon saw why. Sarah's mother was not sitting in her chair, which looked black and shining and terribly empty. Nor was she anywhere else to be seen. Sarah all in black, and Mrs. Spence with a black hat, talked in whispers and disappeared into the wedding-present room. Joseph lay on the big kitchen bed and screamed and screamed and screamed. Nancy stood at the edge of the bed desperately watching him.

"Joseph, you're not to. That's bad!" But Joseph paid no heed; he just paused for a second to find his breath, and waiting to find only a little, he spent it all again on pain or anger. Very soon Mrs. Spence, followed by Sarah, hurried into the kitchen.

"Mercy on 's, Sarah! What ails the child?"

"Him! Och, he's fine. He's aye greetin'."

Mrs. Spence lifted him from the shadow of the curtained bed. "Sarah!" she gasped. "Does he aye look like this?"

"He diz that. Hoo wad ye hae him look? As plump a bairn as ye'll see."

Mrs. Spence looked wildly at him. His little body was enormously puffy; his tiny features were lost in the white balloon of his face. "This child is ill," she said solemnly.

"Hoots, havers, wumman! He gets castor ile ivery day in the warl wide. Hoo cud he ail, I'm askin'?"

"Well, *you* see that he gets no more for a month." Mrs. Spence was angry.

"Hoity toity," said Sarah lightly; and then, "Here's the coffin comin'!" she whispered tensely, her eyes fixed on the window. The baby was laid down on the bed and forgotten. The two women looked in silence for a moment at the men who carried the coffin across the field.

"I thought you'd have had a chesting service, Sarah." Mrs. Spence's voice had an edge of reproof in it.

"It's ower far tae bring Sandy McWhirter twa trips. The minister disna haud by't forbye. 'Superstition,' sez he—in the kirk, min' ye. 'A'll tell ye for why,' sez he. Oot mairches Alecina McFadzean, tossin' her heid. An' that's the last o' the auld kirk for her. 'Superstition,' sez he; an' he tellt us for why. But deed I forget."

Another moment's silence as they watched. "There they're noo. We'll let them chap." There came a knock: 'Chap, chap'—not a gay rat-tat-tat. The symbol of death on the threshold made solemn soft knocking at the door: 'Chap,' pause, 'chap.' Sarah opened to two men and a black coffin. To the men speaking in whispers Sarah whispered back; but Joseph on the big bed screamed and screamed and screamed. Nobody heeded him. He had had his day of importance when nobody had heeded the fat old lady.

There came more quiet knocking at the door, and one after another men in dull clothes whispered and tiptoed through the kitchen to the wedding-present room. Nobody seemed to remember Nancy. She tiptoed after the last of them. The door was half open. She peeped round. There was a man on the bed with his boots off. He was lifting something. It was Sarah's mother, bulgy in a white nightgown. They were putting her in the black thing—like the drawer of a chest— with handles. Nancy stepped forward to see better. "The bairn!" gasped somebody. Mrs. Spence rushed forward to remove her; but Sarah stepped in.

"She maun touch the corp noo," she said firmly.

"Let be, Sarah, let be," whispered Ned hoarsely.

"Noa, she maun touch the corp. It's no' canny tae see an' no' tae touch."

Nancy became the centre of the picture. She was led to the bed, half-fearful, half-proud and altogether curious. Directed by Sarah she gave a little quick tap to the cold fat face that looked more terrible than ever, and then Mrs. Spence took her out through the kitchen into the sunlight. Across the fields in every direction were coming darkly-clad men, and they all came together before the house where stood a shining glass coach and heavy black horses with trailing tails. The door opened and out came men slowly, and the coffin came too. It was slipped into the glass coach; flowers white and stiff as paper were laid on it; slowly the horses started; the men glided together in threes and fours behind it and the little procession oozed from sight. None of the women went with it. The men had to fill in the time of their slow walk; so they talked—of the weather, of the standing corn, of the corn that was stooked, and the length of the straw, and the threshing, and the harvest home, and of the weather again; and in no time Sarah's mother was left in the graveyard with her luggage of wreaths about her.

That was in September. In October back they came, Nancy and Mrs. Spence. This time it was the baby, dead though he was so plump, though he had castor oil every day. They put him in a little white box. They sent him off with flowers too; but in a cab he went—the glass coach was too big—and not so many men behind him, and it was a dark day and windy with the leaves pining on the trees and hedges.

"He's nobbut one of God's angels that was with us awhile," said Sarah, and Nancy wondered if heaven had lots of little Josephs who screamed and screamed and screamed, with God in the midst of them.

Nancy enjoyed it. It was so different. She knew nothing of graves but much of heaven, though this last idea of little Joseph-angels was rather disturbing. But Joseph's coffin, wheeled away down the windy autumn road, went somehow as soon as it was out of sight straight to God in heaven, and there the baby was unpacked, doubtless by God himself; and Sarah's mother had been too. They were dressed in white already, which would save the angels a lot of trouble. There was nothing gloomy in Nancy's picture, but something tremendously exciting. And now there was nothing for it but to go home, and Nancy hated home where there was nobody but herself and Mrs. Spence and where nothing ever happened. All the way home, in the cart, in the train, walking the last bit on greasy pavements under the town lamplight, nothing she saw could give her pleasure. It was as if she walked deeper and deeper into a shadow cast from that grim house at her journey's end.

It was such a depressing house, standing far back from a suburban road, deep in a neglected garden. It told the truth about itself so shamelessly—just that nobody loved it. Nobody lived in it even; for Nancy and Mrs. Spence, skulking in corners of it, could not be said to live in it except as mice did and cockroaches. Yes, it was that kind of a house—cockroachy. Clean enough it must have been: at any rate Mrs. Spence kept its dust on the move; yet it hadn't that clearness of eye that much-loved houses wear.

Tonight Nancy dragged reluctantly along the winding path of earth-trodden gravel between dusty-dark laurels of ragged growth to a lustreless door that had soot-dulled ivy crawling from the wall upon it, so that it looked, not like a neat oblong door that would open slickly and welcome you, but like a ragged hole stopped up firmly that didn't want to be opened.

"Spencie, I hate it. I'm frightened. Nobody has such a horrible house as us." Nancy whispered as if the house might hear.

"Hoots, child," said Mrs. Spence, whose own spirits were dimmed by this homecoming. Being in the house in the evening was one thing—lights on and a fire to poke and jobs to be done—but to come back like this to cold and darkness and scuttling cockroaches, likely enough to crunch one underfoot before the kitchen gas was turned on—well, it wasn't pleasant.

"I've had nearabout enough of this," she muttered as she thrust the key in the lock. She turned it and pushed at the door. It resisted a little. Nancy's eyes grew startled. She gave a small gasping "oh" of terror.

"It's all right, silly," said Mrs. Spence sharply. "It's just some letters and the newspaper jamming it."

Nancy could see the white gleam of papers that had been dropped through the hole in the door and she was slightly reassured. But it was on tiptoe that she went in, close behind her friend. The hall light was put on, the passage light: now for the kitchen. Drat it! There, sure enough, a crunch! At last the kitchen light. And then the front door, that had been left open as a comforting link with the outer world till all was found to be secure, was shut.

Edward Gaitens

A WEE NIP

A Macdonnel party was nearly always an informal affair. Guests were never invited by card or telephone. They just "got to know" and drifted in, irresistibly drawn by the prospect of free drink and uproarious song. John Macdonnel always insisted that there were people in the Gorbals who possessed second-sight in the matter of parties. Fellows like Squinty Traynor, Baldy, Flynn and bowlegged Rab Macpherson and ladies like wee Mrs. Rombach, Tittering Tessie and wee Minnie Milligan—though why she always showed up at parties when she was a Rechabite and never touched a drop, he couldn't understand—could smell a wake or a wedding a mile off and always crept in at the exact moment when there was still plenty of drink going and everybody was too drunk to ask or care if they had been invited.

Sometimes the nucleus of a Macdonnel party was formed in the Ladies' Parlour of a local pub from which Mrs. Macdonnel would emerge with some shawled cronies and confer on the pavement, deciding whether they should continue their tippling in another Ladies' Parlour or in one of their own kitchens. Owing to this erratic behaviour on the part of his wife, Mr. Macdonnel occasionally returned from his day's work to find her absent—when he went round her friends' kitchens in search of her—or at home with several lady friends all jolly and mildly drunk. If he was hungry and in sober mood his icy glare sent all his wife's friends flying like snow in a wintry blast, but if he yearned for spirits he thawed and deferred his displeasure till the following morning when

48

the mere thought of work was a nightmare to his aching head.

Every time Jimmy Macdonnel came home from sea there was a party and a few more after it till his pay of several months was burned right up. Even if Mrs. Macdonnel had been six months teetotal, she couldn't resist taking one wee nip to celebrate her son's return and that wee nip somehow multiplied, had bairns, as she would laughingly tell you herself.

Returning from his last voyage before World War I, Jimmy Macdonnel, after a year's absence as cook on a tramp steamship, was the originator of a famous Macdonnel party. It was a bright July Saturday afternoon when Jimmy unexpectedly arrived. A delicious smell of Irish stew was still hanging around the Macdonnel kitchen. Mrs. Macdonnel was a rare cook and Mr. Macdonnel who loved her cooking had dropped into a smiling drowse, dazed by his enormous meal. At the open window Eddy Macdonnel was seated on the dishboard of the sink muttering to himself the Rules of Syntax out of an English Grammar, asking himself how it was that Donald Hamilton could repeat from memory whole pages of the Grammar and yet couldn't write a grammatical sentence, while he, who could hardly memorize a couple of Rules, could write perfect English with the greatest of ease. But he drove himself to the unpleasant exercise of memorizing, resisting the temptation to bask in the powerful sunshine and listen to the children playing at an old singing-game, The Bonny Hoose O' Airlie O. The children were gathered near the backcourt wash-house, round the robber and his wife. First the little girl sang:

> *Ah'll no' be a robber's wife,*
> *Ah'll no' die wi' your penknife*
> *Ah'll no' be a robber's wife*
> *Doon b' the bonny hoose o' Airlie, O.*

then the boy answered, taking her hand,

> *"Oh you sall be a robber's wife,*
> *An' ye'll die wi' my penknife*
> *You sall be a robber's wife*
> *Doon b' the bonny hoose o' Airlie, O."*

The old ballad tune seemed to come out of the heart of
young Scotland, out of the childhood of his country's life.
Eddy wanted to dream into that bygone poetry. Ach! He
drove his mind again to memorizing the lesson for his night-
school class. Mr. Henderson, the English teacher, had a
biting tongue for lazy students. He turned back the page,
started again, and his muttered Rules mingled with the snores
of his father and his mother's whispers as she sat at the table
scribbling a shopping-list on a scrap of paper and continually
pausing to count the silver in her purse.

Just then there was a knock at the stairhead door and Mrs.
Macdonnel, touching back her greying, reddish hair, rose in a
fluster to open, exclaimed, "My Goad, it's Jimmy!" and returned followed by a slim, dapper young man of twenty-nine,
with bronzed features, in the uniform of a petty-officer of the
Merchant Service and carrying a sailor's kitbag which he
dumped on the floor.

"Did ye no' ken Ah was comin' hame the day?" he asked
resentfully; "Ah sent ye a postcard fae Marsels."

"Och, no son!" said his mother, blaming in her heart those
"forrin' postcairds" which always bewildered her. "Shure yer
da would hiv come tae meet the boat. Ye said the twenty-
seeventh," and she began searching in a midget bureau on the
dresser to prove her words, then she gazed mystified at the
"Carte Postale" with the view of Marseilles Harbour. "Och,
Ah'm haverin'!" she cried, "it says here the seeventeenth!"

"Ach away! Ye're daft!" said Jimmy. "How could ye
mistake a 'one' for a 'two'?"

Mr. Macdonnel woke up, rubbing his eyes, Eddy got down
from the dishboard, closing his Grammar; and they all stared
at Jimmy in silent wonder. He certainly looked trim as a
yacht in his blue reefer suit, white shirt, collar and black tie,

but they weren't amazed at his spruceness nor by his unexpected arrival but by the fact that he stood there as sober as a priest. For ten years Jimmy had been coming home from sea at varying intervals and had never been able to get up the stairs unassisted; and here he was, after a six months voyage, not even giving off a smell of spirits. Mr. Macdonnel put on his glasses to have a better look at him. What was wrong with Jimmy? They wondered if he was ill, then the agonizing thought that he had been robbed occurred simultaneously to the old folk, and Jimmy was about to ask them what they were all looking at when his mother collected herself and embraced him and his father shook his hand, patting his shoulder.

Jimmy flushed with annoyance at his mother's sentiment as he produced from his kitbag a large plug of ship's tobacco for his da, a Spanish shawl of green silk, with big crimson roses on it for his mother, and a coloured plaster-of-paris plaque of Cologne Cathedral for his Aunt Kate, then, blushing slightly, he took his seaman's book from his pocket and showed them the photograph of a young woman. "That's Meg," he said, "Meg Macgregor. She's a fisher-girl. I met her at the herring-boats when ma ship called in at Peterhead."

His mother was delighted with his taste and knew immediately why he had arrived sober. She passed the photograph to her husband, who beamed at it and said heartily, "My, she's a stunner, Jimmy boy! A proper stunner! She'll create a sensation roun' here!" Mr. Macdonnel usually awoke ill-tempered from his after-dinner naps, but his indigestion vanished like magic as he imagined the glorious spree they were going to have on Jimmy's six months' pay; and he swore he had never seen such a beautiful young woman as Meg Macgregor. Then Jimmy startled them all by announcing, as if he was forcing it out of himself: "Meg's awfu' good-livin', mother, an' she's asked me tae stoap drinkin' for the rest o' ma life. Ah've promised her Ah will."

Mr. Macdonnel glared wildly at his son, then gave a sour look at the portrait and, handing it back without a word, rolled down his sleeves and pulled up his braces. He was dumbfounded. What had come over his son Jimmy? Teetotal for the rest of his life! Was he going to lose his head over that silly-faced girl? Mrs. Macdonnel studied Jimmy with plaintive anxiety while he described Meg's beauty and goodness. "Ach, she was made tae be adored b' everybody!" he said, and warned his mother to steer clear of the drink and keep her house in order to receive his beloved, whom he had invited to come and stay with the family.

His mother promised to love Meg as a daughter and silently hoped that the girl would stay at home. She was too old now to be bothered by a healthy young woman with managing ways. Jimmy swore he hadn't touched a drop since he had sailed from Peterhead and described the tortures of his two-days' self-denial so vividly that his father shivered and hurried into the parlour to get his coat and vest. Jimmy said he was finished with the sea and booze; sick of squandering money. He was determined to settle on shore, get married, and spend all his money on Meg's happiness.

A miserly gleam beamed in his mother's eye when he said that and she wondered how much his new devotion would limit his contribution to her purse. Jimmy took a bundle of notes from his inside breast-pocket and handed her thirty pounds, reminding her that she had already drawn advance-sums from his shipping office. Mrs. Macdonnel said he was too kind and offered to return five notes with a drawing-back movement, but Jimmy refused them with a bluff, insincere gesture, for there was a flash of regret in his eye as she tucked the wad in her purse, but, with genuine feeling he invited her and his da out to drink him welcome home. "Ah'll have a lemonade," he said, gazing piously at the ceiling as though at the Holy Grail. His mother thought he was being too harsh with himself. "Shure ye'll hiv a wee nip wi' me an' yer da, son. A wee nip won't kill ye!" she laughed slyly, and Jimmy promised to drink a shandygaff just to please her, sighing with relief when he thought of the dash of beer in the lemonade. He called his father who came in from the parlour wrestling with a white dickey which he was trying to dispose evenly on his chest. "Ah won't keep ye a jiffy, laddie!" he said, facing the mirror and fervently praying that the smell of the pub would restore poor Jimmy to his senses.

As she put on her old brown shawl Mrs. Macdonnel was disappointed at Jimmy's insistence that they should go to an out-of-the-way pub. She wanted to show off her bonny son; he was so braw; so like a captain! She imagined the greetings they would get going down the long street.

"Ay, ye've won hame, Jimmy, boay? My, ye're lookin' fine, mun! Goash, ye oaght tae be a prood wumman the day, Mrs. Macdonnel! Jimmy's a credit tae ye!" and she foretasted the old sweet thrill of envy and flattery. But Jimmy said he would never drink again with the corner-boys. Love had made a new man of him!

When they had all gone out Eddy Macdonnel hurried into the small side bedroom to read the book on PSYCHOLOGY AND MORALS he had borrowed from the Corporation Library. Inspired by Jimmy's miraculous conversion he crouched over the volume, concentrating fiercely on the chapters headed WILL POWER AND SIN, and his heart swelled with a reformer's zeal as he saw himself one day applying all these marvellous laws to the human race, hypnotizing countless millions of people into sobriety.

Three hours later he heard a loud clamour in the street below. Throwing his book on the bed he raised the window and looked over and his uplifted heart sank down, for he saw Jimmy stumbling happily up the street with his Aunt Kate's hat on his head and his arm round his father's neck. They were lustily singing "The Bonny Lass O' Ballochmyle". Mr. Macdonnel's dickey was sticking out like the wings of a moulted swan and large bottles of whisky waggled from the pockets of the two men. Behind them, laughing like witches, came Mrs. Macdonnel and Aunt Kate with the sailor's cap on, followed by six of Jimmy's pals who were carrying between them three large crates of bottled beer.

Eddy closed the window quickly and stared sadly at the wall. Jimmy, the idol of his dream, himself had shattered it!

As he turned into the lobby, Jimmy opened the stairhead door and thrust his pals into the kitchen, which already seemed crowded with only two members of the family. John Macdonnel, now a fair young man of twenty-five, just home from overtime at the shipyards, leant in his oil-stained working clothes against the gas stove, reading about the Celtic and Rangers match in the Glasgow *Evening Times* and regretting that he had missed a hard-fought game which his team had won. With a wild "whoopee" Jimmy embraced his brothers, who smiled with embarrassment. John was proud of Jimmy's prestige with the corner-boys, though he knew it was the worthless esteem for a fool and his money; Eddy saw Jimmy as a grand romantic figure, a great chef who had cooked for a millionaire on his yacht and had seen all the capital cities of the world, and Jimmy's kitbag, lying against a home-made stool by the dresser, stuffed with cook's caps and jackets, radiated the fascination of travel.

Aunt Kate, a tiny, dark woman of remarkable vitality, went kissing all her nephews in turn and the party got into full swing. Liquor was soon winking from tumblers, teacups, egg-cups—anything that could hold drink—and Aunt Kate, while directing the young men to bring chairs from the parlour, sang "A Guid New Year Tae Ane an' A'," disregarding the fact that it was only summer-time, and Jimmy, thinking a nautical song was expected from him, sang "A Life On The Ocean Wave!" in a voice as flat as stale beer that drowned his Aunt's pleasant treble. But somebody shouted that he sang as well as John McCormack and he sat down with a large tumbler of whisky, looking as if he thought so himself.

Then Aunt Kate told everybody about her marvellous meeting with Jimmy whose voice she had heard through the partition as she sat in the Ladies' Parlour in The Rob Roy Arms and Eddy learned how his brother had fallen. Jimmy, it appeared, felt he must toast Meg Macgregor in just one glass of something strong; that dash of beer in lemonade had infuriated his thirst and in a few minutes he had downed

54

several glasses of the right stuff to his sweetheart, proving to his aunt's delight that he was still the same old jovial Jimmy.

John Macdonnel, all this while, was going to and fro, stumbling over out-thrust feet between the small bedroom and kitchen sprucing himself up to go out and meet his girl. From feet to waist he was ready for love. His best brown trousers with shoes to match adorned his lower half, while his torso was still robed in a shirt blackened with shipyard oil and rust. He washed himself at the sink, laughing at his Aunt's story, then turned, drying himself, to argue with his mother about his "clean change". Mrs. Macdonnel waved her cup helplessly, saying she couldn't help the indifference of laundrymen and John implored Eddy to shoot downstairs and find if the family washing had arrived at the receiving-office of the Bonnyburn Laundries.

Visitors kept dropping in for a word with the sailor and delayed their departure while the drinks went round. Rumour had spread the report that Jimmy Macdonnel was home flush with money and a Macdonnel party was always a powerful attraction. The gathering was livening up. Two quart bottles of whisky had been absorbed and beer was frothing against every lip when Eddy returned triumphantly waving a big brown paper parcel in John's direction.

It was at the right psychological moment, when a slight lull in the merriment was threatening, that Rab Macpherson romped from his hiding-place in the doorway into the middle of the kitchen and suddenly burst out singing at the top of his voice:

> *Le—et Kings an' courteers rise an' fa'*
> *This wurrld has minny turns,*
> *But brighter beams abune them a'*
> *The star o' Rabbie Burns!*

Rab's legs were very bow and wee Tommy Mohan, who was talking to his pal John Macdonnel at the sink, sunk down on his hunkers and gazed under his palm, like a sailor looking over the sea, away through Rab's legs all the time he was singing. Everybody was convulsed with laughter and Mrs. Macdonnel was so pleased with Rab, that she got up, still laughing, and with her arm around his neck, gave him a good measure of whisky in a small cream jug.

Suddenly everybody fell silent to listen to Jimmy Macdonnel, who had been up since three that morning and half-asleep was trolling away to himself "The Lass That Made The Bed For Me", and Mrs. Steedman, a big-bosomed Orangewoman, startled the company by shouting, "Good aul' Rabbie Burns! He ken't whit a wumman likes the maist!" There was a roar of laughter at this reminder of the poet's lechery, then Aunt Kate insisted that Mr. Macdonnel should sing "I Dreamt That I Dwelt In Marble Halls", while her sister, Mrs. Macdonnel, asked him for "The Meeting Of The Waters" because it reminded her of their honeymoon in Ireland. Mr. Macdonnel, assisted by the table, swayed to his feet as pompously as Signor Caruso, twirled his moustache, stuck his thumbs behind his lapels, like the buskers of Glasgow backcourts, and "hemmed" very loudly to silence the arguing sisters. He always sang with his eyes closed and when the gaslight shone on his glasses he looked like a man with four eyes, one pair shut, the other brilliantly open. He honestly believed he had a fine tenor voice and with swelled chest he bellowed:

Yes! Let me like a soldier fall, upon some open plain!
Me breast boldly bared to meet the ball
That blots out every stain!

The china shivered on the shelves above the dresser and Eddy Macdonnel, lost in some vision of bravery, stared with pride at his father. Halfway through the ballad, Mr. Macdonnel forgot the words but sang on, "tra-laing" here, pushing in his own words there, and sat down well satisfied to a din of handclaps and stamping feet.

Jimmy was blasted into wakefulness by his father's song and he washed himself sober and led out all the young men to help him buy more drink. When they returned, well-stocked, half an hour later, Mr. Macdonnel had the whole crowd singing.

I'll knock a hole in McCann for knocking a hole in me can!
McCann knew me can was new
I'd only had it a day or two,
I gave McCann me can to fetch me a pint of stout
An' McCann came running in an' said
That me can was running out!

This was Mr. Macdonnel's winning number at every spree and the refrain had echoed several times through the open windows to the street and backcourt before the young men returned. In the comparative silence of clinking bottles and glasses, Jimmy told his laughing guests of the night when he had served up beer in chamber-pots to a party of corner-boys. A dozen chamber-pots were arrayed round the table and twelve youths sat gravely before them while Jimmy muttered a Turkish grace over the beer and told them that was the way the Turks drank their drink and they believed him because he had been six times round the world.

When Aunt Kate had recovered from her delight in this story she asked Eddy to run up and see if her "bonny wee man" was home from the gasworks. Eddy raced up to the top storey, knocked on a door, and started back as his uncle's gargoyle face thrust out at him and barked, "Where's Katey? Am Oi a man or a mouse? B' the Holy Saint Pathrick Oi'll murther the lazy cow!" Eddy said faintly, "Jimmy's home an' we're having a party. Will ye come down?" and Mr. Hewes followed him downstairs muttering threats of vengeance on his wife for neglecting his tea.

The gathering had overflowed into the parlour when Eddy returned with the gasworker behind him; the lobby was crowded with newly-arrived guests listening to Aunt Kate singing "The Irish Emigrant's Farewell"; the eyes of all the women were wet with film-star tears and the singer herself seemed to be seeing a handsome Irish youth as she looked straight at her husband standing in the kitchen doorway and returning her stare with a malignant leer. Aunt Kate filled a large cup with whisky from a bottle on the dresser and, still singing, handed it to him with a mock bow. On similar occasions Mr. Hewes had been known to dash the cup from her hand and walk out and desert her for six months, but this time he seized it, swallowed the drink in one gulp, hitched up his belt and joined the party.

Eddy crushed a way through to his seat on the sink and watched his uncle, who, seated beside Mr. Macdonnel, eyed with hostility every move of his popular wife. There was an excess of spite in Mr. Hewes and he loved to hate people. Time, accident and ill-nature had ruined his face. A livid scar streamed from his thin hair down his right temple to his lip; his broken nose had reset all to one side, his few teeth were black and his little moustache as harsh as barbed wire; and with a blackened sweatrag round his neck he looked like a being from some underworld come to spy on human revels. He was called upon for a song when the applause for his wife had ended, and he stood up and roared, glaring at her:

> *Am Oi a man, or am Oi a mouse*
> *Or am I a common artful dodger?*
> *Oi want to know who is master of my house!*
> *Is ut me or Micky Flanagan the lodger?*

Shouts of "ongcore!" egged him on to sing the verse several times, his glare at his smiling wife intensifying with each repetition. He was suspected of having composed the song himself and the neighbours always knew he was going to desert his wife when he came up the stairs singing it. His whole body was humming like a dynamo after two large cups of Heather Dew and as his wife began chanting an old Irish jig he started to dance. Throwing off his jacket he roared "B' Jasus!" tightened his belt and rolled up his sleeves, revealing thick leather straps round his wrists, and his hobnailed boots beat a rapid deafening tattoo on the spot of floor inside the surrounding feet. His wife's chant became shriller and the whole company began clapping hands, stamping and yelling wild "hoochs!" that drove the little gasworker to frenzy. John Macdonnel, all dressed to go out with a new bowler hat perched on his head, lifted a poker from the grate and thrust it into the dancer's hand. Mr. Hewes tried to twirl it round his head between finger and thumb like a drum-major, then smashed it on the floor in passionate chagrin at his failure. "B' Jasus Oi could dance ye'se all under the table!" he yelled, and with head and torso held stiff and arms working like pistons across his middle, he pranced like an enraged cockerel.

Faster he hopped from heel to heel, still packed with energy after a hard day shovelling in a hot atmosphere; sweat glistened on his grey hair and beaded his blackened cheeks; he twisted his feet in and out in awkward attempts at fancy steps and looked as if he would fly asunder in his efforts to beat the pace of his accompanists; then, with a despairing yell of "B' Jasus!" he stopped suddenly, gasped, "Och, Oi 'm bate!" and hurled dizzily behind foremost into his chair.

It was a hefty piece of furniture but it couldn't stand up to his violence; with a loud crack its four legs splayed out and the gasworker crashed like a slung sack into the hearth, smashing the polished plate-shelf sticking out beneath the oven; his head struck heavily the shining bevel of the range; the snapped chair-back lay over his head, and there was a roar of laughter which stopped when he was seen to lie still among the wreckage.

His wife and Mr. Macdonnel bent over him, but he pushed them away, staggered erect and, shaking himself like a dog after a fight, snatched and swallowed the cup of whisky which Mrs. Macdonnel had poured quickly for him while looking ruefully at her shattered chair and plate-shelf. The blow had hardly affected him and, as Mrs. Hewes anxiously examined his head he pushed her rudely aside, shouting, "B' Jasus! Oi'll give ye'se 'The Enniskillen's Farewell!'" and he roared boastfully the Boer War song of an Irish regiment's departure. Suddenly he realized that attention was diverted from him; someone in the packed lobby was crying, "Here's Big Mary! Make way for Blind Mary!" and Mr. Hewes, grasping his jacket from Mr. Macdonnel's hand, slung it across his shoulder, stared malignantly at everyone and pushed uncivilly out of the house.

The Widow Loughran, who was being guided in by Jerry Delaney and his wife, was a magnificent Irishwoman, well over six feet, round about forty, and round about considerably more at waist and bosom. The habit of raising the head in the manner of the blind made her appear taller and gave her a haughty look, but she was a jolly, kind woman in robust health, and her rosy face and glossy, jet hair, her good-humoured laughter, caused one to forget her blindness. Blind Mary was the wonder of the Gorbals. She drank hard and regularly and stood it better than the toughest men. "Mary's never up nor doon," they said, and she boasted that she had never known a "bad moarnin' " in her life. She also wore a tartan shoulder-shawl of the Gordon clan, a widow's bonnet, and a bright print apron over her skirt. Mrs. Macdonnel led her to a seat and she stood up, her hands searching around for Jerry Delaney when she heard there wasn't a chair for him. He was pushed into her arms and she pulled him into a tight embrace on her ample knees. Mr. Delaney, popularly known as "One-Eyed Jerry" since a flying splinter, at his work as a ship's carpenter, had deprived him of his right eye, was no light weight, but Mary handled him like a baby, and Mrs. Macdonnel shrieked with laughter: "Blind Mary's stole yer man, Bridget!" and Mrs. Delaney, a dark beauty of five-and-thirty, laughed back, "Ach away! She's welcome tae him! Shure they're weel matched wi' yin eye atween them!" This so tickled Mary and Jerry that they almost rolled on the floor with helpless laughter, and Mrs. Macdonnel looked very worried, expecting every minute to see another of her chairs smashed to smithereens.

Aunt Kate had vanished in pursuit of her man and returned at this moment, pale with anger, to announce publicly that he had skedaddled, but that she would set the police at his

heels and make him support her; then she sang in her sweetest
voice, "O My Love Is Like A Red, Red Rose!" followed by
a delicate rendering of "Ae Fond Kiss". But no one was surprised by her instant change from wrath to tenderness, except
young Eddy, who felt that this was his most profitable
"psychological" evening as he watched Blind Mary with her
hands boldly grasping Mr. Delaney's thighs and began
excitedly composing an essay on "Psychology And The
Blind" for his night-school class.

Someone called for a song from Blind Mary, and One-
Eyed Jerry courteously handed her to her feet. She stood
dominating the whole room, protesting that she couldn't sing
a note, but everyone cried: "Strike up, Mary! Ye sing like a
lark!" and she began singing "Bonny Mary O' Argyle" to
the unfailing amazement of young Eddy, who could never
understand why her voice that was so melodious in speech
was so hideous when she sang. In his boyhood Eddy had
always loved to see her in the house, finding a strange sense
of comfort in her strength and cheerful vitality. Coming in
from school his heart had always rippled with delight to see
her gossiping and drinking with his mother and some neighbours. Her rich brogue always welcomed him, "Ach, it's me
wee Edward. Come here, ye darlin'!" and there was always a
penny or sixpenny bit for him, hot from her fat hand, or a bag
of sweets, warm from her placket-pocket, their colours
blushing through the paper. He enjoyed the strong smell of
snuff from her soft fingers when they fondled his hair or read
his face and the smell of her kiss, scented with whisky or
beer, had never repelled him.

Mary had only sung two lines, when she was sensationally
interrupted by Bridget Delaney, who suddenly leapt from
her feet and shrieked indignantly: "Ach, don't talk tae me
aboot legs! Is there a wumman in this house has a better leg
than meself? Tae hell wi' Bonny Mary O' Argyle! I'll show
ye'se the finest leg on the South Side this night!" and she
bent and pulled her stocking down her left leg to the ankle,
whipped up her blue satinette skirt and pulled up a blue leg of

bloomer so fiercely that she revealed a handsome piece of behind. "There ye are!" cried Bridget, holding forth her leg. "Ah defy a wumman among ye'se tae shake as good a wan!"

Blind Mary stood silent and trembling in a strange listening attitude, thinking a fight had begun, and everyone was astounded. Jerry Delaney, blushing with shame, plucked nervously at his bedfellow's skirt, but Bridget pulled it up more tightly and shouted: "Awa'! Ye've seen it oaften enough! Are ye ashamed o' it?" while Jerry told her he had always said she had the finest leg in Glasgow and acted as if he had never beheld such a distressing sight. Beside them a very dozy youth gazed dully at Bridget's fat, white thigh, and from the rose-wreathed wallpaper Pope Pius X, in a cheap print, looked sternly at the sinful limb.

Mrs. Macdonnel hurried her hysterical sister-in-law into the small bedroom, and the only comment on the incident was, "Blimey! Wot a lark!" from Mrs. Bills. Blind Mary asked excitedly what had happened. Some of the ladies, while affecting shocked modesty, trembled with desire to take up Bridget's challenge; but no one could have explained her hysteria, except, perhaps, Mr. Delaney. His one eye always glowed with admiration for a fine woman and he had gazed warmly all evening at Blind Mary. But Bridget's astonishing behaviour was superseded for the moment by the arrival of Wee Danny Quinn "wi' his melodyin'," whom Jimmy Macdonnel himself introduced as the guest of honour.

The street-musician, a pug-nosed, dwarfish Glaswegian, bowlegged and very muscular, drank two large glasses of whisky, wiped his lips and began playing. The mother-o'-pearl keys of his big Lombardi piano-accordion flashed in the gaslight as his fingers danced skilfully among them, and while he leant his ear to the instrument, his little dark eyes looked up with a set smile, like a leprechaun listening to the earth. He played jigs and reels and waltzes; all the furniture in the kitchen was pushed to the wall and all who could find room to crush around were soon dancing through the lobby and back again.

A Wee Nip

It was late in the night, when the dancers had paused for refreshment, that Willie McBride the bookmaker, a six-foot red-headed Highlandman, suddenly reappeared arm-in-arm with his wife, he dressed in her clothes and she in his. They had disappeared for fifteen minutes and affected the change with the connivance of Aunt Kate, who slipped them the key of her house. Mr. McBride had somehow managed to crush his enormous chest into the blouse of his slim wife; between it and the skirt, his shirt looked out, and from the edge of the skirt, which reached his knees, his thick, pink woollen drawers were visible; Mrs. McBride, drowned in his suit, floundered, bowing to the delighted company.

This wild whim of the McBrides heated everyone like an aphrodisiac, and very soon Aunt Kate's but-an'-ben became the dressing-room for the transformation of several ladies and gentlemen. The two Delaneys exchanged clothes and Bridget showed to advantage her splendid legs swelling out her husband's trousers; Aunt Kate retired with a slight youth and reappeared in his fifty-shilling suit as the neatest little man of the evening; then Mrs. Macdonnel walked in disguised as her husband, even to his glasses and cap, and was followed by him gallantly wearing the Spanish shawl, in which, after filling out his wife's blouse with two towels, he danced what he imagined was a Spanish dance and sang a hashed-up version of the "Toreador Song" from *Carmen*.

Danny Quinn's playing became inspired and his volume majestic as he laughed at the dressed-up couples dancing around. The house was throbbing like a battered drum when heavy thumps shook the stairhead door. "It's the polis," cried everyone with amused alarm. Mrs. Macdonnel rushed to open and a soft Irish voice echoed along the lobby: "Ye'se'll have to make less noise. The nayburs is complainin'!"

"Ach, come awa in, Tarry, an' have a wee deoch-an'-doris!" cried Mrs. Macdonnel, holding the door wide for the portly constable who stood amazed at her masculine garb, while Willie McBride was roaring, "Do Ah hear me aul'

freend Boab Finnegan? Come ben an' have a drink, man!
Shure you an' me's had many a dram when yer inspector
wisnae lookin'!" and Mrs. Macdonnel conducted into the
parlour Police-Officer Finnegan followed by a tall, young
Highland officer, a novice in the Force, with finger at chin-
strap and a frown of disapproval. The two policemen were
welcomed with full glasses, and Mr. Finnegan, known all
over The Gorbals as "Tarry Bob" because his hair and big
moustache were black as tar and his heavy jowls became more
saturnine with every shave he had, surveyed the strange
gathering with a clownish smile, while Mr. McBride, the
street bookie, told the company how often he had dodged the
Law by giving Tarry Bob a friendly drink.

In five minutes both policemen sat down and laid their
helmets on the sideboard among the numerous bottles and
fifteen minutes later they had loosened their tunics and were
dancing with the ladies, their heavy boots creating a louder
rumpus than they had come to stop.

Eddy Macdonnel stood in the crowded lobby craning his
head over to watch the lively scene. After a long while he
heard his mother say to Tarry Bob, who was protesting he
must go: "Och, hiv another wee nip! Shure a wee nip won't
kill ye!" then he saw the good-natured policeman drench
himself in beer as he put on his helmet into which some
playful guest had emptied a pint bottle.

Eddy's wits were staggering. "Human behaviour" had
muddled his understanding, and he mooned bewildered into
the kitchen where Jimmy sat half-asleep with a glass of
whisky trembling in his bronzed hand, while opposite him sat
a youth gazing in agony at the glass, expecting to see the
darlin' drink spilled on the floor.

Eddy took Jimmy's glass and placed it on the mantelshelf,
then picked up a postcard that lay face downward on the floor.
It was the picture of Meg Macgregor. He had fallen in love
with the picture himself and he looked at it again through
sentimental eyes that saw her average prettiness as dazzling
beauty. He had been nerving himself to ask Jimmy if he had a

photo of her to spare and was awaiting with adolescent impatience her sensational arrival. "Ye've dropped Meg's photo," he said, holding it up to Jimmy's wavering stare. The sailor thrust it aside. "Take it away!" he said. "Her face scunners me!"

"But it's Meg!" Eddy said. "Meg Macgregor. The girl ye're bringing home to marry!"

" 'Take her away!' I said," cried Jimmy with a royal wave of the hand. "There's nae wumman 'll run ma life for me!" The youth sitting by the table nodded his approval, then stood up and quickly drank off Jimmy's whisky.

Eddy studied his brother for a moment, desperately failing to remember some part of his book on psychology that would explain Jimmy's sudden jaundiced dismissal of Meg Macgregor. Then he drifted solemnly into the lobby, opened the stairhead door and wandered slowly down to the close-mouth. His confused head was ringing with a medley of folk-songs and music-hall choruses and his heart held the streams and hills and the women of the poetry of Robert Burns. He was thinking of Jeannie Lindsay and wishing he might find her standing at her close in South Wellington Street. But it was very late. He hurried round the corner in a queer, emotional tangle of sexual shame and desire, his romantic thoughts of Jeannie mingled with the shameful memory of his mother and the women dressing up in men's clothes and Bridget Delaney pulling up her skirts to her hips to show her bare legs to the men.

Moray McLaren

CHECKMATE

Lord Karnockie was one of those strange characters that only eighteenth-century Edinburgh has been able to produce. He was a judge of the High Court who combined a knowledge of law, and a gusto in its practice, with a love of literature of a rather pedantic kind, a deep knowledge of the more useless classics, a puritan exterior (he was long, lanky and dreich), a capacity for tavern conviviality and a warm heart for his friends—when he felt in the mood to expand it.

Facts, the acquisition of facts, especially in the law and in the history of ancient Greece and Rome, combined with a consumption of claret in what would seem to us these days unbelievable quantities, were his primary personal diversions. He never went to the Assembly dances, not so much because he bothered either to approve or disapprove of them, but simply because that sort of thing bored him. When not drinking, reading or talking, chess was his favourite evening pastime, especially on his circuit in the west, where he had many doughty opponents. Amongst the most formidable of these—indeed he had never managed to defeat him—was young Wattie Stewart. Wattie, too, was a typical product of that century in Scotland. He was a rip-roaring young lairdling who combined debauchery with pedantry. He ruled over his land and his tenants, after a fashion, well. And it was, perhaps, on account of his generosity and curious fitful efficiency that his capacity for producing local bastards and his habit of being drunk for days on end were passed over by the populace

66

and by the kirk session. None the less he was a well-read man, and quick in the intellect. He always defeated Lord Karnockie at chess.

Some of His Lordship's paradoxical qualities have already been described. One remains, however, to be mentioned. It was, to our eyes in these days, particularly detestable. He was a Hanging Judge. In that age and country he was not, of course, peculiar. The humane Lord Kames, the brutal Braxfield, shared this peculiarity with him. So did many others. But his gusto as a hanging judge *was* peculiar. He did not hound his victims to the gallows as did the abominable Braxfield, nor did he pedantically and politely lead them there as did Kames. He laughed, or rather sneered, them in that direction throughout the trial. He ended in silence after the verdict of "Guilty". Then he would permit himself some devastating and cruel witticism which would make even the eighteenth-century law clerks shudder. It was hardly believable that the man who uttered these words was the same long, pawky scholar who could be consulted in his library on any literary point, the jovial lawyer who was wont to sit at the head of the table in Blair's tavern dispensing bumper after bumper of claret to friend and stranger. Yet it was so.

He was a friend and rival of Lord Kames. He used to play chess with him and discuss literature and law with him. They never revealed to each other, however, their common gusto in the execution of the ultimate rites of the Scottish Law. Braxfield would have made no bones about it. He would have gloried in recounting how he had guffawed some poor gomeril to the gallows. The sadism of Kames and Karnockie was of a more exquisite kind. It was not spoken of, still less laughed, belched and guffawed over. It was too private, too delicious, even if its outward manifestations had to be made in a public court. It was their own. They did not speak about it.

Still, there was one thing that Karnockie envied Kames. This was a witticism which he had made while he was condemning a young man who was a noted chess-player—chess

67

was a favourite game in Scotland at that time. Lord Kames
had said, when the jury brought in the verdict of "Guilty",
the two words: "Checkmate, Mattie." This exquisite witticism had quickly circulated in Parliament House, much to the
sardonic amusement of the young advocates—also much to the
chagrin of Lord Karnockie, who wished he had said it himself.

However, there came an opportunity for him to say it, and,
indeed, improve upon it. Lord Karnockie saw it in advance
and relished it, but without any personal malice. The occasion
arose as follows.

Young Wattie Stewart had been involved in a brawl at the
village inn. It was, even for him, extremely disgraceful.
Women, whisky and sharp practice at cards had all been
involved. The affair had ended in a free fight, in which the
young laird had seized a kitchen knife and stabbed one of his
opponents. It had been a rash rather than a deliberate action,
with no more emotional impetus than *braggadoccio* or a desire
to frighten. Nevertheless he had killed a man. The county
would fain have had the whole thing hushed up, but matters
had gone too far. The murdered farmer's wife was clamorous.
There were too many witnesses; and the affair was mixed up
with other disgraceful things which it was impossible to
neglect. Young Wattie Stewart the lairdling was committed
for trial for murder at the circuit. And the judge on circuit was
Lord Karnockie.

It would be wrong to suggest that Karnockie had any
animus against the young man who had so frequently defeated
him at chess. He did not feel any more gusto at the prospect
of condemning him to the gallows than he had on any other
occasion of a like nature. What did, however, tickle his
humour was the prospect of defeating his old opponent with a
final and ineluctable stroke. Moreover he relished the fact
that by merely repeating Lord Kames's words he would be
able to improve upon them. Lord Kames had not been con-
sistently defeated at chess by the man he had condemned to
death.

Karnockie, having endured years of intellectual subjugation at the hands of the prisoner, would be able to extract an even greater gusto from the final move on the board of life and death. He turned the words over on his tongue in the judges' lodgings the night before the trial. He wondered whether he could improve on the form of them in any way to suit the situation. But he decided against it. And taking his whisky toddy to bed with him was soon asleep.

Meanwhile, in the town jail, Wattie Stewart was not feeling much inclined for sleep. He knew perfectly well what his verdict and judgment would be on the morrow. Nor did he in his heart resent the justice of either. Unlike the judge, however, his heart was filled with a bitter hatred for his old chess opponent and claret companion who was to pronounce judgment on him in the morning. Why should he, of all people, have this say on his earthly existence? It was monstrous. He had attended, merely for the sake of amusement, many of Lord Karnockie's circuit trials before. He knew in advance the kind of jeer and sneer with which he would be hustled from the dock as soon as the inevitable verdict had been pronounced. Then an idea came to him. He rang the bell for the turnkey.

Prisons in eighteenth-century Scotland were very different from what they are now. There were no disinfectant baths, clean cells and regulation hard benches. There was, on the one hand, indescribable filth and crowded conditions for the impoverished and vagrant prisoners. On the other hand, those prisoners who could afford it had lodgings (while awaiting trial) that almost amounted to comfortable private rooms. Such a one had Wattie Stewart while awaiting *his* trial. Indeed the turnkey had almost assumed the role of his private servant. He would be sent out for wine, spirits, snuff, food and other provisions, and was well rewarded for his services. He answered Wattie's bell immediately.

"See you here, Nicol," said Wattie; "you know you had to take my overclothes away when I was brought in here. Have you still got them?"

"Ay, I have that, sir."

"Then, Nicol, I'd beg one favour of you. Bring me my green surtout, the one with the velvet lapels. I want to appear the gentleman in court before his lordship tomorrow. Besides, it will be gey cold in court the morn."

"Oh, I couldnae dae that, sir."

"Well then, bring me a bottle of usquebaugh, and we'll discuss the matter over that."

The whisky was brought. Most of it went down Nicol's throat. Silver was exchanged and the green surtout was brought in. Wattie dismissed the turnkey and eagerly felt in the pockets. Yes. What he hoped would be there was still there. In the eighteenth century the searching of well-to-do prisoners was a fairly perfunctory affair. Lord Ferrars had been allowed to keep all his jewels and most of his bed-linen while he was awaiting trial for the murder of his valet!

Wearing his green surtout, the prisoner appeared well at ease in court the next morning. The case was obvious. Scarcely any evidence was brought on the panel's side. The jury were not absent ten minutes. The verdict was as expected.

The judge's lantern jaws dropped and dribbled in the pleasant anticipation of his aphorism. Then he said it:

"Weel, Wattie, I think this is checkmate at last."

"My lord," said Wattie, "I believe that before you pronounce sentence I have the right to a few words?"

"Ay, that is so," said his lordship, smacking his lean lips in the knowledge that these words would not amount to much. "Have your say. It'll be your last."

"Well, my lord, I have often defeated your lordship at the game of chess. You have now been present at my defeat in the game of life and death. Though little you had to do with my defeat save to grin at it. Had your lordship not had the bad taste to refer to a game in which you always lost" (here Karnockie looked a trifle discomposed) "I could not do what I am about to do."

Here he whipped out from the pocket of his green surtout a

70

pistol which had, by the carelessness of the prison authorities, been left there, and fired it at the judge.

The ball struck Lord Karnockie just above the heart. He was not instantly killed. But as he slipped from his judge's chair he knew that he was dying. The crimson of his blood was darker and deeper than the scarlet of his robes. He put his hand to the wetness of his mortal wound and was surprised he had so much blood in him. He had always thought of himself as so thin and arid. Yet even at this supreme moment his good humour did not desert him.

"Weel, Wattie," he gasped, "I reckon it's a drawn game." With that he slipped to the floor. The circuit was at an end.

Naomi Mitchison

IN THE FAMILY

It was in the family to be seeing things that are not meant to
be seen. And it was not nice for them, not at all. They could
have done without seeing the most of what they saw. Mostly
all of them had seen the Lights, one way and another, and his
mother had seen the Funeral itself coming round the head of
the glen, and fine she knew the Bearers, and the Corpse she
could guess, and sure enough that was how it was before the
week was out, but she herself was sick in her bed for the whole
day after it.

If you go far enough back, there was his grandfather's
uncle that was a great piper, and he was coming back over the
hills from a wedding at the far side. It was a good-going
wedding, the way they were in those days, and it had lasted all
of four nights, and they would not have been sparing of the
whisky for their pipers. And as he was coming back by
Knocnashee, the fairies came out from the hill and asked
would he come in a whilie and pipe for them. And he would
have done it sure enough, for the whisky had made him as
bold as a robin, but he was just too drunk to do justice to his
own pipes, so he said he would come to them another day.
He never did, and indeed, he died in his bed. But he was in a
terrible fear all his life afterwards in case they would mind on
what he had said. And there was a kind of fear on all the
family, in case it might be remembered on one of them, and he
would need to keep the promise of the old piper.

His father had a young sister, Janet, a terrible bonny lassie
she was, with a high colour on her. But there was a thing went

72

wrong and the doctor could not say right what it was, so he was for sending her to the hospital in Glasgow. Well then, the evening before she was to go, she was walking up by the old well, and who should she see but the fairy woman. And the fairy woman warned her and better warned her not to go to the hospital, walking beside her all the while without movement of her feet, the way it is with the fairy folk. And the lassie came back and she was gey put about and she said she would not go. So they sent for the doctor to tell him of it, but he was wild affronted and said he had it all arranged and go she must or the great doctors in Glasgow would have his head off. So the lassie grat and her mother grat, but the end of it was they could not go against the doctor, and the poor lassie went to the hospital and died there.

So the rest of them said to themselves that if ever they were to get a warning they would bide by it. But for long enough it did not come. His father, Donald MacMillan, had a wee glimpse of the fairies one time; he was under-keeper at the Castle and he was coming back in the early morning from setting his traps on the hill and as he came down by the back road the fairies were riding round the castle, wee dark folk on white ponies with a glitter of gold on the bridle. But he held his tongue about it, for it is not an under-keeper's place to be seeing the fairies belonging to the castle ones. And he did not like it, no, not at all, and after that he volunteered for the Army, and it was ten years before he came back.

But Angus himself had seen not a thing. And he was apt to say there was nothing at all in it, and when his sister Effie came back from a dance one night in a terrible fright and saying that a ghost had walked with her all the way from the cross-roads, he was not believing her. For the thing is this. You may know well enough that something has happened. But, gin the Kirk is against it, and the schools, and the newspapers and the wireless forby, you will find it hard enough to believe your own eyes and ears. And the other thing is, that, with yon kind of sights, it is never the same twice. I will see a thing one way and you will see it another, but maybe it is the same in itself. Yet it might be the Ministers are in the right of it and we should not be speaking of such things at all.

But, however that may be, Angus was a well-doing laddie. He was driving one of the Forestry lorries and he cared for his lorry the same as it was a horse. He was for ever cleaning and oiling it and putting in a wee thing here or there and never once did he have an accident on the road. And he was a Church member and in the choir and he was not drinking scarcely at all except maybe now and then, and he was going with a lassie that was in the choir too, and she was in the alto line and he was in the tenor. And not one of the family had seen an unchancy thing for years now, and his sister Effie married and with three bairns and indeed she was inclined to laugh at the story of her own ghost now. For it had mistaken her surely, the poor thing, since all it had been after from her was the lend of a horse and cart, and it turned out afterwards that it was an old soul from one of the crofts at the head of the glen and he had died more than a year back and terrible put about over this same thing and so he had needed to come back.

He had the Gaelic, had Angus, not so as to read excepting it might be some easy kind of song, but well enough to speak a bit and to know what was said to him. This was mostly because his father and mother would be speaking the Gaelic to one another across the table the way the bairns would not be understanding them, and Angus was that angry at this when he was a wee fellow that he started to learn the Gaelic out of pure devilment to know what his elders would be saying.

Well, the choir had been practising all winter and the time came when they were to go over and give a concert in aid of the church funds at Auchandrum, and there was to be a dance after. They would hire a bus and it would be just fine, with all the folk singing away to pass the time on the road and going back with the lasses, and indeed Angus was mostly sure that Peigi MacLean—for that was his lassie's name—would be sitting beside him at the back, though she would not promise.

Then it came on to two days before, and Angus had

finished up and parked his lorry at the saw-mill with a tarpaulin over her, and he was taking the short cut home
through the larches and by the old well that nobody went to
now, since there was a fine new County Council water supply
at that side of the village and some of the houses with bath-
rooms even. There was a woman sitting by the side of the
well and at first he thought she was a summer visitor and
maybe a painter or that, the way she had a long green cloak
of an old-fashioned kind that our own womenfolk would
never be wearing. But as he came nearer she stood, and he
saw that she was going to speak to himself and a kind of
uneasiness came at him that got suddenly worse when she
spoke to him by name and that in the Gaelic. So he got a grip
on the monkey wrench that he was taking back to the house
and he answered her and she began to walk by his side and he
saw that there was no movement of her feet under the green
cloak and for a while he could not anyways listen to what she
was saying, with the blood pouring in spate through him and
the sweat standing out on his forehead and the greatest fear
on him lest she should reach out her hand and touch his own.

But after a whilie it came to him that she was speaking
about the choir and their journey to Auchandrum and she was
warning him, that he must not, above all, let Peigi go on the
bus, or there would be no happiness for him all his life long.
And he tried wild to speak, but he could not get his mouth
round the words for a time. At last he said in the Gaelic:
"How are you telling me this, woman of the Sidhe?"

She said: "It is because of the friendship between ourselves
and your grandfather's uncle that was a good piper and a
kindly man, drunk or sober, and I am telling you for your
great good. Angus, son of Donald."

So he said: "How will I know if it is true?"

She smiled, and some way it was a sweet smile, but far off,
since she had the face and body of a young lassie, yet her look
was that of an old, old woman, beyond love or hate. She said:
"I will show a sign on the thing you hold in your hand, and
believe you me, Angus!"

And he looked full into her eyes, for the fear was beginning to leave him, but as he did that he began to see the young larches behind her on the hillside, and in a short while it was clear through her he was looking and nothing at all to show where she had been, only the sweat cold on his face. So he went home and said nothing, and his mother brought in the tea, and suddenly she laughed and asked him what kind of a job at all had he been doing on his lorry, for there was the monkey-wrench lying over on the press, and it was wreathed round with the bonny wild honeysuckle.

Well, he thought and he better thought, and he worked the talk round till his mother began to speak of her good sister Janet, who had not been let take the warning, but had died in the Glasgow hospital, and he thought it would be a wild thing if the like of thon were to happen to his own lassie through his fault. So when he had washed he went over to the choir practice and there sure enough was Peigi. So on the way back he was speaking to her, begging her not to go to the concert. But she was not listening to him at all, for she thought he was on for some kind of devilment and she said goodnight to him, kind of sharp.

Well, the next day he was hashing and fashing away at it and in the evening again he went over to Peigi's folks' house and he got the talk round to warnings, so that she would be prepared, and then, as she was seeing him to the gate, he told her how it had been. Well, she was terrible put about and at first she was not believing him, and then she was, but she had her dance dress washed and ironed and what would the rest of the lasses say? And there could be nothing in it and nobody believed in such blethers nowadays. And the more Angus pled and swat, the more reasons Peigi was finding not to be heeding him at all and the more she needed to say to herself that he had maybe been drinking and if she were to do what he asked, all the folk would be speaking of it and she was not to be made a clown of by Angus or any other lad, and it would be a great dance after the concert and was Angus not coming to be her partner?

"If you go, I will go, Peigi," said Angus, "for if there is a danger coming to you, I would soonest be there."

So he went to his bed and he tried to tell himself that none of this was real; but it was beyond him not to believe, and indeed in his sleeping he was seeing the fairy woman just as plain, and she speaking to him again. And in the morning it was on him wild to keep Peigi from the concert, yet all the forenoon he could not think of a way. But towards four he was taking back the lorry empty to the saw-mill and he saw Peigi on the road going for a message for her mother. He cried on her to come up beside him and he would give her a lift along, and up she came. But when he got to the cross-roads he put on speed and swung his lorry round and up the glen. "What in God's name are you up to, Angus!" said Peigi, and held on tight.

"I am taking you away from the concert," said Angus, and he did not look at her, but only at the road ahead of him.

"Well then, I will scream!" said Peigi.

"It will not help you any," said Angus, "and maybe least said is soonest mended. And indeed I am terribly sorry, Peigi, but it is on me to do this. And you had best not try to snatch at the steering wheel, Peigi, for I would need to hit you and I amna wanting to."

So Peigi sat as far as she could from him in the cab of the lorry, and they never passed another car, but only an old farm cart or so, and Angus hooted and put on all speed and there was nothing she could do, and by and by she cried a little because she was thinking of the dance dress and the nice evening she would be missing, and what in all the world could she say to the rest of the choir?

But Angus was watching his petrol gauge. He was ten miles out of the village now, and he swung round on to a side road that went up past the common grazing towards some old quarries. There would be no chance of Peigi hailing a car and getting a lift back on a road the like of this. And they went bumping up along the old tracks and it was near six and the bus would be starting for Auchandrum in half an hour. At last

F

he stopped the lorry at the mouth of one of the quarries and he said: "I am that spited, Peigi, but I know well I am in the right of it."

Peigi said nothing and when he tried to come near her she snatched herself away. So there they sat and no pleasure in it for either of them, but well they knew what would be said of them in the village. And forby that, Angus was thinking how it would be when he did not bring his lorry back to the saw-mill. He liked his job with the Forestry fine, but this way he would be leaving it with no good character. And the more he thought, the blacker things looked ahead of him, and sudden he began to wonder if the fairy woman had played a trick on him. And it was a terrible thought, yon.

So he started up his engine again and he backed and turned and came down cannily in second and Peigi beside him as cross as a sack of weasels. "Will you no' speak to me at all, Peigi?" he asked, as they came out into the glen road down towards the village.

"I will never speak to you again!" she said, and a terrible hurt feeling came over his heart and he hated the fairy woman and the warning and all the two days and nights of it. So that way they came down to the village. "Do you not take me to the house!" said Peigi suddenly, "leave you me here and maybe—och, maybe they'll not know and there could be time to think of a thing to say!"

He stopped the lorry and jumped out to help her down, but she had jumped clear, and when he came to her she gave a cry and started to run down the road. So he did not follow until she was out of sight and he knew she would take the back road by old Donnie's hen house.

As he came down to the post office he saw a ring of folk round the telephone kiosk and his own brother cried on him to stop and he jumped out. "Is it yourself, Angus!" his brother shouted and seized him by the two hands and there were tears streaming out of his eyes and then he said, "Did Peigi go with the choir?"

"She did not," said Angus and there was her father shaking

78

him by the hands as well, and it all came out there had been an accident to the bus and three or four folk hurt bad and mostly all cut with the glass and they had just heard it on the telephone, but they werena just sure who was on it. And Angus found himself going off into a wild silly kind of laughing and he could not stop himself any. So he got back into the lorry and drove off to the saw-mill and parked her, and then he started to clean her and polish her, for he did not know what the Forester would say, and he might be getting his books and he might never be back in the cab of his lorry.

Sure enough, while he was at it, up came the Forester, for he had been terrible put about when Angus MacMillan never brought in the lorry, and he mostly so dependable, and the Forester had his own bosses over him. "So this is you at last!" said the Forester. "And what have you to say?"

But Angus found no words for he could not begin to speak of a fairy woman. At last he kicked at the tyre of the lorry and said: "I am terrible sorry, Duncan, and I have not hurt her any, and—and I will pay for the petrol."

"I will need to think what to do about this," said the Forester, "for I cannot have such a carry-on with my lorries. I will see you in the morning." So Angus said never a word, but home he went, and his own folk speaking about nothing but the accident and the lucky he was to be out of it. They knew that Peigi MacLean had not been in it, but they did not know yet that she had been with him. One of his chums had a leg broken, and another was bleeding from his inside and the doctor up with him, and Peigi's young sister had a terrible nasty cut on her head and it was a wonder nobody was killed. Angus went off to his bed and he was terrible tired, but some way he could not sleep. And at least he said to himself, it was a true warning, and I took it, and the fairy has not tricked me. So he got out of his bed and felt for his flash, and he walked around in his shirt looking for any one thing that was worth giving as a gift. And there seemed to be nothing. For what would a fairy do with the set of cuff links he won at the Nursing Association raffle or the printed letter that had come with his Welcome Home money or the bottle of port he was saving up for Effie's new bairn's christening, or his good boots, even? But at last he came on a thing and it was a wee kind of medal that his father had worn at his watch chain and his father before him, and it might have belonged to the piper for that matter. He did not know was it silver or not and he gave it a rub on his sleeve. And he went out in his bare feet, and his shirt blowing round his legs, and up to the well, and the queer thing was he kind of half wanted to see the fairy woman, but there was no breath at all of her. So he threw the wee medal into the well and he stood and he said a kind of half prayer, and he came stumbling back down the path with the stones sore on his feet, but after that he slept as quiet as a herring in a barrel.

But the next morning he went down to the saw-mill and the Forester sent for him to his wee office with the papers and the telephone and the bundles of axes and saw blades. But still he could say nothing, and after a time the Forester said in an angry kind of way that if he had no excuse then he was sacked. But at that Angus had to speak and out it came, the whole story, and halfway through the Forester got up and shut the door of his office. At the end he said: "There is folks that would shut you up in the Asylum for the like of yon, Angus."

"But it is not touched I am!" said Angus anxiously.

"I know plenty that would think it," said the Forester. "So it was a green cloak she was wearing, yon one? Aye, aye. It is fortunate altogether that you have the Gaelic. But I am wondering wild what would the Minister say."

"You will not tell him, Duncan!" said Angus. But he knew that the Minister was no great favourite with the Forester, on account he had complained that the noise of the saw-mill was stopping him from composing his sermons, and everyone in the place knew that the half of them came out of books.

The Forester said nothing to this, and Angus stood first on one foot and then on the other. At last the Forester said: "Are you for marrying Peigi?"

80

"I am, surely," said Angus, "but I am no' just so sure of herself. I amna sure if she will speak to me, even."

"Well," said the Forester, "you had better be asking her and that way you will keep this story in the one family and maybe it will stay quietest so, for it doesna do to be speaking of such things."

"I just darena ask her and that it is the truth," said Angus.

"Well," said the Forester, "if you are marrying Peigi MacLean I will overlook this and keep you on, but if you havena the courage, then you can take your books and off with you and best if you go away out of the place altogether." And Angus went stumbling out the door of the wee office, and the Forester took two new axe heads out of the store and checked them off.

Word had got about of how Angus and Peigi had passed the evening of the concert, and Angus getting plenty from his mates of what could be done with a nice lassie in the cab of a lorry or in the back of it even, and they all thinking it was for badness he had taken her away and kind of half proud of him. But the accident to the bus had more to it, so the talk went over to that, and glad enough was Angus.

After his tea he went over to the MacLean's house, and there was father MacLean staking his peas, and Angus asked after Peigi's sister, and the district nurse was in with her, and then he spoke of the great growth on the peas. At last old MacLean said: "What is this I hear about yourself and Peigi, Angus MacMillan?"

Angus said: "It is true enough she came for a drive in my lorry, but it wasna for anything bad."

"You are telling me that," said old MacLean and he began to fill his pipe, "but you were away for three hours and what could you find to be speaking about? So I must ask you, what were you doing?"

"I was driving the lorry mostly," said Angus, "and Peigi wasna speaking to me, she was that cross."

"Then I will ask you, why did you drive the lorry with my daughter in it?"

Then Angus cleared his throat and said in a kind of loud voice: "I had a warning that Peigi was not to go with the choir."

Mr. MacLean said nothing for a time, but scraped his boot on the edge of a spade and puffed away at his pipe, and at last he said: "I was hearing just that. And she would have been killed, likely, if she had been in the bus."

"I was thinking so," said Angus in a half whisper. For she would have been next to her sister and most likely on the outside next to the glass. And then the District Nurse came out of the house and said cheerily that the lassie was going on fine, and now she must be off to the others and what a carry-on she was having with them all. And she started her wee car and drove off.

"Well, well," said Mr. MacLean, "it is in your family to be seeing things. And things are mostly unchancy. But this time it was the great chance for my own lassie. Aye, aye. You will be wanting to see Peigi, likely?"

"It is what I would like most in the world," said Angus, "but——"

"Well, come you in," said Mr. MacLean, "and we will say no more over this matter of the warning." They went into the house together. Peigi was there, washing her sister's frock that had been spoilt a bit. Her father said: "I will go through and see your sister."

Peigi went on slapping and scrubbing away at the dress, letting on she did not see there was a soul there.

After a time Angus said: "Are you speaking to me, Peigi?"

"Ach well——" she said, "I might."

"Duncan was at me over me taking the lorry," said Angus.

"Was he now? And I am sure he was quite right. You should not be taking things without leave."

"He spoke the way he might be giving me my books, Peigi."

Peigi let the frock fall back into the lather. "The dirty clown! How could he do that on you?"

"Well," said Angus, "he was only kind of half believing

me, maybe. If he were to believe me right I am thinking there would be nothing said. Ach, Peigi, he would believe me if he thought I had done it because I loved you true! He was asking were you and I to be married, Peigi. But I was saying I daredna ask you."

"How?" she said.

"Och well, if you hadna been speaking to me, it would have been kind of difficult, Peigi."

Peigi was flicking the suds off her fingers. She said into the air: "Isn't it wild now, to think of the nice time we could have been having on the hillside and we just ourselves, if only you had explained the thing right to me at the first!"

"Indeed and I did my best!" said Angus.

"Aye, but I was not knowing then that the bus would have this accident, and how would anyone with a grain of sense believe you, Angus? But we will not speak any more of this warning nor anything to do with it, because I am thinking we will have plenty else to speak about."

Alexander Reid

THE KITTEN

The feet were tramping directly towards her. In the hot darkness under the tarpaulin the cat cuffed a kitten to silence and listened intently.

She could hear the scruffling and scratching of hens about the straw-littered yard; the muffled grumbling of the turning churn in the dairy; the faint clink and jangle of harness from the stable—drowsy, comfortable, reassuring noises through which the clang of the iron-shod boots on the cobbles broke ominously.

The boots ground to a halt, and three holes in the cover, brilliant diamond-points of light, went suddenly black. Couching, the cat waited, then sneezed and drew back as the tarpaulin was thrown up and glaring white sunlight struck at her eyes.

She stood over her kittens, the fur of her back bristling and the pupils of her eyes narrowed to pin-points. A kitten mewed plaintively.

For a moment, the hired man stared stupidly at his discovery, then turned towards the stable and called harshly: "Hi, Maister! Here a wee."

A second pair of boots clattered across the yard, and the face of the farmer, elderly, dark and taciturn, turned down on the cats.

"So that's whaur she's been," commented the newcomer slowly.

He bent down to count the kittens and the cat struck at him, scoring a red furrow across the back of his wrist. He caught

her by the neck and flung her roughly aside. Mewing she
came back and began to lick her kittens. The Master turned
away.

"Get rid of them," he ordered. "There's ower mony cats
aboot this place."

"Aye, Maister," said the hired man.

Catching the mother he carried her, struggling and swearing, to the stable, flung her in, and latched the door. From the
loft he secured an old potato sack and with this in his hand
returned to the kittens.

There were five, and he noticed their tigerish markings
without comprehending as, one by one, he caught them and
thrust them into the bag. They were old enough to struggle,
spitting, clawing and biting at his fingers.

Throwing the bag over his shoulder he stumped down the
hill to the burn, stopping twice on the way to wipe the sweat
that trickled down his face and neck, rising in beads between
the roots of his lint-white hair.

Behind him, the buildings of the farm-steading shimmered
in the heat. The few trees on the slope raised dry, brittle
branches towards a sky bleached almost white. The smell of
the farm, mingled with peat-reek, dung, cattle, milk, and the
dark tang of the soil, was strong in his nostrils, and when he
halted there was no sound but his own breathing and the
liquid burbling of the burn.

Throwing the sack on the bank, he stepped into the stream.
The water was low, and grasping a great boulder in the bed
of the burn he strained to lift it, intending to make a pool.

He felt no reluctance at performing the execution. He had
no feelings about the matter. He had drowned kittens before.
He would drown them again.

Panting with his exertion, the hired man cupped water
between his hands and dashed it over his face and neck in a
glistening shower. Then he turned to the sack and its
prisoners.

He was in time to catch the second kitten as it struggled out
of the bag. Thrusting it back and twisting the mouth of the

sack close, he went after the other. Hurrying on the sun-browned grass, treacherous as ice, he slipped and fell head-long, but grasped the runaway in his outflung hand.

It writhed round immediately and sank needle-sharp teeth into his thumb so that he grunted with pain and shook it from him. Unhurt, it fell by a clump of whins and took cover beneath them.

The hired man, his stolidity shaken by frustration tried to follow. The whins were thick and, scratched for his pains, he drew back, swearing flatly, without colour or passion.

Stooping, he could see the eyes of the kitten staring at him from the shadows under the whins. Its back was arched, its fur erect, its mouth open, and its thin lips drawn back over its tiny white teeth.

The hired man saw, again without understanding, the beginnings of tufts on the flattened ears. In his dull mind he felt a dark resentment at this creature which defied him. Rising, he passed his hand up his face in heavy thought, then slithering down to the stream, he began to gather stones. With an armful of small water-washed pebbles he returned to the whins.

First he strove to strike at the kitten from above. The roof of the whins was matted and resilient. The stones could not penetrate it. He flung straight then—to maim or kill—but the angle was difficult and only one missile reached its mark, rebounding from the ground and striking the kitten a glancing blow on the shoulder.

Kneeling, his last stone gone, the hired man watched, the red in his face deepening and thin threads of crimson rising in the whites of his eyes as the blood mounted to his head. A red glow of anger was spreading through his brain. His mouth worked and twisted to an ugly rent.

"Wait—wait," he cried hoarsely, and, turning, ran heavily up the slope to the trees. He swung his whole weight on a low-hanging branch, snapping it off with a crack like a gun-shot.

Seated on the warm, short turf, the hired man prepared his

weapon, paring at the end of the branch till the point was sharp as a dagger. When it was ready he knelt on his left knee and swung the branch to find the balance. The kitten was almost caught.

The savage lance-thrust would have skewered its body as a trout is spiked on the beak of a heron, but the point, slung too low, caught in a fibrous root and snapped off short. Impotently the man jabbed with his broken weapon while the kitten retreated disdainfully to the opposite fringe of the whins.

In the slow-moving mind of the hired man the need to destroy the kitten had become an obsession. Intent on this victim, he forgot the others abandoned by the burn side; forgot the passage of time, and the hard labour of the day behind him. The kitten, in his distorted mind, had grown to a monstrous thing, centring all the frustrations of a brutish existence. He craved to kill. . . .

But so far the honours lay with the antagonist.

In a sudden flash of fury the man made a second bodily assault on the whins and a second time retired defeated.

He sat down on the grass to consider the next move as the first breath of the breeze wandered up the hill. As though that were the signal, in the last moments of the sun, a lark rose, close at hand, and mounted the sky on the flood of its own melody.

The man drank in the coolness thankfully, and, taking a pipe from his pocket, lit the embers of tobacco in the bowl. He flung the match from him, still alight, and a dragon's tongue of amber flame ran over the dry grass before the breeze, reached a bare patch of sand and flickered out. Watching it, the hired man knitted his brows and remembered the heather-burning, and mountain hares that ran before the scarlet terror. And he looked at the whins.

The first match blew out in the freshening wind, but at the second the bush burst into crackling flame.

The whins were alight on the leeward side and burned slowly against the wind. Smoke rose thickly, and sparks and lighted shivers of wood sailed off on the wind to light new fires on the grass of the hillside.

Coughing as the pungent smoke entered his lungs, the man circled the clump till the fire was between him and the farm. He could see the kitten giving ground slowly before the flame. He thought for a moment of lighting this side of the clump also and trapping it between two fires; took his matches from his pocket, hesitated, and replaced them. He could wait.

Slowly, very slowly, the kitten backed towards him. The wind fought for it, delaying, almost holding the advance of the fire through the whins.

Showers of sparks leaped up from the bushes that crackled and spluttered as they burned, but louder than the crackling of the whins, from the farm on the slope of the hill, came another noise—the clamour of voices. The hired man walked clear of the smoke that obscured his view and stared up the hill.

The thatch of the farmhouse, dry as tinder, was aflare.

Gaping, he saw the flames spread to the roof of the byre, to the stables; saw the farmer running the horses to safety, and heard the thunder of hooves as the scared cattle, turned loose, rushed from the yard. He saw a roof collapse in an uprush of smoke and sparks, while a kitten, whose sire was a wild cat, passed out of the whins unnoticed and took refuge in a deserted burrow.

From there, with cold, defiant eyes, it regarded the hired man steadfastly.

Neil M. Gunn

THE TAX-GATHERER

"Blast it," he muttered angrily. "Where is the accursed place?"

He looked at the map again spread before him on the steering-wheel. Yes, it should be just here. There was the cross-roads. He threw a glance round the glass of his small saloon car and saw a man's head bobbing beyond the hedge. At once he got out and walked along the side of the road.

"Excuse me," he cried. The face looked at him over the hedge. "Excuse me, but can you tell me where Mrs. Martha Williamson stays?"

"Mrs. Who?"

"Mrs. Martha Williamson."

"No," said the face slowly, and moved away. He followed it for a few paces to a gap in the hedge. "No," said the man again, and turned to call a spaniel out of the turnips. He had a gun under his arm and was obviously a gamekeeper.

"Well, she lives about here, at Ivy Cottage."

"Ivy Cottage? Do you mean the tinkers?" And the gamekeeper regarded him thoughtfully.

"Yes. I suppose so."

"I see," said the gamekeeper, looking away. "Turn up to your right at the cross-roads there and you'll see it standing back from the road."

He thanked the gamekeeper and set off, walking quickly so that he needn't think too much about his task, for it was new to him.

When he saw the cottage, over amongst some bushes with

a rank growth of nettles at one end, he thought it a miserable place, but when he came close to the peeling limewash, the torn-down ivy, the sagging roof, the broken stone doorstep thick with trampled mud, he saw that it was a wretched hovel.

The door stood half-open, stuck. He knocked on it and listened to the acute silence. He knocked again firmly and thought he heard thin whisperings. He did not like the hushed fear in the sounds, and was just about to knock peremptorily when there was a shuffling, and, quietly as an apparition, a woman was there.

She stood twisted, lax, a slim, rather tall figure, with a face the colour of the old limewash. She clung to the edge of the door in a manner unhumanly pathetic, and looked at him out of dark, soft eyes.

"Are you Mrs. Williamson?"

After a moment she said, "Yes."

"Well, I've come about that dog. Have you taken out the licence yet?"

"No."

"Well, it's like this," he said, glancing away from her. "We don't want to get you into trouble. But the police reported to us that you had the dog. Now, you can't have a dog without paying a licence. You know that. So, in all the circumstances, the authorities decided that if you paid a compromise fine of seven-and-six, and took out the licence, no more would be said about it. You would not be taken to court." He looked at her again, and saw no less than five small heads poking round her ragged dark skirt. "We don't want you to get into trouble," he said. "But you've got to pay by Friday—or you'll be summonsed. There's no way out."

She did not speak, stood there unmoving, clinging to the door, a feminine creature waiting dumbly for the blow.

"Have you a husband?" he asked.

"Yes," she said, after a moment.

"Where is he?"

"I don't know," she answered, in her soft, hopeless voice. He wanted to ask her if he had left her for good, but could not, and this irritated him, so he said calmly, "Well, that's the position, as you know. I was passing, and, seeing we had got no word of your payment, I thought I'd drop in and warn you. We don't want to take you to court. So my advice to you is to pay up—and at once, or it will be too late."

She did not answer. As he was about to turn away the dregs of his irritation got the better of him. "Why on earth did you want to keep the dog, anyway?"

"We tried to put him away, but he wouldn't go," she said.

His brows gathered. "Oh, well, it's up to you," he replied coldly, and he turned and strode back to his car. Slamming the door after him, he gripped the wheel, but could not, at the last instant, press the self-starter. He swore to himself in a furious rage. Damn it all, what concern was it of his? None at all. As a public official he had to do his job. It was nothing to him. If a person wanted to enjoy the luxury of keeping a dog, he or she had to pay for it. That's all. And he looked for the self-starter, but, with his finger on the button, again could not press it. He twisted in his seat. Fifteen bob! he thought. Go back and slip her fifteen bob? Am I mad? He pressed the self-starter and set the engine off in an unnecessary roar. As he turned at the cross-roads he hesitated before shoving the gear lever into first, then shoved it and set off. If a fellow was to start paying public fines where would it end? Sentimental? Absolutely.

By the following Tuesday it was clear she had not paid.

"The case will go on," said his chief in the office.

"It's a hard case," he answered. "She won't be able to pay." His voice was calm and official.

"She'll have to pay—one way or the other," answered his chief, with the usual trace of official satire in his voice.

"She's got a lot of kids," said the young man.

"Has she?" said the chief. "Perhaps she could not help having them—but the dog is another matter." He smiled, and glanced at the young man, who awkwardly smiled back.

There was nothing unkindly in the chief's attitude, merely a complete absence of feeling. He was dealing with "a file", and had no sympathy for anyone who tried to evade the law. He prosecuted with lucid care, and back in his office smiled with satisfaction when he got a conviction. For to fail in getting a conviction was to be inept in his duty. Those above him frowned upon such ineptitude.

All the same, the young man felt miserable. If he hadn't gone to the cottage it would have been all right. But the chief had had no unnecessary desire for a court case—particularly one of those hard cases that might get into the press. Not that that mattered really, for the law had to be carried out. Than false sentiment against the law of the land there could, properly regarded, be nothing more reprehensible—because it was so easy to indulge.

"By the way," said the chief, as he was turning away, "I see the dog has been shot. You didn't mention that?"

"No. I——" He had forgotten to ask the woman if the dog was still with her. "I—as a matter of fact, I didn't think about it, seeing it was a police report, and therefore no evidence from us needed."

"Quite so," said his chief reticently, as he turned to his file.

"Who shot it?" the young man could not help asking.

"A gamekeeper, apparently."

The young man withdrew, bit on his embarrassment at evoking the chief's "reticence", and thought of the gamekeeper who might believe that if the dog was shot nothing more could be done about the case. As if the liability would thereby be wiped out! As if it would make the slightest difference to the case!

In his own room he remembered the gamekeeper and his curious look. Decent of him all the same to have tried to help. If the children's faces had been sallow and hollow from underfeeding, what could the dog have got? Nothing, unless——The thought dawned: the gamekeeper had probably shot the brute without being asked. Poaching rabbits and game? Perhaps the mainstay of the family? He laughed in his nostrils. When you're down you're right down, down and out. Absolutely. With a final snort of satire, he took some papers from the "pending" cover and tried to concentrate on an old woman's application for a pension. It seemed quite straightforward, though he would have to investigate her circumstances. Then he saw the children's faces again.

He had hardly been conscious of looking at them at the time. In fact, after that first glance of surprise he had very definitely not looked at them. The oldest was a girl of nine or ten, thin and watery, fragile, with her mother's incredible pallor and black eyes. The stare from those considering eyes, blank and dumb, and yet wary. They didn't appeal: trust could not touch them; they waited, just waited, for—the only hope—something less than the worst.

And the little fellow of seven or eight—sandy hair, inflamed eyelids, and that something about the expression, the thick, half-open mouth, suggesting the mental deficient. Obviously from the father's side, physically. The father had deserted them. Was perhaps in quod somewhere else, for they had only recently returned from their travels to the cottage. How did they manage even to live in it without being turned out? But the police would have that in hand as well! There was something too soft about the woman. She would never face up to her husband. When he was drunk, her softness would irritate him; he would clout her one. She was feckless. Her body had slumped into a pliant line, utterly hopeless, against the door. All at once he saw the line as graceful, and this unexpected vision added the last touch to derision.

The young man had observed in his life already that if his mind was keen on some subject he would come across references to it in the oddest places, in books dealing with quite other matters, from the most unlikely people. But this, carefully considered, was not altogether fortuitous. For example, when the old woman who had applied for the Old Age Pension asked him if he would have a cup of tea, he hesitated, not because he particularly wanted to have a cup of tea, but because he vaguely wanted to speak to her about the ways of tinkers, for Ivy Cottage was little more than a mile away.

His hesitation, however, the hesitation of an important

G

official who had arrived in a motor-car and upon whom the granting of her pension depended (as she thought), excited her so much that before she quite knew what she was doing she was on her knees before the fire, flapping the dull peat embers with her apron, for she did not like, in front of him, to bend her old grey head and blow the embers to a flame. As he was watching her she suddenly stopped flapping, with an expression of almost ludicrous dismay, and mumbled something about not having meant to do that. At once he was interested, for clearly there was something involved beyond mere politeness. The old folk in this northern land, he had found, were usually very polite, and he liked their ways and curious beliefs. The fact that they had a Gaelic language of their own attracted him, for he was himself a student of French, and, he believed, somewhat of an authority on Balzac.

Fortunately for the old lady, a sprightly tongue of flame ran up the dry peat at that moment, and she swung the kettle over it. "Now it won't be long," she said, carefully backing up the flame with more peat.

She was a quick-witted, bright-eyed old woman, and as she hurried to and fro getting the tea things on the table they chatted pleasantly. Presently, when she seated herself and began to pour the tea, he asked her in the friendliest way why she had stopped flapping her apron.

She glanced at him and then said, "Och, just an old woman's way."

But he would not have that, and rallied her. "Come, now, there was something more to it than that."

And at last she said: "It's just an old story in this part of the world and likely it will not be true. But I will tell it to you, seeing you say you like stories of the kind, but you will have to take it as you get it, for that's the way I got it myself, more years ago now than I can remember. It is a story about our Lord at the time of His crucifixion. You will remember that when our Lord was being crucified they nailed Him to the Cross. But before they could do that they needed the nails, and the nails were not in it. So they tried to get the nails made, but no one would make them. They asked the Roman soldiers to make them, but they would not. Perhaps it was not their business to make the nails. Anyway, they would not make them. So they asked the Jews to make the nails, but they would not make them either. No, they would not make them. No one would make the nails that were needed to crucify our Lord. And when they were stuck now, and did not know what to do, who should they see coming along but a tinker with his little leather apron on him. So they asked him if he would make the nails. And he said yes, he would make them. And to make the nails he needed a fire. So a fire was made, but it would not go very well, so he bent down in front of it and flapped it with his leather apron. In that way the fire went and the nails were made. And so it came about that the tinkers became wanderers, and were never liked by the people of the world anywhere. And that's the story."

When at last he drove away from the old woman's house he came to the cross-roads and, a few yards beyond, drew up. This is the place, he thought, and he felt it about him, gripped the wheel hard, and sat still. Irritation began to get the better of him. Anyone could see he was a fool. He got out and stretched his legs and lit a cigarette. There was no one in the turnip field, no one anywhere. All at once he walked back quickly to the cross-roads, turned right, and again saw the cottage. It was looking at him with a still, lopsided, idiotic expression. His flesh quickened and drew taut in cool anger. He threw the cigarette away, emptied his mind, and came to the door, which was exactly as it had been before, half open and stuck.

When he had knocked once, and no one answered, he felt like retreating, so he knocked very loudly the second time, and the woman materialized. There was no other word for it. There she was, with the graceful twist in her dejected body, attached to the edge of the door. Was she expecting the blow? Was there something not so much antagonistic as withdrawn, prepared to endure, in the pathos of her attitude? She knew how to wait, in any case.

"I see you didn't pay," he said.

She did not answer. She could not have been more than thirty.

"Well, you have got to appear before the court now," he asserted, and added, with a lighthearted brutality, "or the police will come and fetch you. Hadn't you the money to pay?" And he looked at her.

"No," she said, looking back at him.

"So you hadn't the money," he said, glancing away with the smile of official satire. "And what are you going to do now—go to prison?"

The children were poking their heads round her skirts again. Their fragility appeared extreme, possibly because they were unwashed. Obviously they were famished.

She did not answer.

"Look here," he said, "this is no business of mine." He took out his pocket-book. His hands shook as he extracted a pound note. "Here's something for you. That'll pay for every-thing. The only thing I want you *never* to do is to mention that I gave it to you. Do you understand?"

She could not answer for looking at the pound note. If he had been afraid of a rush of gratitude he might have saved himself the worry. She took it stupidly and glanced at him as if there might be a trick in all this somewhere. Then he saw a stirring in her eyes, a woman's divination of character, a slow welling of understanding in the black deeps. It was pathetic.

"That's all right," he said, and turned away as if she had thanked him.

When he got back into his car he felt better. That was all over, anyway. She was just stupid, a weak, stupid woman who had got trodden down. Tough luck on her. But she certainly wouldn't give him away. Perhaps he ought to have em-phasized that part of it more? By God, I would never live it down in the office! Never! He began to laugh as he bowled along. He felt he could trust her. She was not the sort to give anything away. Too frightened. Experience had taught her how to hold her tongue before the all-important males of the world—not to mention the all-important females! She knew the old conspiracy all right and then some! His mirth increased. That he had felt he could not afford the pound—a pound is a pound, by heavens!—added now to the fun of the whole affair.

He did not go to court. After all, he might feel embarrassed; and the silly woman might, if she saw him, turn to him or depend on him or something. Moreover, he did not know how these affairs were conducted. So far it had not been his business. Besides, he disliked the whole idea of court proceedings. Time enough for that when he *had* to turn up.

Before lunch the chief came into his room for some papers. The young man repressed his excitement, for he had been wondering how the case had gone, having, only a few minutes before, remembered the possibility of court expenses. He could not bring himself to ask the result, but the chief, as he was going out, paused and said: "That woman from Ivy Cottage, the dog case, she was convicted."

"Oh. I'm glad you got the case through."

"Yes. A silly woman. The bench was very considerate in the circumstances. Didn't put on any extra fine. No expenses. Take out the licence and pay the seven-and-six compromise fine—or five days. She was asked if she could pay. She said no. So they gave her time to pay."

The young man regarded the point of his pen. "So she's off again," he said, with official humour.

"No. She elected to go to prison. She put the bench rather in a difficulty, but she was obdurate."

"You mean—they've put her in prison?"

"Presumably. There was no other course at the time."

"But the children—what'll happen to them?"

"No doubt the police will give the facts to the Inspector of Poor. It's up to the local authorities now. We wash our hands of it. If people will keep dogs they must know what to expect!" He smiled dryly and withdrew.

The young man sat back in his chair and licked his dry lips. She had cheated him. She had . . . she preferred . . . let him think. Clearly the pound mattered more than the five days. His money she would have left with the eldest girl, or some of it, with instructions what to buy and how to feed the children. She would have said to the eldest girl, "I'll be away for a few days, but don't worry, I'll be back. And meantime . . ."

But no, she would tell the eldest everything, by the pressure of instinct, of reality. That would bring the eldest into it; make her feel responsible for the young ones. And food . . . food . . . the overriding avid interest in food. Food—it was everything. The picture formed in his mind of the mother taking leave of her children.

It was pretty hellish, really. By God, he thought, we're as hard as nails. He threw his pen down, shoved his chair back, and strolled to the window.

The people passed on the pavement, each for himself or herself, upright, straight as nails, straight as spikes.

He turned from them, looked at his watch, feeling weary and gloomy, and decided he might as well go home to lunch, though it was not yet ten minutes to one. Automatically taking the white towel from its nail on the far side of the cupboard, he went out to wash his hands.

Winifred Duke

THE HALLOWE'EN PARTY

I'm aye ane for a ploy. I dinna mind whit the excuse is, whether it's a weddin', or a tea-party, or Hogmanay, or a Public Holiday. It's a' the same tae me. I like fine gettin' the invitation, an' thinkin' oot whit I'll wear, an' gangin' when the time comes, an' talkin' aboot it aifterwards wi' ither bodies. It's richt he'rtenin', ye ken, tae meet yer friends, forby haein' a meal in anither hoose, wi' nae washin'-up ava.

Hallowe'en's a great time for parties in Carlonie. It's no' only the young folks, mind ye, but we auld yins get grand fun oot o' it. O' course I'm lang past bobbin' for aipples, an' sic-like folly, but a Hallowe'en tea is no' juist the same as an ordinary ane. There's a queer-like feelin', as though ye micht meet a ghaist roond the corner gaein' hame, an' it's fine the way ye sometimes get yer wish.

Last Hallowe'en we had a party at Mrs. Robieson's. Hae I no' tell't ye aboot her afore? She's a Carlonie body, but she marriet an' went away, an' when she cam' back she was a widow, wi' nae family. She aye said she'd like tae dee in Carlonie, but I hope we'll keep her beside us a whilie yet. I canna think o' Carlonie wantin' Mrs. Robieson.

When Hallowe'en was comin' near she speired at me aboot gi'en' a party. It was no' for the bairns or the young yins, she says, but she was for haein' folks like hersel', an' whit did I suggest they should dae? "There'll be yersel', o' course," says she. "I'm dependin' on ye to see me through, an' there's Mrs. Sturrock. She's lonely since Phemie marriet, an' she was tellin' me she's to hae her sister frae Inverness beside her for a week then, so that'll be fower, countin' oorsel's. An' can ye suggest ony ithers?"

"Whit aboot Miss Todd?" I says. "She's a richt cheery body."

"Ay," says Mrs. Robieson. "We'll hae Miss Todd, an' I was thinkin' o' Mrs. Fraser. Her an' me's billies, an' the rest a' ken her. That's six. We could hae mair, though. My table'll seat eight at a pinch."

I thocht a bittie, an' then I suggested Miss Grieve. I saw Mrs. Robieson's face fa', an' I didna wonder, for a ploy wi' Miss Grieve's no muckle fun.

There's some folks seem born sour, an' puir Miss Grieve was ane o' them. I'm no' sayin' she hadna had a hard life, but, maircy me! so hae maist o' us, an' we dinna gang aboot wi' faces as lang as Leith Walk because o' it. I never mind Miss Grieve bein' pleased wi' onything, an' I've ken't her for forty odd years. Gin it was fine, she'd say the fairmers wantit rain, an' when it rained she'd tell ye we never saw the sun in oor climate, an' o' course it was wet because she'd planned a big washin'. Folks focht shy o' her, wi' her grievances an' her trick o' buryin' a'body, so she was left oot o' a'thing. When a trip or a party was bein' planned they aye said: "Och! we'll na hae Miss Grieve. She'll spoil it a'."

"Miss Grieve?" says Mrs. Robieson till me noo. "No' me."

"She's richt lonely," I says.

"It's her ain fault," says Mrs. Robieson. "I ken she's poor an' stays by her lane, but folks has nae use ava for a body that's aye grumblin'. There's Miss Todd. She's no' even as weel-aff as Miss Grieve, but she's got a smile an' a pleasant word for ye, an' friends is aye wantin' her. Miss Grieve would wreck ony party, an' ye ken that fine."

I says, aye, Mrs. Robieson's richt, but a grand ploy like a Hallowe'en party would maybe cheer up Miss Grieve. "I'll sit next her," I says, "an' she can grumble as muckle as she chooses. It'll gang intil ane ear an' oot at the ither. So that mak's seven. Whit are ye gaein' tae dae wi' us?"

"Well, there's the tea," she says. "I mean tae gi' ye a richt guid spread, an' aifterwards we can hae games. There's aye cairds, an' maybe some o' us can start somethin' new. An' bein' Hallowe'en we can peel aipples, an' crack nuts, an' it's guid fun, though we're past wishin' for a handsome husband or tae win the Derby sweep."

It was a' settled, an' we each got oor invitation in plenty time to buy a new frock gin we needed yin, an' we a' accepted, an' was lookin' forward tae it, I can tell ye. Mrs. Robieson aye gi'es her friends a pleasant evenin', an' there was a lot o' talk aboot it in Carlonie. Whenever we met a body we ken't they'd say: "An' whit are ye daein' at Hallowe'en?" an' we'd reply: "Och! gaein' till Mrs. Robieson's party."

I'd promised to come roond early an' gi' her a hand. She was a verra guid manager, Mrs. Robieson, an' when I arrived a'thing was weel forward. My! the tea-table lookit bonny. She'd pit coloured paper serviettes on each plate, an' there was a pot o' bulbs in the middle o' the cloth, an' her best chiny an' silver. I thinks till mysel' that gin we eat hauf o' whit she's provided we'll be needin' an ambulance tae get us hame, but when I tell't her this she juist lauchs. It was cauld weather, she reminds me, an' we was gettin' oor tea an' supper in ane, so she hoped we'd a' bring guid appetites.

"An' whit can I dae to help?" I says.

"Weel, it's a' ready, thank ye," says she. "But ye micht wash a few extra cuppies, juist tae hae them in case, an' unpack thon wee cakes. I'm feart o' filin' my skirt wi' the cream, they're sae awfae sticky."

I did that, an' she says as soon as the folks is a' arrived she'll slip oot an' infuse the tea, gin I'll keep them talkin'. I says wi' pleasure, an' had she ony plans for aifter tea?

"Ay," says she, lookin' rale pleased. "I found that Mrs. Sturrock's sister is a great yin for tellin' fortunes. We'll get her to read oor cuppies, an' she'll maybe dae it wi' the cairds as weel."

"That'll be grand," I says. "Och! there's a ring."

"I'll gang," she says. "It's Mrs. Fraser. I can see thon red hat o' hers."

Mrs. Fraser it was, an' she'd come early on account o' haein' tae leave in guid time for her bus as she stays aboot twa miles oot-by Carlonie. The rest wasna lang aifter her. We a' tuk' aff oor things in Mrs. Robieson's bedroom, an' had a keek at each ither's dresses, an' then we went doon till the parlour. They was a' admirin' the table when Mrs. Robieson says: "But whaur's Miss Grieve?"

"She's late," says Mrs. Sturrock. "An' she's nearer than the lave o' us."

"She's comin', though," says Miss Todd. "I met her this mornin' an' she was sayin' it was safe tae rain, her rheumatics was sae bad, but she'd mak' the effort no' tae disappoint ye, Mrs. Robieson."

"That'll be her," says Mrs. Robieson. "She aye rings like tae break the bell."

"I'll let her in," I says, "an' ye mak' the tea."

Miss Grieve was standin' on the doorstep, lookin' at the bell as though it had bitten her. When I opened the door she says she'd rung three times, an' naebody cam', but it didna maitter whether she caught her deith o' cauld waitin' in sic a wind. I says I'm richt sorry, but I cam' directly I heard the bell, an' would she come away. She got in six grumbles at least on the stairs, an' mair in the bedroom. I tried to cheer her up by tellin' her we was a' tae hae oor fortunes tell't, but she says it's past the time for her to get ony guid luck.

"Fortune-tellin' at oor ages!" she says. "An' ye ken fine the minister doesna approve. Besides, it's richt scarin'. Gin ye're tell't somethin' guid, ye ken it's a' havers, an' yet ye're disappointit when it doesna come aff, an' gin it's bad luck promised, ye're lookin' oot for it a' the time."

"It's richt guid fun," I says, but she starts tellin' me aboot a gipsy her sister consulted, wha tell't her she'd never mairry, an' sure eneuch she never did. I says that wasna the gipsy's blame, an' she got awfae vexed an' says did I mean tae insult her puir sister?

"No' me," I says. "Come away doon, Miss Grieve, an' ye'll feel fine aifter yer tea."

"Ither folks' food aye gi'es me indigestion," she says. "An' I doot I've ta'en a chill a'ready, standin' on thon step. The wind's like a knife."

"It's grand weather for the back-end," I says.

"Ay, but it's winter next week," says she, "an' it'll be six months afore we see the sun."

I tuk' her doon, an' she tells a' the ithers aboot hoo she got perished waitin' on her ring bein' answered, an' when Mrs. Sturrock introduced her sister Miss Grieve says she reminds her o' her puir cousin Kirsty wha died o' cancer last Noo Year. "A big, fine-lookin' woman," she says. "She'd three operations, but they couldna save her. Ye're the marrows o' her, Mrs. Scott."

"We'd better tak' oor teas," says Mrs. Robieson, for puir Mrs. Scott was lookin' like tae greet, an' I ken't fine oor hostess was richt vexed wi' me for insistin' on her invitin' Miss Grieve. I sat next till her, wi' Miss Todd on my ither side, an' Miss Todd startit tellin' us aboot whit she'd over- heard the minister's wife sayin' till Sandy Craig, the odd man, an' when we'd dune lauchin' the cups went roond, an' we a' began on a richt guid tea.

Ye'd think that'd cheer up maist dour bodies, but no' Miss Grieve. She sent back her cuppie three times, first because it was ower strong, an' then because it was ower weak, an' finally because Mrs. Robieson had pit sugar ben, an' she ken't fine Miss Grieve never tuk' sugar. That startit her aff on a' the folks she minded wha had kill't themsel's through eatin' things they shouldna, an' it fair tuk' away my appetite. She tell't Mrs. Scott doon the table a' aboot her cousin Kirsty's three operations, an' added that it would hae been fower gin the puir thing hadna deid. When Miss Todd got her aff operations she was back till her ain chill, an' speired at me aboot the price o' funerals an' lairs. Then Mrs. Sturrock cut her thumb instead o' the slice o' pie she was for, an' that set Miss Grieve aff on blood-poisonin'.

103

"It's awfae dangerous, a wee cut," she says. "If I was ye, Mrs. Sturrock, I'd ca' at the doctor's on my way hame."

"Ay, ye would," says Mrs. Sturrock, an' I didna blame her for bein' sae short-spoken. Miss Grieve had fair spoilt oor appetites wi' her talk o' operations an' funerals, an' noo she was as guid as tellin' Mrs. Sturrock that her ain would be the next in Carlonie.

"It's just naethin'," says Mrs. Scott. "Mrs. Robieson, may I tak' a liberty an' speir for the recipe for this jelly? It's richt tasty."

"It's my ain mak'," says Mrs. Robieson. "My mither made it afore me, an' I aye gang by her ingredients. Ye'll tak' anither helpin', I hope? An' Mrs. Fraser's plate's toom. I beg yer pardon, Mrs. Fraser. Noo, whit are ye for? The cream cakes cam' frae Dundee. Ay, try yin. That's richt. An' anither cuppie tea?"

"It's no' safe tae eat cream that's traivelled," says Miss Grieve. "Ye dinna ken whether it was pit intil a clean vessel. That reminds me, I heard an awfae story a week syne aboot a dairy. It's the yin whaur ye get yer milk," she tells me. "A friend o' mine saw whit happened there wi' her verra ain eyes."

I tell't her I was no' wantin' tae hear aboot it, an' she sat back, richt offended. For a while she was sulkin', an' the rest o' us made up for lost time an' enjoyed oor teas wi'oot bein' warned we was eatin' ower muckle, or the wrang things, or they'd disagree wi' us, or we'd eaten too fast. The table looked a sicht by the time we'd finished, but, as Mrs. Robieson said, it showed we'd likit fine whit she'd gi'ed us. I ken I did.

Aifter tea I lent a hand wi' clearin' the things away, an' then we a' sat roond the fire, crackin'. Mrs. Robieson produced a basket o' bonny red aipples, an' it was richt guid fun peelin' them an' throwin' the peel ower oor shoulders tae mak' oor sweethe'rts' initials. Miss Todd came in for eneuch chaff when hers was a B every time. Mrs. Sturrock tell't her

Birse, the mairket gairdener, maun be meant, but Miss Todd juist gi'ed a lauch an' shook her heid.

"It's a' nonsense," says Miss Grieve. "I ken't a young lassie, an' she gaed till a Hallowe'en party, an' her aipple-peel cam' oot every time in a W. She thocht it meant she'd get a laddie ca'ed William or Walter, but nae sic thing. On the way hame she met an auld mannie wha tried to kiss her, an' she ran away an' fell doon an' broke her nose, an' she was sic a fricht for the lave o' her days she got naebody ava."

Mrs. Robieson says maybe the auld mannie's name began wi' a W, an' in ony case breakin' her nose had naething tae dae wi' the Hallowe'en party. Miss Todd says she'd like fine tae hae her fortune tell't, an' will Mrs. Scott dae her? Mrs. Scott says ay, wi' pleasure, an' oot wi' her pack o' cairds. We a' sat munchin' oor aipples, an' Miss Grieve, aifter tellin' us that aipples was bad at the end o' a meal, an' gi'en' us the history o' a friend o' hers wha swallowed a pip wi' awfae consequences, was as interested as ony o' us.

"Ye'll get a letter," says Mrs. Scott. "It's comin' across watter. An' there's guid news in it. An' ye'll hae somethin' new. I dinna ken whit it is, but I see a blue thing. Maybe it's a hat?"

Miss Todd says she'd a hat in her mind, an' her new winter coat was blue, so verra likely that'd be it. The end o' her fortune was richt pleasant, wi' her wish comin' till her, an' guid health, an' friends a' roond. Then Mrs. Robieson an' me was baith dune in turn, an' there was plenty nice things waitin' for us. She was tae hae a change o' times, an' a present in three days, an' I was tae hear o' money for me, an' a parcel wi' my wish. Mrs. Sturrock said her sister'd tell't her fortune afore they cam' oot, so she'd no' be dune again, an' Mrs. Fraser had had to leave aifter tea tae get her bus, so that left Miss Grieve.

"I dinna believe in it," says she.

"Och! come on," says Mrs. Robieson. "It's a' part o' the fun."

"I never get my wish wi' thon things," says Miss Grieve.

"Maybe yer luck'll change this time," says Mrs. Sturrock. "Bella's awfae guid at it."

Mrs. Scott spread oot the cairds an' tell't Miss Grieve she saw her wish comin' till her. It would be through a fair-haired lassie. "Div ye ken onybody wi' fair hair? She's close till ye, Miss Grieve. Maybe it's a relation."

"There's my niece Peggy," says Miss Grieve. "She's red-heided. But, losh! she'd na dae onythin' for her puir auld auntie. A richt selfish wee besom, like a' young folks these days."

"They're no' sae black as they're paintit," says Miss Todd. "An' ye'll get yer wish. Is na that fine noo?"

"I'll believe in it when it's here," says Miss Grieve.

Mrs. Scott tell't her that she didna see onythin' else comin' for her, forby a postcaird next week. She says that'll be frae the sweep, disappointin' her as usual, but it canna be helpit. Then we a' roasted nuts, an' had fine fun watchin' them crack. Aifter that we a' tell't ghaist-stories an' speired riddles, an' Mrs. Robieson gi'ed us mair tea an' cakes, an' then it was time for hame. We a' says till her it had been a richt nice Hallowe'en party, an' we'd fair enjoyed oorsel's. Miss Grieve said it was awfae dangerous tae gang oot o' a hot room intil the cauld nicht air, but naebody heedit, an' we didna catch a chill amang us, no' even her, wi' a' her croakin'.

A week later I met her, richt weel-dressed, an' lookin' quite important. She tell't me she couldna bide as she'd a train tae catch. "I'm for Dundee," she says. "An' gin ye see Mrs. Sturrock, tell her tae tell her sister when she's writin' till her that her fortune's come true. I've gotten my wish."

I says I was fine an' pleased tae hear that, an' micht I speir whit it was? Miss Grieve looks quite blate.

"Ye'll no' lauch?" says she.

"No' me," I says.

"Weel, it's a permanent wave," she says. "I've aye wantit yin, an' I wished for it, never thinkin' I'd get it, they're sae expensive. An' whit div ye think? Last Wednesday I had a letter frae Peggy, my niece, ye ken, an' it seems the lassie's won a competition in ane o' the papers, an' the prize was a permanent wave. Peggy's been permed quite lately, so she says will I tak' it instead o' her, an' I've my appointment booked, an' it's tae be dune in Dundee this aifternoon."

"Weel, that's fine," I says. "A permanent wave will juist set ye, Miss Grieve. An' ye see it cam' aboot that ye got yer wish through a fair-haired lassie aifter a'. Yon Mrs. Scott was richt."

"Ay," says Miss Grieve. "They're grand things, Hallowe'en parties. I'm no sure I shall na gi' yin mysel' next year."

Ruthven Todd

THE BIG WHEEL

The blight had hit the potatoes and they were very small, a
plentiful crop but only the size of peas. Duggie Cameron
found it was as much as he could do to raise the rent; his two
stirks, both good blue-grey heifers eighteen months old, only
brought in six-pound-ten each and there was the auctioneer's
commission to take off that.

He was working at the lobsters as well, but the weather was
squally and often he couldn't get out for a week, and then he
found some of the pots smashed and others drifted and lost.
He used to come in, quite often, with only half a dozen lobsters, and perhaps a few crabs, from his fifty-six pots; he had
to keep the catch, in a box moored in the port, until he had
three or four dozen and they used to die on him. When, at
last, he had collected enough, the post-car took a couple of
bob off him for carrying them up the island, then another
shilling went to the boat for taking them to the mainland, and
ten or twelve bob more to the railway, by which time, as like
as not, another three or four were dead, and the remainder
might bring in only a shilling apiece at Billingsgate.

Duggie and his wife, Morag, talked it over and decided
that the only way to keep going was to get the parish poor-
inspector to recommend them for the care of a half-wit; so
Morag, with her tongue working on the words in her cheek
as she wrote, respectfully hoped that Mr. MacLean would get
for them the charge of a mentally deficient boy. At least, they
decided, however bad a worker he might be, they would get
fourteen bob a week, regularly, for his keep, and it wouldn't

cost any more to feed him than it did at present to feed the two of them and Lachie, their seven-year-old boy.

Sandy Johnstone came from Tobermory. His mother was a tinker woman, and she, who should have known, wasn't certain as to which of three men was his father, and so was forced to give him her own name, but she was dead a long time and they had sent Sandy to an institution in Dundee, where he learned to chew tobacco and to swear.

Mr. MacLean met him off the *Lochinvar*, where he was under the care of one of the Public Assistance officials from Oban. He had come all the way up to Oban in charge of several different guards. Mr. MacLean gave him a good meal of fried eggs and ham, but Sandy couldn't eat it because he had been sick off the end of Lismore, so he got a packet of cigarettes instead and a box of matches—a new box, really full.

The driver and Mr. MacLean sat in front and Sandy was in the back where he bounced around like a pea in a bottle, and smoked and sang and watched the long grey road curl round the ends of the lochs and the bases of the mountains. It was dark before they reached Tor Mor and Sandy saw the light, blinking under the shadow of a heavy hill, for a long time before they reached it.

After Mr. MacLean and the driver had had tea and had driven off again to Salen, the Camerons gave Sandy a boiled salt saithe, a big cup of tea and a bit of scone with syrup on it. The fish was bony and he didn't like it much, and anyway he was tired, so Duggie helped him to carry his chest up the stairs, and put him into the room where he was to sleep. The ceiling of the room sloped down nearly to the floor and he bumped his head on it several times while he was undressing They had given him some new shirts before he left the institu tion, and the one he had on had lovely wide purple stripes on it and was nice and cool against his skin, all smooth against him; it was nice to sleep in, and the white light of the full moon was cool also, and he was very tired and hoped that they wouldn't make him work too hard.

2

They did make Sandy work pretty hard, and Lachie was for ever pestering the life out of him; but there was one good thing anyway, Duggie wouldn't take him out to the lobsters again after the first time when he was sick all the way and was no use at all. So Duggie went out to the Carrick Mor after his pots, while Sandy had to stay at home and clean the byre and wash potatoes, and also had to scrub the kitchen out, for Morag said:

"What's the use of having the boy, if we don't get the work out of him?"

Lachie was lame and besides being twisted outside Sandy thought his inside must have been squint as well. He used to tell tales on Sandy; he'd go and say that Sandy had been swearing at him and had called him bad names; then Duggie would come with his cromag and chase Sandy, who would swear at him and say he would go and tell the doctor; but he knew that it was no good going to the doctor, because he'd been once and the doctor hadn't listened to him and had told him to go home—the doctor stuck by the people that weren't insured and would pay him when they were ill, rather than to the ones he got paid for in any case.

One day Duggie went to the stable to see the mare that was heavy with foal, to see if she was near her time, and he found that she'd cast it and it was lying dead at her feet, among the dung; and he thought that Sandy had given her a fright, so he gave him a frightful slanging. Then Lachie said he saw Sandy hit her, which was a lie for he'd done no such thing, and Duggie hit him with the hoe and made him cry. So Sandy hated Lachie and would have liked to have hit him with the graip, but he was afraid that when they found out Duggie would come after him with the gun.

3

Sandy sat on the edge of the dung-midden, playing his

mouth-organ: the khaki breeches he had got from his parish were torn at the knees and his tacketty boots were worn out— the piece of tin from a pail of sheep-dip that Duggie had mended them with was cold against his toes, because Morag hadn't darned the holes in his stockings for a long time. But Sandy didn't mind that, because he had a big chew of bogie-roll that he had got off Duncan, the postman, the night before, and its being in his waistcoat pocket made him warm inside.

It was "Daisy Bell" Sandy was playing on his mouth-organ, he liked "Daisy" but used to get muddled up with other tunes when he played it, but he kept on trying until Lachie came up and wanted the mouth-organ. Sandy wouldn't let him have it till Duggie came and told him to give it to the kid as he wouldn't harm it. So Sandy gave it to him and he did break it and pulled all the thin yellow tin bits off its inside. Poor Sandy had no more mouth-organs, so he had to whistle instead. But he didn't like that little brat. He thought how nice it would be if Lachie was dead and then he could play his mouth-organ and no one could take it away and break it. After all, it was a new one too, with nice bumpy letters on the side of it, and it was mean of Lachie to break it.

One day Mr. MacLean came and gave Sandy new boots and breeches and ten Capstans and a new penny, not a wee white one but only a big brown one. Sandy hid the big penny in the wash-house but put the Capstans in his jacket pocket and went to chop the turnips for the stirks, with a cigarette going full blast; he chopped the swedes into a tea-chest with an old scythe-blade; only if he wasn't careful, he used to cut his fingers because the chopper was very shoogly. When he had the box full, Duggie, who was back from his pots in a bad fettle because he'd only got three lobsters and a crab, told him he was lazy and had better hurry up and clear the byre out. Sandy went inside and the cow's breath had made it very hot so he took off his jacket and hung it on the stakes. When he was busy brushing the far end, Lachie came in and saw the jacket and pulled it down and began to look through the pockets; he didn't get the brown penny because Sandy had it hidden, but he found the packet of Capstans and took them out and made a row of dead soldiers with them in the wet gutter at the cows' tails, then he went home for a piece as Morag was baking.

When Sandy came back he found all his cigarettes spoiled, he tried to chew one, after peeling the soggy paper off it, but it tasted of ammonia so he spat it out. He thought it would be a good thing if the old cart-wheel in the fank fell on top of Lachie and killed him, then there would be a funeral and they might give Sandy a glass of whisky like they did at his old mother's funeral and, even if they did find out, all they could do would be to send him back to the institution, where he'd get a new mouth-organ, with nice shiny silver bumpy letters on it, and heaps of Capstans.

He went and looked at the wheel. It was standing up against the sheep-pen and was very heavy; the iron boss was broken and Duggie had put it there until he found one that would fit: it was badly balanced and Sandy saw that it would take only a little push to knock it over. Then he went back to the byre and went on brushing, it was very hard to make a good job of it: Duggie wouldn't give him a proper brush from a shop, but only a bundle of birch twigs tied together with a bit of lacing-wire off the garden fence. The wire scratched Sandy's hand and made it bleed, it didn't bleed so red as the pig did when they stuck the stabbing-knife in its throat; perhaps his blood was blacker because it had to ooze through an extra skin of dung on his hand. He swept the gutter and the walk and then started to shake up the cows' bedding with the graip until Lachie, who wouldn't leave him in peace, came in and wanted the graip but he didn't get it till he got the big hay-fork and stuck it in Sandy's backside.

Sandy gave him the graip and went to the wash-house and got the penny his inspector gave him. Then he went up to the fank and put the penny down in front of the wheel, after which he clambered into the sheep-pen and squatted down. Lachie took a long time to come, but at last Sandy heard him calling:

"Where are you, Sandy? Come an' wash the pigs' petatoes!"

So Sandy said:

"What is it? Sandy's in the fank."

Sandy watched Lachie coming up the road, he took a long time. He stopped to look at a frog in the ditch and squashed it with a big stone.

He saw the new penny and said:

"Ha, ha, I got Sandy's penny."

He bent down to pick it up but Sandy gave the wheel a big push and it hit Lachie's head. He lay very still, just like a bag of potatoes.

Sandy climbed over the pen and picked up his penny. He found a small chew of bogie-roll in his pocket and went down to the byre to bed the cows.

R. B. Cunninghame-Graham

BEATTOCK FOR MOFFAT

The bustle on the Euston platform stopped for an instant to let the men who carried him to the third-class compartment pass along the train. Gaunt and emaciated, he looked just at death's door, and, as they propped him in the carriage between two pillows, he faintly said, "Jock, do ye think I'll live as far as Moffat? I should na' like to die in London in the smoke."

His cockney wife, drying her tears with a cheap hemstitched pocket-handkerchief, her scanty town-bred hair looking like wisps of tow beneath her hat, bought from some window in which each individual article was marked at seven-and-sixpence, could only sob. His brother, with the country sun and wind burn still upon his face, and his huge hands hanging like hams in front of him, made answer.

"Andra'," he said, "gin ye last as far as Beattock, we'll gie ye a braw hurl back to the farm, syne the bask air, ye ken, and the milk, and, and—but can ye last as far as Beattock, Andra'?"

The sick man, sitting with the cold sweat upon his face, his shrunken limbs looking like sticks inside his ill-made black slop suit, after considering the proposition on its merits, looked up, and said, "I should na' like to bet I feel fair boss, God knows; but there, the mischief of it is, he will na' tell ye, so that, as ye may say, his knowlidge has na' commercial value. I ken I look as gash as Garscadden. Ye mind, Jock, in the braw auld times, when the auld laird just slipped awa', whiles they were birlin' at the clairet. A braw death, Jock . . .

114

do ye think it'll be rainin' aboot Ecclefechan? Aye . . . sure to
be rainin' aboot Lockerbie. Nae Christians there, Jock, a'
Johnstones and Jardines, ye mind?"

The wife, who had been occupied with an air cushion and,
having lost the bellows, had been blowing into it till her
cheeks seemed almost bursting, and her false teeth were
loosened in her head, left off her toil to ask her husband "If 'e
could pick a bit of something, a pork pie, or a nice sausage
roll, or something tasty," which she could fetch from the
refreshment room. The invalid having declined to eat, and his
brother having drawn from his pocket a dirty bag, in which
were peppermints, gave him a "drop", telling him that he
"minded he aye used to like them weel, when the meenister
had fairly got into his prelection in the auld kirk, outby."

The train slid almost imperceptibly away, the passengers
upon the platform looking after it with that half-foolish, half-
astonished look with which men watch a disappearing train.
Then a few sandwich papers rose with the dust almost to the
level of the platform, sank again, the clock struck twelve,
and the station fell into a half quiescence, like a volcano in the
interval between the lava showers. Inside the third-class
carriage all was quiet until the lights of Harrow shone upon
the left, when the sick man, turning himself with difficulty,
said, "Good-bye, Harrow-on-the-Hill. I aye liked Harrow
for the hill's sake, tho' ye can scarcely ca' yon wee bit mound
a hill, Jean."

His wife who, even in her grief, still smarted under the
Scotch variant of her name, which all her life she had pronounced as "Jayne", and who, true Cockney as she was,
bounded her world within the lines of Plaistow, Peckham
Rye, the Welsh 'Arp ('Endon way), and Willesden, moved
uncomfortably at the depreciation of the chief mountain in her
cosmos, but held her peace. Loving her husband in a sort of
half-antagonistic fashion, born of the difference of type between the hard, unyielding, yet humorous and sentimental
Lowland Scot, and the conglomerate of all races of the island
which meet in London, and produce the weedy, shallow

breed, almost incapable of reproduction, and yet high strung and nervous, there had arisen between them that intangible veil of misconception which, though not excluding love, is yet impervious to respect. Each saw the other's failings, or, perhaps, thought the good qualities which each possessed were faults, for usually men judge each other by their good points, which, seen through prejudice of race, religion, and surroundings, appear to them defects.

The brother, who but a week ago had left his farm unwillingly, just when the "neeps were wantin' heughin and a feck o' things requirin' to be done, forby a puckle sheep waitin' for keelin'," to come and see his brother for the last time, sat in that dour and seeming apathetic attitude which falls upon the country man, torn from his daily toil, and plunged into a town. Most things in London, during the brief intervals he had passed away from the sick bed, seemed foolish to him, and of a nature such as a self-respecting Moffat man, in the hebdomadal enjoyment of the "prelections" of a Free Church minister, could not authorize.

"Man, saw ye e'er a carter sittin' on his cart, and drivin' at a trot, instead o' walkin' in a proper manner alangside his horse?" had been his first remark.

The short-tailed sheep dogs, and the way they worked, the inferior quality of the cart horses, their shoes with hardly any calkins worth the name, all was repugnant to him.

On Sabbath, too, he had received a shock, for, after walking miles to sit under the "brither of the U.P. minister at Symington," he had found Erastian hymn books in the pews and noticed with stern reprobation that the congregation stood to sing, and that instead of sitting solidly whilst the "man wrastled in prayer", stooped forward in the fashion called the Nonconformist lounge.

His troubled spirit had received refreshment from the sermon, which, though short, and extending to but some five-and-forty minutes, had still been powerful, for he said:

"When yon wee, shilpit meenister—brither, ye ken, of rantin' Ferguson, out by Symington—shook the congregation

ower the pit mouth, ye could hae fancied that the very sowls
in hell just girned. Man, he garred the very stour to flee
aboot the kirk, and, hadna' the big book been weel brass
banded, he would hae dang the haricles fair oot."

So the train slipped past Watford, swaying round the
curves like a gigantic serpent, and jolting at the facing points
as a horse "pecks" in his gallop at an obstruction in the
ground.

The moon shone brightly into the compartment extinguish-
ing the flickering of the half-candle-power electric light. Rug-
by, the station all lit up, and with its platforms occupied but
by a few belated passengers, all muffled up like race horses taking their exercise, flashed past. They slipped through Cannock
Chase, which stretches down with heath and firs, clear brawling streams, and birch trees, an outpost of the north lost in the
midland clay. They crossed the oily Trent, flowing through
alder copses, and with its backwaters all overgrown with
lilies, like an "aguapey" in Paraguay or in Brazil.

The sick man, wrapped in cheap rugs, and sitting like Guy
Fawkes, in the half comic, half pathetic way that sick folk sit,
making them sport for fools, and, at the same time, moisten-
ing the eye of the judicious, who reflect that they themselves
may one day sit as they do, bereft of all the dignity of strength,
looked listlessly at nothing as the train sped on. His loving,
tactless wife, whose cheap "sized" handkerchief had long
since become a rag with mopping up her tears, endeavoured
to bring round her husband's thoughts to paradise, which she
conceived a sort of music-hall, where angels sat with their
wings folded, listening to sentimental songs.

Her brother-in-law, reared on the fiery faith of Moffat
Calvinism, eyed her with great disfavour, as a terrier eyes a
rat imprisoned in a cage.

"Jean wumman," he burst out, "to hear ye talk, I would
jist think your meenister had been a perfectly illeeterate man,
pairadise here, pairadise there; what do ye think a man like
Andra' could dae daunderin' aboot a gairden naked, pu'in
soor aipples frae the trees?"

Cockney and Scotch conceit, impervious alike to outside criticism, and each so bolstered in its pride as to be quite incapable of seeing that anything existed outside the purlieus of their sight, would soon have made the carriage into a battlefield, had not the husband, with the authority of approaching death, put in his word.

"Whist, Jeanie wumman. Jock, dae ye no ken that the Odium-Theologicum is just a curse—pairadise—set ye baith up—pairadise. I dinna' even richtly ken if I can last as far as Beattock."

Stafford, its iron furnaces belching out flames, which burned red holes into the night, seemed to approach, rather than be approached, so smoothly ran the train. The mingled moonlight and the glare of ironworks lit the canal beside the railway, and from the water rose white vapours as from Styx or Periphlegethon. Through Cheshire ran the train, its timbered houses showing ghostly in the frost which coated all the carriage windows, and rendered them opaque. Preston, the Catholic city, lay silent in the night, its river babbling through the public park, and then the hills of Lancashire loomed lofty in the night. Past Garstang, with its water-lily-covered ponds, Garstang where, in the days gone by, Catholic squires, against their will, were forced on Sundays to "take wine" in church on pain of fine, the puffing serpent slid.

The talk inside the carriage had given place to sleep, that is, the brother-in-law and wife slept fitfully, but the sick man looked out, counting the miles to Moffat, and speculating on his strength. Big drops of sweat stood on his forehead, and his breath came double, whistling through his lungs.

They passed by Lancaster, skirting the sea on which the moon shone bright, setting the fishing boats in silver as they lay scarcely moving on the waves. Then, so to speak, the train set its face up against Shap Fell, and, puffing heavily, drew up into the hills, the scattered grey stone houses of the north, flanked by their gnarled and twisted ash trees, hanging upon the edge of the streams, as lonely, and as cut off from the world (except the passing train) as if they had been in Central

Africa. The moorland roads, winding amongst the heather, showed that the feet of generations had marked them out, and not the line, spade, and theodolite, with all the circumstance of modern road makers. They, too, looked white and unearthly in the moonlight, and now and then a sheep, aroused by the snorting of the train, moved from the heather into the middle of the road, and stood there motionless, its shadow filling the narrow track, and flickering on the heather at the edge.

The keen and penetrating air of the hills and night roused the two sleepers, and they began to talk, after the Scottish fashion, of the funeral, before the anticipated corpse.

"Ye ken, we've got a braw new hearse outby, sort of Epescopalian lookin', wi' gless a' roond, so's ye can see the kist. Very conceity too, they mak' the hearses noo-a-days. I min' when they were jist auld sort o' ruckly boxes, awfu' licht, ye ken upon the springs, and just went dodderin' alang, the body swinging to and fro, as if it would flee richt oot. The roads, ye ken, were no nigh and so richtly metalled in thae days."

The subject of the conversation took it cheerfully, expressing pleasure at the advance of progress as typified in the new hearse, hoping his brother had a decent "stan' o' black", and looking at his death, after the fashion of his kind, as it were something outside himself, a fact indeed, on which, at the same time, he could express himself with confidence as being in some measure interested. His wife, not being Scotch, took quite another view, and seemed to think that the mere mention of the word was impious, or, at the least, of such a nature as to bring on immediate dissolution, holding the English theory that unpleasant things should not be mentioned, and that, by this means, they can be kept at bay. Half from affection, half from the inborn love of cant, inseparable from the true Anglo-Saxon, she endeavoured to persuade her husband that he looked better, and yet would mend, once in his native air.

"At Moffit, ye'd 'ave the benefit of the 'ill breezes, and

that 'ere country milk, which never 'as no cream in it, but 'olesome, as you say. Why yuss, in about eight days at Moffit, you'll be as 'earty as you ever was. Yuss, you will, you take my word."

Like a true Londoner, she did not talk religion, being too thin in mind and body even to have grasped the dogma of any of the sects. Her heaven a music 'all, her paradise to see the King drive through the streets, her literary pleasure to read lies in newspapers, or pore on novelettes, which showed her the pure elevated lives of duchesses, placing the knaves and prostitutes within the limits of her own class; which view of life she accepted as quite natural, and as a thing ordained to be by the bright stars who write.

Just at the Summit they stopped an instant to let a goods train pass, and, in a faint voice, the consumptive said, "I'd almost lay a wager now I'd last to Moffat, Jock. The Shap, ye ken, I aye looked at as the beginning of the run home. The hills, ye ken, are sort o' heartsome. No that they're bonny hills like Moffat hills, na', na', ill-shapen sort of things, just like Borunty tatties, awfu' puir names, too, Shap Fell and Rowland Edge, Hutton Roof Crags and Arnside Fell; heard ever onybody sich-like names for hills? Naething to fill the mooth; man, the Scotch hills jist grap ye in the mooth for a' the world like speerits."

They stopped at Penrith, which the old castle walls make even meaner, in the cold morning light, than other stations look. Little Salkeld, and Armathwaite, Cotehill, and Scotby, all rushed past, and the train, slackening, stopped with a jerk upon the platform, at Carlisle. The sleepy porters bawled out "change for Maryport", some drovers slouched into carriages, kicking their dogs before them, and, slamming to the doors, exchanged the time of day with others of their tribe, all carrying ash or hazel sticks, all red-faced and keen-eyed, their caps all crumpled, and their great-coat tails all creased, as if their wearers had lain down to sleep full dressed, so as to lose no time in getting to the labours of the day. The old red sandstone church, with something of a castle in its look, as well befits a shrine close to a frontier where in days gone by the priest had need to watch and pray, frowned on the passing train, and on the manufactories, whose banked-up fires sent poisonous fumes into the air, withering the trees which, in the public park, a careful council had hedged round about with wire.

The Eden ran from bank to bank, its water swirling past as wildly as when "the Bauld Buccleugh" and his Moss Troopers, bearing the "Kinmount" fettered in their midst, plunged in and passed it, whilst the keen Lord Scroope stood on the brink amazed and motionless. Gretna, so close to England, and yet a thousand miles away in speech and feeling, found the sands now flying through the glass. All through the mosses which once were the "Debateable Land" on which the moss troopers of the clan Graeme were used to hide the cattle stolen from the "auncient enemy", the now repatriated Scotchman murmured feebly "that it was bonny scenery" although a drearier prospect of "moss hags" and stunted birch trees is not to be found. At Ecclefechan he just raised his head, and faintly spoke of "yon auld carle, Carlyle, ye ken, a dour thrawn body, but a gran' pheelosopher," and then lapsed into silence, broken by frequent struggles to take breath.

His wife and brother sat still, and eyed him as a cow watches a locomotive engine pass, amazed and helpless, and he himself had but the strength to whisper, "Jock, I'm dune, I'll no see Moffat, blast it, yon smoke, ye ken, yon London smoke has been ower muckle for ma lungs."

The tearful, helpless wife, not able even to pump up the harmful and unnecessary conventional lie, which, after all, consoles only the liar, sat pale and limp, chewing the fingers of her Berlin gloves. Upon the weather-beaten cheek of Jock glistened a tear, which he brushed off as angrily as if it had been a wasp.

"Aye, Andra'," he said, "I would hae liket awfu' weel that ye should win to Moffat. Man, the rowan trees are a' in bloom, and there's a bonny breer upon the corn—aye, ou aye, the reid bogs are lookin' gran' the year—but, Andra', I'll tak ye east to the auld kirk-yaird, ye'll no' ken onything aboot it, but we'll hae a heartsome funeral."

Lockerbie seemed to fly towards them, and the dying Andra' smiled as his brother pointed out the place and said, "Ye mind, there are no ony Christians in it," and answered, "Aye, I mind, naething but Jardines," as he fought for breath.

The death dews gathered on his forehead as the train shot by Nethercleugh, passed Wamphray and Dinwoodie, and with a jerk pulled up at Beattock just at the summit of the pass.

So in the cold spring morning light, the fine rain beating on the platform, as the wife and brother got their almost speechless care out of the carriage, the brother whispered, "Dam't, ye've done it, Andra', here's Beattock; I'll tak' ye east to Moffat yet to dee."

But on the platform, huddled on the bench to which he had been brought, Andra' sat speechless and dying in the rain. The doors banged to, the guard stepped in lightly as the train flew past, and a belated porter shouted, "Beattock, Beattock for Moffat," and then, summoning his last strength, Andra' smiled, and whispered faintly in his brother's ear, "Aye, Beattock—for Moffat!" Then his head fell back, and a faint bloody foam oozed from his pallid lips. His wife stood crying helplessly, the rain beating upon the flowers of her cheap hat, rendering it shapeless and ridiculous. But Jock, drawing out a bottle, took a short dram and saying, "Andra', man, ye made a richt gude fecht o' it," snorted an instant in a red pocket-handkerchief, and calling up a boy, said, "Rin, Jamie, to the toon, and tell McNicol to send up and fetch a corp." Then, after helping to remove the body to the waiting-room, walked out into the rain, and, whistling "Corn Rigs" quietly between his teeth, lit up his pipe, and muttered as he smoked, "A richt gude fecht—man, aye, ou aye, a game yin Andra', puir felly. Weel, weel, he'll hae a braw hurl onyway in the new Moffat hearse."

Robin Jenkins

FLOWERS

At the door of the little school Miss Laing frowned at her
seven scholars off to gather flowers.

"Can I trust you?" she asked.

"Yes, miss," they chorused, except one.

Miss Laing pointed a chubby stern finger at the red-eyed
dissenter.

"Now, Margaret, I want no more nonsense from you."
She gazed with professional intentness at the small sulky girl
with the red ribbon in her hair. "Do you understand?"

Huffishly, Margaret nodded.

"That's a good girl. Now off with you. Come back at once
when I ring the bell."

As the teacher stood at the door in the heat and brilliance of
the sun, watching the children scamper to the gate, a great
roar was heard growing louder and louder until in front, low
over the sea loch, with the pilots clearly visible, three fighter
aeroplanes in camouflage paint flashed into view, flying with
exhilarating swiftness and power.

Miss Laing was exhilarated. She waved her hand wildly.

"There they are, children," she cried. "There are the true
flowers of our country, the most precious, the most beautiful.
Wave to them."

The children were startled and even a little alarmed by her
excessive white-haired enthusiasm. Aeroplanes were now

commonplace on the loch. Canna Rock was used for bombing practice. That was why almost every day they had all to promise solemnly, with their hands on their Bibles, never to go down to the shore.

Then the aeroplanes were gone again and their roar faded until a bee buzzing by was louder.

"Remember," cried Miss Laing. "Be very careful."

Margaret halted in the shade of a tall pine and watched the others hurrying towards the fields at Laggan under the larch wood, away from the sea. She sneered as she saw how Roderick McKenzie's long thin lassie-like legs twinkled under his torn kilt; he had his little sister Morag by the hand. They all gabbled to one another in Gaelic, mysterious and hateful to her Lowland ears.

Tears came into her eyes. She looked about her and saw, with aversion, the bell heather streaming like fire along the top of the dyke, the red branches and velvety foliage of the pine overhead, and the tiny school with its queer high roof. She wished to see the shops, houses, tramcars of home. She wished this summer afternoon to be playing in Mathieson Street with her friends Belzie Carruthers and Janet Morrison. She didn't want to be here in the Highlands staying with Aunt Sheena. She didn't want to be safe from bombs.

It was silly anyhow picking wild flowers in the hot sunshine. Miss Laing would just show off by telling their names, and then she'd either throw them out or else put them into a vase where in a day they'd wither.

Suddenly she jumped up over the dyke and ran across the heather. She didn't crouch nor try to hide. She didn't care if Miss Laing was spying on her. She didn't care either that she was breaking a sacred promise.

The sea was in sight with gold and silver spangles swimming in it like wonderful swans when she abruptly stopped, drawing in her breath in astonishment and awe. On a rock lay neatly coiled a smaller adder, green with gold and black zigzag markings; its little head, eyes shut, formed the apex of the coil. It lay sunning itself, camouflaged against the background of greeny-grey lichened stone and gently waving fronds of bracken.

She didn't know what to do. Adders, Miss Laing had warned them, were dangerous and must always be avoided. There was plenty of room for her to creep safely past. But she hesitated, and the snake awoke, conscious of her presence. It raised its head high, glancing quickly round. She saw its tiny eyes and its black tongue spitting in and out.

Suddenly it seemed to represent not only that detestable alien country but her own wickedness in disobeying. Furiously she lifted a stone and threw it. The snake hissed and slithered away. She snatched up a stick of hazel and stepped in pursuit, striking again and again though she felt sick with fear and hatred. A lucky blow crushed its head against a stone and blood trickled from its mouth; but it still hissed and slithered on, escaping into the bracken. She stood gazing at the speck of blood and scraped it with her stick. She was amazed because she hadn't thought a snake would have red blood in it.

She became aware of a yellow flower at her feet. Like the serpent it seemed hateful for some reason she could not understand, and she was about to trample on it when, unaccountably, its beauty, harmlessness, and its loneliness there amidst the tall brackens, moved her instead to stoop, tenderly pluck it, and hold it against her cheek.

Such obscure intensity of feeling was a new experience for her, and she stood gazing in fascination and guilt along the seaweeded rock and white sand. A black and white bird with long red legs and beak rose up with shrill cries. She watched it in fear. Then she looked again at a sandy corner among the rocks. Perhaps she might be able to paddle there. Would there be any unexploded bombs or ferocious crabs or stinging jellyfish?

She came down the bank cautiously and, flower in hand, walked slowly across the beach. The cool salty breeze was pleasant on her face and legs. More birds rose and screamed. She waited till they were gone.

When she crept round the boulder that shut off the sandy nook she stopped, surprised and embarrassed. It had never occurred to her there might be someone there.

Two men were lying stretched out on the sand in the shallow glittering water.

It was a strange place to lie, especially as they seemed to have their clothes on. She watched them moving gently with the waves' push. The water surely must be very warm. Certainly the sun struck it with a great blaze, forcing her to shade her eyes with her hand.

Smiling shyly, uncertain of her welcome, she started to walk over to them.

She paused again suddenly when she was close enough to see they wore airmen's clothing: they had the huge fur-lined boots, though one of them seemed to have only one boot on. They gave no sign at all that they knew she was there. Further along the beach the red-beaked birds screamed again. She walked a step or two nearer, then rigidly halted. Her scalp tingled and her whole body seemed frozen in the cold bright sea. In her hand the yellow flower was crushed into a green and black mess.

One of the airmen, with fair hair, had no face at all: while the other's face was half gone, and what remained was un-recognizable as human. The one with the single boot had only one leg; the fingers of his right hand, flung out in the shallow water, were gleaming bones. A sweet nasty smell mingled with the tang of the sea.

Screaming she turned and raced back. Frenzied eagerness to shock Miss Laing with the news of her discovery drove her on as much as the horror itself. But as she made to clamber up the bank she became aware of the crushed flower in her hand. Weeping and yelling, she rubbed it madly on the grass.

Lewis Grassic Gibbon

SMEDDUM[1]

She'd had nine of a family in her time, Mistress Menzies, and brought the nine of them up, forby—some near by the scruff of the neck, you would say. They were sniftering and weakly, two-three of the bairns, sniftering in their cradles to get into their coffins; but she'd shake them to life, and dose them with salts and feed them up till they couldn't but live. And she'd plonk one down—finishing the wiping of the creature's neb or the unco dosing of an ill bit stomach or the binding of a broken head—with a look on her face as much as to say *Die on me now and see what you'll get!*

Big-boned she was by her fortieth year, like a big roan mare, and *If ever she was bonny 'twas in Noah's time*, Jock Menzies, her eldest son, would say. She'd reddish hair and a high, skeugh nose, and a hand that skelped her way through life; and if ever a soul had seen her at rest when the dark was done and the day was come he'd died of the shock and never let on.

For from morn till night she was at it, work, work, on that ill bit croft that sloped to the sea. When there wasn't a mist on the cold, stone parks there was more than likely the wheep of the rain, wheeling and dripping in from the sea that soughed and plashed by the land's stiff edge. Kinneff lay north, and at night in the south, if the sky was clear on the gloaming's edge, you'd see in that sky the Bervie lights come suddenly lit, far and away, with the quiet about you as you stood and looked, nothing to hear but a sea-bird's cry.

[1] *Smeddum* is defined by the Scots dictionaries as meaning "mettle, spirit, liveliness," but the best synonym is the colloquial "guts".

But feint the much time to look or to listen had Margaret
Menzies of Tocherty toun. Day blinked and Meg did the
same, and was out, up out of her bed, and about the house,
making the porridge and rousting the bairns, and out to the
byre to milk the three kye, the morning growing out in the
east and a wind like a hail of knives from the hills. Syne back
to the kitchen again she would be, and catch Jock, her eldest,
a clout in the lug that he hadn't roused up his sisters and
brothers; and rouse them herself, and feed them and scold,
pull up their breeks and straighten their frocks, and polish
their shoes and set their caps straight. *Off you get and see
you're not late,* she would cry, *and see you behave yourselves at the
school. And tell the Dominie I'll be down the night to ask him
what the mischief he meant by leathering Jeannie and her not well.*

They'd cry *Ay, Mother,* and go trotting away, a fair flock of
the creatures, their faces red-scoured. Her own as red, like a
meikle roan mare's, Meg'd turn at the door and go prancing
in; and then at last, by the closet-bed, lean over and shake her
man half-awake. *Come on, then, Willie, it's time you were up.*

And he'd groan and say *Is't?* and crawl out at last, a little
bit thing like a weasel, Will Menzies, though some said that
weasels were decent beside him. He was drinking himself into
the grave, folk said, as coarse a little brute as you'd meet,
bone-lazy forby, and as sly as sin. Rampageous and ill with
her tongue though she was, you couldn't but pity a woman
like Meg tied up for life to a thing like *that.* But she'd more
than a soft side still to the creature, she'd half-skelp the backside from any of the bairns she found in the telling of a small
bit lie; but when Menzies would come paiching in of a noon
and groan that he fair was tashed with his work, he'd mended
all the ley fence that day and he doubted he'd need to be off
to his bed—when he'd told her that and had ta'en to the
blankets, and maybe in less than the space of an hour she'd
hold out for the kye and see that he'd lied, the fence neither
mended nor letten a-be, she'd just purse up her meikle wide
mouth and say nothing, her eyes with a glint as though she
half-laughed. And when he came drunken home from a mart

she'd shoo the children out of the room, and take off his clothes and put him to bed, with an extra nip to keep off a chill.

She did half his work in the Tocherty parks, she'd yoke up the horse and the sholtie together, and kilt up her skirts till you'd see her great legs, and cry *Wissh!* like a man and turn a fair drill, the sea-gulls cawing in a cloud behind, the wind in her hair and the sea beyond. And Menzies with his sly-like eyes would be off on some drunken ploy to Kinneff or Stonehive. Man, you couldn't but think as you saw that steer it was well that there was a thing like marriage, folk held together and couldn't get apart; else a black look-out it well would be for the fusionless creature of Tocherty toun.

Well, he drank himself to his grave at last, less smell on the earth if maybe more in it. But she broke down and wept, it was awful to see, Meg Menzies weeping like a stricken horse, her eyes on the dead, quiet face of her man. And she ran from the house, she was gone all that night, though the bairns cried and cried her name up and down the parks in the sound of the sea. But next morning they found her back in their midst, brisk as ever, like a great-boned mare, ordering here and directing there, and a fine feed set the next day for the folk that came to the funeral of her orra man.

She'd four of the bairns at home when he died, the rest were in kitchen-service or fee'd, she'd seen to the settling of the queans herself; and twice when two of them had come home, complaining-like of their mistresses' ways, she'd thrashen the queans and taken them back—near scared the life from the doctor's wife, her that was mistress to young Jean Menzies. *I've skelped the lassie and brought you her back. But don't you ill-use her, or I'll skelp you as well.*

There was a fair speak about that at the time, Meg Menzies and the vulgar words she had used, folk told that she'd even said what was the place where she'd skelp the bit doctor's wife. And faith! that fair must have been a sore shock to the doctor's wife that was that genteel she'd never believed she'd a place like that.

Be that as it might, her man new dead, Meg wouldn't hear of leaving the toun. It was harvest then and she drove the reaper up and down the long, clanging clay rigs by the sea, she'd jump down smart at the head of a bout and go gathering and binding swift as the wind, syne wheel in the horse to the cutting again. She led the stooks with her bairns to help, you'd see them at night a drowsing cluster under the moon on the harvesting cart.

And through that year and into the next and so till the speak died down in the Howe Meg Menzies worked the Tocherty toun; and faith, her crops came none so ill. She rode to the mart at Stonehive when she must, on the old box-cart, the old horse in the shafts, the cart behind with a sheep for sale or a birn of old hens that had finished with laying. And a butcher once tried to make a bit joke. *That's a sheep like yourself, fell long in the tooth.* And Meg answered up, neighing like a horse, and all heard: *Faith, then, if you've got a spite against teeth I've a clucking hen in the cart outbye. It's as toothless and senseless as you are, near.*

Then word got about of her eldest son, Jock Menzies that was fee'd up Allardyce way. The creature of a loon had had fair a conceit since he'd won a prize at a ploughing match— not for his ploughing, but for good looks; and the queans about were as daft as himself, he'd only to nod and they came to his heel; and the stories told they came further than that. Well, Meg'd heard the stories and paid no heed, till the last one came, she was fell quick then.

Soon's she heard it she hove out the old bit bike that her daughter Kathie had bought for herself, and got on the thing and went cycling away down through the Bervie braes in that spring, the sun was out and the land lay green with a blink of mist that was blue on the hills, as she came to the toun where Jock was fee'd she saw him out in a park by the road, ploughing, the black loam smooth like a ribbon turning and wheeling at the tail of the plough. Another billy came ploughing behind, Meg Menzies watched till they reached the rig-end, her great chest heaving like a meikle roan's, her eyes on the shape of the furrows they made. And they drew to the end and drew the horse out, and Jock cried *Ay*, and she answered back *Ay*, and looked at the drill, and gave a bit snort, *If your looks win prizes, your ploughing never will.*

Jock laughed, *Fegs, then, I'll not greet for that*, and chirked to his horses and turned them about. But she cried him *Just bide a minute, my lad. What's this I hear about you and Ag Grant?*

He drew up short then, and turned right red, the other childe as well, and they both gave a laugh, as plough-childes do when you mention a quean they've known over-well in more ways than one. And Meg snapped *It's an answer I want, not a cockerel's cackle: I can hear that at home on my own dunghill. What are you to do about Ag and her pleiter?*

And Jock said *Nothing*, impudent as you like, and next minute Meg was in over the dyke and had hold of his lug and shook him and it till the other childe ran and caught at her nieve. *Faith, mistress, you'll have his lug off!* he cried. But Meg Menzies turned like a mare on new grass, *Keep off or I'll have yours off as well!*

So he kept off and watched, fair a story he'd to tell when he rode out that night to go courting his quean. For Meg held to the lug till it near came off and Jock swore that he'd put things right with Ag Grant. She let go the lug then and looked at him grim: *See that you do and get married right quick, you're the like that needs loaded with a birn of bairns—to keep you out of the jail, I jaloose. It needs smeddum to be either right coarse or right kind.*

They were wed before the month was well out, Meg found them a cottar house to settle and gave them a bed and a press she had, and two-three more sticks from Tocherty toun. And she herself led the wedding dance, the minister in her arms, a small bit childe; and 'twas then as she whirled him about the room, he looked like a rat in the teeth of a tyke, that he thanked her for seeing Ag out of her soss, *There's nothing like a marriage for redding things up.* And Meg Menzies said *EH?* and then she said *Ay*, but queer-like, he supposed she'd no thought of the thing. Syne she slipped off to sprinkle thorns in the bed and to hang below it the great handbell that the bothy-billies took with them to every bit marriage.

Well, that was Jock married and at last off her hands. But she'd plenty left still, Dod, Kathleen and Jim that were still at school, Kathie a limner that alone tongued her mother, Jeannie that next led trouble to her door. She'd been found at her place, the doctor's it was, stealing some money and they sent her home. Syne news of the thing got into Stone-hive, the police came out and tormented her sore, she swore she never had stolen a meck, and Meg swore with her, she was black with rage. And folk laughed right hearty, fegs! that was a clout for meikle Meg Menzies, her daughter a thief!

But it didn't last long, it was only three days when folk saw the doctor drive up in his car. And out he jumped and went striding through the close and met face to face with Meg at the door. And he cried *Well, mistress, I've come over for Jeannie*. And she glared at him over her high, skeugh nose, *Ay, have you so then? And why, may I speir?*

So he told her why, the money they'd missed had been found at last in a press by the door; somebody or other had left it there, when paying a grocer or such at the door. And Jeannie—he'd come over to take Jean back.

But Meg glared. *Ay, well, you've made another mistake. Out of this, you and your thieving suspicions together!* The doctor turned red, *You're making a miserable error*—and Meg said *I'll make you mince-meat in a minute.*

So he didn't wait that, she didn't watch him go, but went ben to the kitchen, where Jeannie was sitting, her face chalk-white as she'd heard them speak. And what happened then a story went round, Jim carried it to school, and it soon spread out, Meg sank in a chair, they thought she was greeting; syne she raised up her head and they saw she was laughing, near as fearsome the one as the other, they thought. *Have you any cigarettes?* she snapped sudden at Jean, and Jean quavered *No*, and Meg glowered at her cold. *Don't sit there*

and lie. Gang bring them to me. And Jean brought them, her
mother took the pack in her hand. *Give's hold of a match till I
light up the thing. Maybe smoke'll do good for the crow that I got
in the throat last night by the doctor's house.*

Well, in less than a month she'd got rid of Jean—packed off
to Brechin the quean was, and soon got married to a creature
there—some clerk that would have left her sore in the lurch
but that Meg went down to the place on her bike, and there,
so the story went, kicked the childe so that he couldn't sit
down for a fortnight, near. No doubt that was just a bit lie
that they told, but faith! Meg Menzies had herself to blame,
the reputation she'd gotten in the Howe, folk said, *She'll meet
with a sore heart yet.* But devil a sore was there to be seen,
Jeannie was married and was fair genteel.

Kathleen was next to leave home at the term. She was tall,
like Meg, and with red hair as well, but a thin fine face, long
eyes blue-grey like the hills on a hot day, and a mouth with
lips you thought over thick. And she cried *Ah well, I'm off
then, mother.* And Meg cried *See you behave yourself.* And
Kathleen cried *Maybe; I'm not at school now.*

Meg stood and stared after the slip of a quean, you'd have
thought her half-angry, half near to laughing, as she watched
that figure, so slender and trig, with its shoulders square-set,
slide down the hill on the wheeling bike, swallows were
dipping and flying by Kinneff, she looked light and free as a
swallow herself, the quean, as she biked away from her home,
she turned at the bend and waved and whistled, she whistled
like a loon and as loud, did Kath.

Jim was the next to leave from the school, he bided at home
and he took no fee, a quiet-like loon, and he worked the toun,
and, wonder of wonders, Meg took a rest. Folk said that age
was telling a bit on even Meg Menzies at last. The grocer
made hints at that one night, and Meg answered up smart as
ever of old: *Damn the age! But I've finished the trauchle of the
bairns at last, the most of them married or still over young. I'm
as swack as ever I was, my lad. But I've just got the notion to
be a bit sweir.*

Well, she'd hardly begun on that notion when faith! ill the news that came up to the place from Segget. Kathleen her quean that was fee'd down there, she'd ta'en up with some coarse old childe in a bank, he'd left his wife, they were off together, and she but a bare sixteen years old.

And that proved the truth of what folk were saying, Meg Menzies she hardly paid heed to the news, just gave a bit laugh like a neighing horse and went on with the work of park and byre, cool as you please—ay, getting fell old.

No more was heard of the quean or the man till a two years or more had passed and then word came up to the Tocherty someone had seen her—and where do you think? Out on a boat that was coming from Australia. She was working as stewardess on that bit boat, and the childe that saw her was young John Robb, an emigrant back from his uncle's farm, near starved to death he had been down there. She hadn't met in with him near till the end, the boat close to Southampton the evening they met. And she'd known him at once, though he not her, she'd cried *John Robb?* and he'd answered back *Ay?* and looked at her canny in case it might be the creature was looking for a tip from him. Syne she'd laughed *Don't you know me, then, you gowk? I'm Kathie Menzies you knew long syne—it was me ran off with the banker from Segget!*

He was clean dumbfounded, young Robb, and he gaped, and then they shook hands and she spoke some more, though she hadn't much time, they were serving up dinner for the first-class folk, aye dirt that are ready to eat and to drink. *If ever you get near to Tocherty toun tell Meg I'll get home and see her some time. Ta-ta!* And then she was off with a smile, young Robb he stood and he stared where she'd been, he thought her the bonniest thing that he'd seen all the weary weeks that he'd been from home.

And this was the tale that he brought to Tocherty, Meg sat and listened and smoked like a tink, forby herself there was young Jim there, and Jock and his wife and their three bit bairns, he'd fair changed with marriage, had young Jock Menzies. For no sooner had he taken Ag Grant to his bed than he'd started to save, grown mean as dirt, in a three-four years he's finished with feeing, now he rented a fell big farm himself, well stocked it was, and he fee'd two men. Jock himself had grown thin in a way, like his father but worse his bothy childes said, old Menzies at least could take a bit dram and get lost to the world but the son was that mean he might drink rat-poison and take no harm, 'twould feel at home in a stomach like his.

Well, that was Jock, and he sat and heard the story of Kath and her say on the boat. *Ay, still a coarse bitch, I have not a doubt. Well if she never comes back to the Mearns, in Segget you cannot but redden with shame when a body will ask "Was Kath Menzies your sister?"*

And Ag, she'd grown a great sumph of a woman, she nodded to that, it was only too true, a sore thing it was on decent bit folks that they should have any relations like Kath.

But Meg just sat there and smoked and said never a word, as though she thought nothing worth a yea or a nay. Young Robb had fair ta'en a fancy to Kath and he near boiled up when he heard Jock speak, him and the wife that he'd married from her shame. So he left them short and went raging home, and wished for one that Kath would come back, a summer noon as he cycled home, snipe were calling in the Auchindreich moor where the cattle stood with their tails a-switch, the Grampians rising far and behind, Kinraddie spread like a map for show, its ledges veiled in a mist from the sun. You felt on that day a wild, daft unease, man, beast and bird: as though something were missing and lost from the world, and Kath was the thing that John Robb missed, she'd something in her that minded a man of a house that was builded upon a hill.

Folk thought that maybe the last they would hear of young Kath Menzies and her ill-gettèd ways. So fair stammygastered they were with the news she'd come back to the Mearns, she was down in Stonehive, in a grocer's shop, as calm as could be, selling out tea and cheese and such-like with no blush of shame on her face at all, to decent women that were properly wed and had never looked on men but their own, and only on them with their braces buttoned.

It just showed you the way that the world was going to allow an ill quean like that in a shop, some folk protested to the creature that owned it, but he just shook his head, *Ah well, she works fine; and what else she does is no business of mine.* So you well might guess there was more than business between the man and Kath Menzies, like.

And Meg heard the news and went into Stonehive, driving her sholtie, and stopped at the shop. And some in the shop knew who she was and minded the things she had done long syne to other bit bairns of hers that went wrong; and they waited with their breaths held up with delight. But all that Meg did was to nod to Kath *Ay, well, then, it's you—Ay, mother, just that—Two pounds of syrup and see that it's good.*

And not another word passed between them, Meg Menzies that once would have ta'en such a quean and skelped her to rights before you could wink. Going home from Stonehive she stopped by the farm where young Robb was fee'd, he was out in the hayfield coling the hay, and she nodded to him grim, with her high horse face. *What's this that I hear about you and Kath Menzies?*

He turned right red, but he wasn't ashamed. *I've no idea— though I hope it's the worse——It fell near is——Then I wish it was true, she might marry me, then, as I've prigged her to do.*

Oh, have you so, then? said Meg, and drove home, as though the whole matter was a nothing to her.

But next Tuesday the postman brought a bit note, from Kathie it was to her mother at Tocherty. *Dear mother, John Robb's going out to Canada and wants me to marry him and go with him. I've told him instead I'll go with him and see what he's like as a man—and then marry him at leisure, if I feel in the mood. But he's hardly any money, and we want to borrow some, so he and I are coming over on Sunday. I hope that you'll have dumpling for tea. Your own daughter, Kath.*

Well, Meg passed that letter over to Jim, he glowered at it

dour, *I know—near all the Howe's heard. What are you going to do, now, mother?*

But Meg just lighted a cigarette and said nothing, she'd smoked like a tink since that steer with Jean. There was promise of strange on-goings at Tocherty by the time that the Sabbath day was come. For Jock came there on a visit as well, him and his wife, and besides him was Jeannie, her that had married the clerk down in Brechin, and she brought the bit creature, he fair was a toff; and he stepped like a cat through the sharn in the close; and when he had heard the story of Kath, her and her plan and John Robb and all, he was shocked near to death, and so was his wife. And Jock Menzies gaped and gave a mean laugh. *Ay, coarse to the bone, ill-gettèd I'd say if it wasn't that we came of the same bit stock. Ah well, she'll fair have to tramp to Canada, eh mother?—if she's looking for money from you.*

And Meg answered quiet *No, I wouldn't say that. I've the money all ready for them when they come.*

You could hear the sea plashing down soft on the rocks, there was such a dead silence in Tocherty house. And then Jock habbered like a cock with fits *What, give silver to one who does as she likes, and won't marry as you made the rest of us marry? Give silver to one who's no more than a——*

And he called his sister an ill name enough, and Meg sat and smoked looking over the parks. *Ay, just that. You see, she takes after myself.*

And Jeannie squeaked *How?* and Meg answered her quiet: *She's fit to be free and to make her own choice the same as myself and the same kind of choice. There was none of the rest of you fit to do that, you'd to marry or burn, so I married you quick. But Kath and me could afford to find out. It all depends if you've smeddum or not.*

She stood up then and put her cigarette out, and looked at the gaping gowks she had mothered. *I never married your father, you see. I could never make up my mind about Will. But maybe our Kath will find something surer. . . . Here's her and her man coming up the road.*

Dorothy K. Haynes

THE HEAD

The joug, the iron collar of penitence, was fastened to the church wall, four feet from the ground. It was too low for a tall man. He could neither stand nor sit, nor even lean in comfort. The gaolers forced him down by the shoulders, and the two semi-circles of iron, cold and heavy, were padlocked round his throat. Then, half squatting, cramped already, he was left to the mob.

The first missile struck him—a wet cloth, which had soaked all night in the kennel. Its stinking folds wrapped him for a moment—as he jerked it off, the iron collar bit into his neck. An old woman, yattering and mumbling like a witch, emptied a pan of slops over his clothes, and he bit his tongue as he tried to duck from a clod of turf. They threw anything, anything which could soil or hurt him, stones, rotten food, and dirty water, till at last he sagged and nearly fainted; then they left him, for there was no fun to be had from a man who could no longer feel.

The sun was beating on to him, and he could not turn his eyes away. Above him, a steeple soared naked in the glare, and somewhere, behind him, a shadow steeple lay bent and prostrate on the roadway, and halfway up the opposite wall. The street was empty, the uneven roofs climbing like steps and stairs, up and up in a jumble of gables and chimney pots. Round his feet was a mass of filth and offal, and his clothing stank with what had dried on him. He eased his neck, and tried to move his legs to support himself more easily. At least, the crowd had gone; now there was the rest of the day to be borne, with the pain of his cramped body and bleeding face. He would have to endure the long burning hours till evening came, when they would free him, and he could stretch his legs, and maybe bathe his wounds and bruises before he crept home.

He did not turn his eyes when he heard the clop of hoofs from the Westport, or the sound of a crowd following. Better to wait, and not anticipate what was to come. He closed his eyes, as the noise came nearer, the steps beating about him, the voices indistinct in their gabble. Then the man on horseback roused him with a deep, jovial hail.

"Hey, there, thief! Here's one to keep you company. Here's a friend for ye!" He edged his horse nearer to the wall, and unwrapped a stained, stiff sacking which rested on his saddle. The thief looked dumbly, his eyes screwed against the light. Inside the wrapping was a human head, hacked off raggedly, the eyes wide open, like grapes ready to burst.

He said nothing. He only stared at the head, and the man on the horse laughed roughly. "English," he said. "We'll see how he likes the view of Scotland frae the top o' the kirk. We'll keep him nearer the ground for the first day, though. The town will mebbe want to see him a bittie clearer."

The crowds were clamouring round the horse, pushing one another for a near view of the horror. The rider cursed, and cleared a path with his powerful voice. "Out the way, there, *out* the way! Plenty of room for you all!" He was in a high, roaring humour, aloft in the saddle, pleased to be the centre of attention. It was a long time since the town had had such a trophy, and he made the most of his position, playing with the head, delaying the moment when he would display it fully.

At the Cross, just in front of the joug and pillory, was an iron spike, a little taller than a man. It was here that the heads or limbs of traitors and enemies were hoisted for public scorn, before being removed to a higher and more exalted position. Once there had been a leg, once a hand, which beckoned to the sky with a bent finger. Now the man on the horse cast away the bloodied sack, and held up the head like an offering. He hesitated. There seemed to be some doubt as to the best way of securing it; then, not wishing to show any inefficiency, he jabbed the neck stump on to the spike, and left it impaled.

The crowd soon tired of the curiosity, sooner than they had tired of baiting the man in the joug. They came to stare, bringing their children, and pointing upwards at the gory thing. Soon, however, they drifted away. There were more pleasant places to spend a summer afternoon, more pleasant things to see. The thief was left alone again, with the street bare and empty before him, and the shadow steeple soon veering round with the sun.

A curtain lifted in a window near the church, and a face peered out, milky white against the pane. All the other houses seemed dead, shut up against the dust and the glare. He was a tenant of an empty town, with only the head to keep him company. He could not keep his eyes from it. Looking at it now, in the harsh sunlight, he saw it more clearly than in the quick glimpse he had had before it was hoisted. It was not a young head. The hair on top, standing up like rushes, was grey, and the skin was bristly and pale, bled white. The mouth was open in surprise, a black slit, the eyes dull and bulging. He wondered how the man had died. Perhaps he had gasped and grimaced as a sword entered his body. Certainly he had not been beheaded in one swift blow. The neck was too ragged, too mangled, the bungled effort of one with more zeal than aptitude.

An Englishman; an enemy. And here they were, side by side, held up to ridicule in the same town. A crow flapped a ragged wing over the church, wheeled, dipped, and circled nearer. It swooped near the head, its beak poised to peck, and the man in the joug called hoarsely, his voice not unlike the voice of the crow. The bird veered off, and again the curtain moved in the house near the church, and a woman's face glanced and retreated quickly. The man could not turn his head to see properly, but he sensed the furtive interest, the curiosity, the disgust, and perhaps the pity. He wanted to think about her, cool in her clean house, calm and kind and

140

feminine; but his mind would not obey him. His interest was all bound up in the head.

He had, for a moment, been afraid of it, afraid lest the crow should strike, and pierce the grape-coloured eyes, or batter its beak on the bony skull. It became very urgent to him that the head should be protected, horrible as it was. It was like a friend to him, goggling with its startled stare, quiet and unmoving in its sufferings. He was so absorbed in it that he forgot his own pain, the numbing crick in his back, the stiff agony of bending legs. His eyes no longer sought the broad sweeping street, or the sun—mellowed jumble of gables. He could see no farther than the head, stuck on its spike. Tomorrow it would rot high among the gargoyles; today, he prayed, it would be left unmolested. Surely the birds would have pity on it for one day!

And then the fly came, a large bluebottle, buzzing a stale, flat song in the heat. "Not on me!" he prayed. "Not on me!" Tethered, unable to move, it would have tortured him to screaming. But the fly only circled and droned, then made straight for the severed head. It settled, buzzed, and returned, settling on the bruised brow. The man watched it, fascinated. It began to creep, slowly, slowly, faltering over every blemish, darting in black, swift rushes, flying off in short circles to creep and creep again. The man flexed his face in sympathy, following the insect's progress with agony. It halted for a long time on an eyelid, poised like a plump currant, then crawled across the bulged eyeball. The man's eyes winked and watered, the fly teased him, hovering on the brink of every aperture, flying off, buzzing madly, but always returning; always, always returning.

The sun shifted, the shadow steeple shifted another point. The man did not notice. His back, his legs, his chafed wrists were all forgotten. All his feelings were centred in his face, and his face twitched and contorted with the borrowed agonies of the face opposite. The black fly went creeping, creeping over a lip, into the black pit of the mouth, and the man spat, his tongue dry, like leather. The fly explored a

141   K

nostril, and he sneezed till the iron cut into his neck again. It ran along a bloodstain into the ear, and he suffered till it trailed out again, creeping, creeping in sudden darts and pauses. He wept aloud. Sweat ran down his face, and he closed his eyes, so that he would not see; but always he had to look again, because his imagination teased him with the buzz and creep and the horrible fancies of his mind.

He was surprised when they came to set him free. He had forgotten that, sometime, they would let him go. The keys jingled, the collar swung back in two halves. "Hey, steady!" said the gaoler, not unkindly. He walked off, swinging his keys, and the man staggered, and sank to the ground. His legs were too cramped to hold him, and his neck swelled so that he thought he would choke.

The shadow of the steeple was in front of the church now, the sun soft and red. Smoke drifted above the roofs, the quiet haze of fires in summer. The house by the church opened its door, and the woman came out at last, hastily, as if half ashamed of her mercy. She had a basin in her hand, and warm water, and a square of soft white cloth. "Here," she said quickly, "bathe your poor face before you go home. Leave the basin, and I'll take it in when you've finished. You'll manage yourself?"

He nodded, too spent to thank her, or to watch her hurry away. He lay for a long time before he could move. At last he dragged himself erect, and bent to the basin. The water was cool now, fresh and cool and soothing. He lifted the cloth, dripping wet over his soiled hand. Slowly and stiffly he limped over to the spike, muttering to himself, "There, there," hardly knowing what he was saying. His dry lips cracked in a smile as, with fumbling, gentle fingers, he wiped the face of the dead.

J. F. Hendry

THE DISINHERITED

A ray of sun, from behind a cloud, opened out on a small figure in a suit of blue Harris tweed, hastening desperately along the empty streets, between the shadowing tenements, to reach the haven of church before the bell stopped ringing. A pale ghost, with bloodless lips sailed past the dark-blue windows of Templeton's the Grocers, Benson's the Newsagents, and the Hill Café, now and then, as it ran, staring backward, appalled, at a reflection in their window-blinds. A cap bit deep into the brow, and a spotted bow-tie pointed to five past seven. There was no time to adjust them.

—— Dong! Ding-dong! Ding-dong!—— sang the chimes, their echoes washing in waves of monotonous warning up the High Street, where a yellow cat stood lazily stropping itself against a chalk-fringed wall.

—— Dong! Ding-dong!—— and then, surprisingly, in a sudden giddy recoil, stopped altogether. Sawney broke into a run as he tackled the cobbled hill.

"What's the hurry?" called Big Sneddon, the policeman, from across the street. "Ye're awfu' religious all of a sudden, or are ye off to a fire? The Bad Fire?——"

He broke down into raucous laughter at his own wit, but the face which was turned on him was so full of savagery, and something else besides, that it would have silenced anyone, let alone Big Sneddon, the handcuff-king. The angular blue figure straightened at once, and gazed thoughtfully after Sawney, now racing uphill, but it was not the expression alone in the latter's face that had sobered him. "Poor Devil," he said aloud, "he's for it all right."

Panting as he arrived at the door, Sawney paused for a moment or two, feeling as breathless as the bells. He turned to the east, but only for the wind, and, taking off his bonnet, waved it once or twice before his face, to dry the sweat.

"Late! Curse it," he coughed, then plunged, like a man in a dream, through the open portals of the Kirk.

In their pew, the family were sitting waiting for him. He walked down the aisle, conscious of their hostile stares, and saw his mother's face grow slowly purple. He was wearing high, narrow boots of red ox-hide, which creaked as he walked, and now seemed about to crack, though this was hardly a cause for anger. His father, however, to his surprise, blew his nose loudly in his handkerchief, and Jimmy, his brother, sniggered outright, in the aisle. It was just like Jimmy to snigger. He had neither tact nor sympathy. He needed a doing!

Grinning sheepishly to several of his mother's stairhead acquaintances, he took his place beside her on the cushion, and a long and vicious hair entered his leg. He squirmed.

"How dare ye," hissed his mother. "Sawney, how dare ye drag me down like this! Never, never, will I be able to live doon the disgrace ye've brought upon me this day!"

Why this should be so was not immediately clear to Sawney, since, just then, in a river of robes, the Minister entered through a side-door and flowed up the stairs that led to the pulpit. You would have thought he was going to his execution, the majestic way he walked up.

These ruminations were cut short by a fierce dig in the ribs. "Ye're finished, dae ye hear? I want no part of ye from now on! Oh, wait till I get ye outside," his mother moaned in whispering, inarticulate rage, one eye on the pulpit where the Minister was opening the Book—"I'll skivver the liver out o' ye, ye impiddent young deevil! Look at ye, look at your face!"

His father's impassive stare, Jimmy's noble contempt, his mother's passion and the amused glances of young girls,

peeping over the tops of their hymn-books, at last forced
Sawney actually to feel his face, which had in fact, now that
his attention had been drawn to it, begun to seem slightly
puffy.

Only then, as the congregation, without warning, stood up
like a forest to sing the opening hymn: "Be Strong in the
Fight!" did it dawn on Sawney's horror-stricken conscience
that he had come to church, to attend morning service, with
two black eyes.

They swelled up till he could scarcely see. Miserably he sat
as though in a cage, exposed to amusement, curiosity and
scorn, his hands thrust between his knees, out of sight, to still
their convulsive bird-like movements of escape.

Whenever he turned to look at her, he met the fixed glare
of his mother, or heard the words: "Vagabond! Scamp!——"

He grued when he thought of the end of the service, when
he would have to face her tigerish wrath, out there in the
bright sunlight. Surely this enforced silence would do something to calm her down? Instead, it only served to deepen her
shame.

"The disgrace!" she said, drawing her breath, and looking
round, her back stiff.

Sheepishly, he grinned again and looked at his father, who
pushed forward his white moustache and stolidly gazed at the
pulpit.

Once more, he was in disgrace. He had always been in disgrace ever since, a boy in striped pants, called "Zebra" by his
unfeeling friends, he had left school for the last time and
kicked his books high in the air over the wall into Sighthill
Cemetery. The only prize he had ever had in his life, was a
book called *No and Where to Say It*, and that was for regular
attendance at the Highland Society School. It was a good
book. It told you about the perils of life for a young man, and
how easy it was, after the first weak "Yes" to evil com-
panions, to go on saying "Yes", and end up gambling, drinking, going with women and spending your substance, or
breaking your mother's heart.

"You'll break my heart!" she hissed now. "You and your wild hooligan freens!——"

He had learned to say "No" from that book. Surely *he* could not be breaking his mother's heart? He did not drink. He did not gamble. All he did was box every Sunday morning in the stables behind Possil Quarry.

He was not, Sawney told himself, in the habit of grousing, but what chance had he ever had? Instead of meditating now on his sins, as he should have done, or trying to remember exactly what it was that Joseph had taken with him from Pharaoh's palace, he began to think of his own upbringing. An old man, who had once been an agricultural labourer, wearing a lum hat wanting a crown, had stood like a clown in the cobbled backyard of the house in Grafton Street when he was born, his patron saint, an industrial troubadour, singing in beggared chivalry. In token of the day of infinite jest it was, he played on a flute that through his mother's dreams had drowned the sound of the traffic, and now and then quavered a thoroughly commercial chorus:

Balloons and windmills for jelly jars!

Amid that great conglomeration of city streets, blocks of tenements, unsightly factories, and engineering shops, intricate as the network of railways imposed on the town without so much as a by-your-leave, without planning of any sort, and with no principles at all save those of immediate and substantial gain, there was no one to suckle the child except the midwife, a stout buxom woman, timeless as one of the Furies, as it lay blinking in the bed on the wall.

Outside his room lay the rampant scenery of loch and mountain, but Campsie and Lennoxtown were as far away, for the child, as the life his ancestors had once led among these former fields. Their miles had been transformed into money. Nearer were the forests of poverty broken down into the fuel and ash of coal-depots and yards. Nearer were the foliage and sky of hoardings, blossoming enormous letters and pictures, a mythology of commerce, whose gods and demons waited to invade his fairyland. Nearer were the woodland paths of tram-lines and railways. An iron song of bells and sirens stilled the birds. He had been born into a cage.

Nomadic crime had settled on these steppes. Where once the total police force had consisted of Sergeant Oliver and Constable Walker, now twenty-six officers and men were required to keep what they called "the peace", a force larger than that of other equally populated areas further south—such as Ayr.

His self-pity was cut rudely short.

A thunder of shuffling presaged the "skailing" of the kirk. The congregation relaxed and allowed itself the luxury of starched smiles.

Sawney rose, and filtered slowly and shamefully, out into the bright sunlight, feeling more forsaken, more forlorn than ever.

Outside, little groups stood discussing the sermon, waiting for friends, inspecting each other's dress, or gossiping. Mrs. Anderson sailed past them, her ears burning, imagining that behind her she could hear suppressed laughter, scandalous allegations and even criminal threats.

She waited until she had reached the comparative neutrality of the pavement, then she spun round on her son, who had been dragging behind like an unwilling puppy.

"How did it happen? Who did it to ye? It serves ye right!" she said in one breath.

"It wasna my fault, honest! He hit me first."

"Who? I'll never, *never* forgive ye for this, I swear!"

"Dukes Kinnaird. He was sparring. He's to fight the English champion tomorrow. They asked me to go a couple of rounds with him."

"Did ye?" asked the white-haired old man who was his father, stuffing thick black down into his pipe and trying to look angry, in support of his wife.

"It was only supposed to be a spar," pleaded Sawney, "but all of a sudden he hit me right between the eyes. I saw he was coming for a knock-out, the dirty dog."

147

"Don't dare use that language in front of me. On a Sunday, too!"

"What happened?" his father asked.

"I let go with my left and crossed with my right. He went back over the ropes into a bath of hot water."

The old man laughed. His wife turned on him. "That's enough of you! Well, I'm for no more of it. Ye can come hame and pack yer things. I don't want ye in my hoose. Ye'll end up on the end of a rope one day, I tell ye."

For all his waywardness, Sawney was genuinely appalled. Leave home? Where would he go? He'd be a laughing stock. He knew his mother, the auld wife, was hard, but only now was he beginning to realize just how hard. She seemed to have no affection for him left.

"Ye'll pack your things and away this very night!" she said.

He looked at the auld wife to see if she meant it. Her collar stood high on her scrawny neck, and her hat, with one feather on it, made her seem a comical figure, in her anger.

"Why can't you be liker your brother?" his father asked in a low voice. "He never gets into any scrapes."

"We canny all be in the Post Office," said Sawney.

"He's a well-behaved lad. It's a pity ye werena liker him. He'll do weel for himself."

Sawney did not doubt it. He had never denied that his brother was a very worthy man, a gentleman, and different altogether from himself. It had seemed natural to him, even as a boy, that he should have to fight Jimmy's battles, although Jimmy was older than he was, in the days when fights really were fights. Many a "jelly-nose" he had awarded boys at school to save his brother's reputation and the family honour, but it never occurred to him to talk about it, or to think there was any particular merit in it. Jimmy was the meritorious one. He never got into scrapes, never fought, never squabbled. Such things were beneath him. He read books until they wafted him into the Post Office, and now he was a Sorter— to Sawney, one of the intellectuals.

As they walked down Hillkirk Road, Mrs. Anderson bowing in enforced silence, and screwing up her eyes in what she imagined to be a smile to her neighbours, he had to step on to the pavement to avoid a horse and cart, which with a great grinding of the brake was proceeding downhill. It reminded him of early escapades, which really, he thought, had been enough to break even his mother's stout heart. Had he been younger, he would almost certainly have jumped on the back of that same lorry. He had always done so, until the fatal day when he slipped and the wheel went over his leg, breaking it. He had then had to spend six weeks in bed. What a delight it had been to get out again!

He could still remember that afternoon as clearly as this one. It had been such heaven to run about with his leg out of plaster of Paris, that he must have gone slightly mad. Another lorry passed, and forgetting his mother's injunctions, he had darted after it as soon as he was out of the close-mouth. Leaning on the back with his stomach, he heaved himself up, putting one foot on the rear-axle as he did so. To his horror, his foot slipped and slid through between the spokes. He had howled, for the bone was broken, for the second time. Then, far more scared of his mother than of what had happened to his foot, he had limped upstairs into the close, and sat for three-quarters of an hour on the stairhead lavatory seat, white and sick, gazing at the blood on his leg and hoping somehow it would heal before he had to go in. It did not heal, and he had had a thrashing on top of the ordeal.

Now they were in Springburn Road and Mrs. Anderson could give something like full vent to her fury.

"I've a good mind to belt yer ear!" she said. "If you were half a man you'd dae it!" she concluded to her husband.

"But he's a man!" protested the latter. "He's past that!" Then, seeing the ruthlessness in his wife's features, he came to a firm resolve.

"All right," he said, "I'll take him in hand myself."

"You will," she repeated, "and he'll go this very night, don't forget!"

"How could you do it? To me? Your own mother? Don't I work and slave for ye? Haven't I always worked and slaved to bring you up in decency?"

She was working herself up into a frenzy, starting a "flyting", and Sawney sought for a way of escape, any way of escape.

"You told me to come to Church, so I came!" he parried.

"You came! You came did ye? Do ye know what the neighbours will be saying this verry meenit? Do ye?"

"Excuse me, mither," he said, "there's Rob across the street. I want to talk to him. See you later!"

As he dashed across the roadway to Rob, he heard his mother's last few words hurtle after him.

"Ye can come and fetch yer things when ye're ready!"

It was late when Sawney finally arrived home, having put off the evil hour as long as he possibly could. The door was locked. But it was not the first time he had been locked out, and he knew what to do. Prising open the bedroom window, he climbed up and firmly grasped the aspidistra plant he knew stood there, so that it should not fall over. Then, stepping in, he advanced with it in his arms, through the darkness, into the middle of the room. There was a loud crash.

He had walked bang into the half-open door. Now the fat was in the fire! For a second there was silence, then:

"Come here!" thundered his father's voice from the kitchen.

Walking awkwardly through, the plant still in his hand, he saw the old man standing firmly by the gas-bracket, in his shirt-sleeves, with his cap on.

"I've come to get my things," he said sullenly. "—— are they upstairs?"

"A fine time to come in I must say! Yer things? I've done all *your* packing, my lad! There's nothing left for you to do. It's all here for you to take!"

He had never seen his father so determined before. It was an unpleasant shock. He had no idea where he would go in the middle of the night, unless to Rob's. He saw his father peer forward, as though to read his mood, and an unreasoning anger took hold of him:

"I'm not going to give up boxing because of her," he said defiantly. "Where are my things?"

"Ye can do whatever ye like. It's up to you," was the answer. "Your things? How many things dae ye think ye've got, beyond what ye stand up in, ye pauper? There's your things, the lot of them!"

He nodded towards the mantelpiece. Sawney's eyes followed.

"There's only a matchbox there!" he said.

His father's features relaxed. "I ken that," he answered, knocking out his pipe, "but it's big enough to hold a' *you* own!"

They stared at each other, and ruefully smiled.

His father put his fingers on the gas-bracket.

"Try not to upset your mother again!" he said. "Are you a' right?"

"All right," said Sawney, about to speak, but his father had already turned down the gas and the little kitchen was in complete darkness.

By the red glare of the fire they made their way to bed.

A. J. Cronin

THE PROVOST'S TALE

It was Hogmanay night—eve of Scotland's greatest feast—
and at the Philosophical Club of Levenford a full assembly
prepared to see the New Year in. Members relaxed in the
presence of their guests, and, abandoning all thought of pro-
found debate, consented to pass the hours in amicable inter-
course. Many songs had been sung and many stories told, and
in between the talk flowed easily. Then, midway through the
evening, a lull fell within the bright and cheerful room. Old
John Leckie had spoken.

Leckie, who had been Provost of the Borough more than
thirty years ago, was now an aged, taciturn man of eighty,
who came to the club only on special occasions—to honour it
with the presence of its oldest member. Then he would sit in
his special corner—silent, dignified, and apparently remote.

But at the right moment he would speak, and now, cutting
across a conversation which maligned a recent change in the
Levenford weather, he had said:

"You're speaking about the thaw. Well, I can tell ye a
story about a thaw that happened lang syne, and it was and
it wasna to do with the weather."

A polite murmur of encouragement rose from the gathering, at which he paused, took his pipe from his lips, fixed a
rheumy, reminiscent eye upon his listeners, and held them
as he spoke.

There's not many here this night will mind of Martha
Lang, but in her time no woman in this Borough was better

152

kenned. About the back end of last century she kept a small
tobacconist's shop at the corner of Church Street and Dobbie's
Loan.

'Twas all done away with, that property, when they
widened the road to fetch the tram-cars to the toun more nor
twenty year ago; but anyway, that was where Martha had her
shop.

"Black Martha" some called her, and others "Bible
Martha", but that was aye behind her back, for none
would dare to take a liberty with Martha Lang before her
face.

She wasn't a tall body—rather to the contrar', in fact. Her
hair was dark, and clenched back tight from her brow, and she
was aye dressed plain as plain in a black serge goun, so that
you might think she was a woman you'd never look twice at.

Ay, like a shadow she was in the dimness of her own shop,
but her spirit was no shadow. She had a look on her pale,
narrow face that struck you and daunted you—a kind of tight-
lipped, bitter look it was, and it burned out of her dark
browed eye like fire. Some folks were feared of her and many
hated her, but all agreed that she was a just and righteous
woman. Ay, she was a saved woman, and the proud look of it
was in her eye.

The shop wasna muckle to look at. Its window was small
with panes of greenish blown glass, and that low it seemed to
courie doun beneath the figure of an East Indianman that
stuck out above it; and all that it held was three yellow
canisters that stood solemn-like in a row. The door was stiff,
and went "ping" when ye opened it.

Inside, the place was murky. 'Twas like an auld apothe-
cary's shop with its counter and small brass scale and its row
of blue and white delf jars, but 'twas silent, somehow, and
severe—too cold in winter, too hot in summer—a place not
made to linger in.

Next to the shop was the kitchen of Martha's house. It had
a window that opened to Dobbie's Loan and one in the divid-
ing wall—a kind of keek-hole, ye might say—that let ye see

from the shop to the kitchen or the other way about, as the case might be.

The kitchen was just ordinar'. A big dresser against the wall with blue china on it, three pewter covers hanging on the wall with the fire in the range glinting on them dourly, a wag-at-the-wall clock, twa texts, a table scrubbed to a driven whiteness, some straight chairs, and a long, low, horsehair sofa—that made up the tale of the furnishings. And out of the room a flight of narrow steps arose, steep as any ladder, to the twa bedrooms above.

At the time I'm speaking of Martha's husband had been dead and coffined and buried these fifteen years. A long time! She had been left with one bairn, a boy called Geordie. He was three year auld when Martha was widowed, and so she had the upbringin' of him. And bring him up she did! Strict wasna the name for the way she handled him. Never a glint of human affection kindled her bleak eye. To those that dared tax her on the matter, she had the answer pat, and she would throw Ecclesiastes xii and 8 right intil their teeth. Ay, bitter and harsh she was with him in everything.

Well, that was Martha and her son, and at the time the fearsome thing I'm going to speak of came about Geordie was turned eighteen years auld. He was a strapping lad, with wide shoulders and arms that dangled doun into his big red hands; and he had a pleasant, open face. Yet a kind of saft and simple look was in the face, as though some of the spunk had been leathered out of him when he was younger. An apprentice engineer he was, learning his trade in the shipyard.

'Twas the winter of 1895. A black frost had grippit the land. The roads were like iron; the pond was bearing; twal' degrees it was some nights; in the morning a skin of ice on the ewer, and your brose cauld before ye supped them.

Twa days before Christmas, I was in Martha's shop for my ounce of the usual about half-past six in the evening, when Geordie came out of the kitchen. Whenever Martha set eye on him she put doun the lid on the jar sharp.

"Where are ye going?" says she, in the hard way she had.

"I thought I would take a turn doun to the pond," he answered mild-like, ye ken. He had his skates swingin' by the straps in his hand.

"Were ye not out last night?" quoth she again, "and can ye find no more profitable work to do?"

He made some excuse about the exercise being fine, but all the time her glower never lifted. Then all at once she shifted her eyes. It was as if the sight of him scaurried her.

"Be in before the clock chaps nine, then," she said sternly, "and watch the company ye keep."

Well, Geordie trots out, and as his way was mine we went doun the road together. For all the cold it was a braw night. The lamps in the street had white rings round their globes like hoar; the moon was in its first quarter, and it was pinned high up in the velvet sky like a brooch; the jingle of Geordie's skates—they had been his father's, mind ye, and that was how he came by them—made fine, clear music.

He was fond of the skating, ye see, and he was a bonny, bonny skater. Sure enough, there was none to equal him in Levenford. At the corner of the Common we said good-nicht, and off he went to the ice, and home I went to my own fireside.

I didna see Geordie for twa or three days. Christmas went by, and all the time the frost continued. It couldna last like that was what folks said, stamping their feet as they talked for a short second at the Cross; it would crack quick, like all these bitter frosts. But last it did. Hard and fast it lasted, and at the middle of the week word came through from Darroch that the Loch was frozen over, a thing that hadna happened for near enough seven year.

Well, on that same day I was in Martha's shop. Earlier than my usual, I was, and the Yard horn had just blown for half-past five. I had pouched my ounce, and paid for't, and was just having twa words with Martha—not that I took much pleasure in that, but as Provost then it behoved me more than ordinar' to keep on the richt side of Martha's bitter tongue.

She was at her endless knitting ahint the counter, and I was standin' in the far corner, when "Ping!" the door swings open, and Geordie comes in. I was in the shadow, more nor less, and so full was he of what he was going to say that he didn't see me, and straight out he bursts, "The Loch's frozen, mother, and there's grand ice as far as Ardmurren island."

"And what benefit is that to you or to me?" raps out Martha, knit, knitting away.

Geordie looked doun at his big boots, glaikit-like.

"There's the race," he jerks out.

"The race!" quoth she, sharp, as though she doubted her own hearing. And she lays doun the knitting, and looks straight at him with a black stare.

"You know, mother, for the Winton Antlers," Geordie went fumblin' on. "They're wantin' me to gang in. Do ye not mind about it?"

Now I kenned what Geordie was driving at. The race ower the ice, he meant, from Markinch, round the island of Ardmurren, and back again. 'Twas a historic race, open to the countryside, instituted by the fourth Earl of Winton lang syne—some say 'twas first done when Rob Roy was in his prime—and the Earl had gien a kind of trophy for the prize, a head of antlers mounted on oak, above a silver shield. Though 'twas seldom that it could take place, the auld custom had been keepit up and some made muckle o't.

Anyway, I could see that Martha jaloused what her son meant, for she looked at him fiercely, and cried, "Have ye taken leave of your senses?"

"But I'm picked as the best in the toun," Geordie explained, "and it's on Hogmanay Saturday. I needna miss my work. It's—it's an honour."

"Honour, forsooth," bursts out Martha. "Black dishonour, ye should say. Are ye still a bairn, that ye know not what this thing is? A meeting for the godless of the countryside! Brawling and drunkenness, amangst corrupt and sinful men. And, above all, a race, with the workers of iniquity wagerin' siller upon the winner. Oh! I have mind of it from my younger days before the grace came to me."

She made an effort, and calmed herself.

"No, no! You'll be party to no such mockery in the fair face of God's daylight."

"But, mother, I'll gamble none and I'll drink none," Geordie pleaded. "I'm only wantin' to skate for the toun."

"Can ye touch pitch and remain undefiled?" cries Martha.

Geordie's lip hung doun like a bairn's.

"What way are ye so doun on me?" he mumbled. "You treat me like I was a dog."

A spasm tightened Martha's face.

"Go in!" she cried loudly, pointing to the kitchen. "You'll go to no race! And black, burning shame on you that would dare to lift your voice against your mother!"

He gien her a kind of dejeckit look, and, for all his size, put down his head and went shouldering off as she had bid him. When he had gane, Martha drew in her breath between her teeth. Her face was grey, yet kind of triumphant, like the face of a woman that chastises herself and draws out o't a bitter ecstasy.

Well, the week went on, and so did the frost, and towards the week's end it seemed to stiffen its grasp like the last spasm of a dying man. On the eve of Hogmanay a few thin snowflakes came waverin' doun out of the numb sky. Folks prophesied a white end for the auld year, but the morning of the year's last day broke clear, and all that was left of the snow was some that had sifted into corners and crannies like sugar. The sun came up, round and red, as if 'twere shamed for staying so long away. But as it mounted higher in the sky it shone bright and bonny.

'Twas the day of the race, this, mark ye. Though I hadna much interest in the matter, what with one thing and another —the day being so braw and the feel of Hogmanay in the air—when Bailie Weir asked me to drive up to Markinch with him in his new gig I said I'd go. And so we set out after dinner. We came to Markinch all too soon. The single street of the village—by ordinar' so empty a dog could sleep safe in the middle o't—was black with folks moving and laughing and pushing on to the rough white ice that edged the shore.

Hereabouts on the frozen loch they had put up some booths, and round about these stalls the crowd was gathered, in fine fettle, ye may guess.

Near enough two hundred folks were clustered on the ice—a large gathering considering, and a gathering not without its notables.

When the time of the race drew near, the gaiety and excitement louped up the higher. At three o'clock the competitors came out from their tent on to the clear space which formed the starting point—six young men, the picked skaters of the district—and began to skate about, sweeping in circles, and taking short dashes up the course to loosen their limbs.

I tell ye plump and plain that when I saw them my eyes near drappit out of my heid, for there amangst them was Geordie. I could scarcely credit it, but so it was. Geordie Lang was there! He had a queer, nervous air about him, as if he was gey and sorry he was there. I've told ye he was a big, saft lad, and now there was a scared, muddled look on him as if he didna know how in all the world he had got to Markinch.

Anyway, the Bailie and myself went ower and spoke to Geordie.

"How do you feel for it, Geordie?" Weir speired. I hadna let on to Weir about what I knew, and he wasna a customer of Martha's in any case.

"I'm not bad, thank ye, Mister Weir," says Geordie, in a pithless voice.

"Are ye all set? Ye couldna have a better day for't."

"Day or no day, I'll never win it," said Geordie, in the same fushionless manner.

The Bailie laughed, and slapped Geordie on the back.

"It's half the battle to have gotten round your mother," said I, quiet-like. "I was feared she wouldna let ye come."

Geordie made no reply. He heard me but pretended not to; but I saw his sandy eyebrows gie a quick twitch. I kenned then that he had slipped out his gear and rin awa' to the race against Martha's will. And so it was. He had just come on straight from his work, and hadna been home for his dinner.

Fond, fond of the skating was Geordie, ye see. But losh! I felt heart sorry for the lad, thinkin' on the kind of homecoming he wad have, win or no win, with the Antlers or without them.

In the meantime Weir was speaking.

"Watch yourself when you're roundin' the island," counselled the Bailie, pointing his finger. "Don't swing too wide or you'll lose distance."

The three of us looked towards Ardmurren, which rose like a dark hillock in a wide deserted plain. Three miles away it was, out in the middle of the loch, but in that bright light it showed so clear we could near see the scarlet clusters upon the distant holly trees.

"And keep well up the middle," continued the Bailie, waving his hand as though he kenned all about it. "You'll get the smoothest ice there."

Geordie nodded his head listlessly, as though to say, "I'm in for it now, anyway," but what he did say was, "I'll do my best. I can do no more."

"Good luck to ye then, lad," cried Weir; and as Geordie moved off what could I do but say the same?

Well, by this time they were preparing for the start, the six men lined up—they had drawn their places by pulling straws —the crowd quiet and eager. Geordie was leanin' forward with his lips thegither, and I could see the cold sweat on his brow. Right reason or none, it gied me a grue to look at him. I could hardly keep my eyes off him.

Twa of the other skaters I kenned by name. The man in the middle—Big Callum, they called him—was an athlete who had won medals for tossing the caber, no less, at the Luss Games and he didna seem to be carin' a bit. And next to him was Dewar, a lang strip of a callant who was tightening his belt and chewing tobacco to steady himself. The other three lads at the end of the line were not accounted to have muckle chance, but by the looks of them they were going to try.

Well, they were ready at last. Colquhoun, the keeper, who was starting the race, put his shot-gun to his shoulder, and raised the muzzle towards the sky. The crowd held its breath.

159

"Are ye ready, lads?" shouts Colquhoun. I saw Geordie clench his teeth, and knot up his big red hands, then "Bang!" went the gun. The skates crunched into the ice. They were off.

The crowd roared. The start was a good one, and the six lads shot doun the course spaced even, in a straight rank. Ower the broad open space they swept, skimming like a flight of birds across a glassy sea, and the screel of their skates had a sound like the whistle of wings.

"A fine, fair start!" shouted someone. "There's nothing in it."

No, there was nothing in it, for the first mile; then in a gradual kind of fashion Callum began to draw away from the rest. He wasna a bonny skater but he was powerful, and he lunged forrit with savage thrusts of his strong legs.

"Callum's ahead! He's got it by ten yards!" bawled out the head-keeper, who had his glass to his eye.

The cry of Callum was ta'en up.

"Dewar's second!" shouted Colquhoun again, "and the rest a' bunched thegither!"

Well, they went like this for another mile; then they drew near to Ardmurren, driving to it like an arrow to the target. They were there, in a long column now, out of which the six of them flashed round in turn. A kind of sigh, like a sough of wind, swept up from the crowd as they swept out of sight. Then there was a fresh yell as the first man swung into view. "Callum's round first! Callum's ahead!"

Aside me Bailie Weir was on his tiptoes. A red-faced man at the best of times, he was purple now.

"Did ye notice?" he cried at me. "Lang took the best o' the bend. He's inside now, like I telled him."

Away, far, far, I could see that Geordie was lyin' third, behind Dewar and Callum. The pace was ower good for the rest of them. They had tailed a long distance behind. But Geordie was goin' well, with an easy swing of his lanky legs. There's no doubt but that he was a bonny, bonny skater.

All the time the crowd was in a regular stir; but somehow I didna feel excited. Something hung ower me; I couldna just explain what it was or how it was, but half-troubled I felt and half-feared.

Well, on they came, getting nearer and nearer. Half-way home, ye could see, even at the distance, that Callum was tiring. Dewar was pressing him, close on his heels, coming up with the short, running style he had. Callum spurted but couldna shake the other off. Neck and neck Dewar and Callum came tearin' along. Then Callum began to flag. The crowd was in a fever—the one half crying Callum's name and the other Dewar's—so ta'en up with the twa o' them, they forgot about Geordie. But the Bailie had his eye on Lang.

"Look at him, will ye?" he bawls out. "He's coming up!" And sure enough Geordie lengthened his lang legs, and up he came like a clap of wind.

The folks from Levenford that wanted their man to win went wild with excitement.

"Geordie!" they roared. "Come on, Geordie! Come on!"

Well, Geordie couldna hear them, but he did come on, and before ye could blink an eye he flew past both Callum and Dewar, so quick that they seemed to drop backwards from him. Twa, five, ten yards ahead he was. Ay, at a mile from home he was near twenty yards to the fore.

"Geordie! Geordie Lang!" roared the crowd, cheering and tossing their bonnets.

Well, as I have told ye—and the stricken truth it is—midst all the shoutin' I had a sore oppression on me. And the louder they shouted the waur it grew. Whether it was the thought of Martha or that strange look on Geordie's face, I canna tell, but, as God's my witness, I had the cold fear that something awfu' was going to come about. And come about it did.

At the half-mile from home, when Geordie was away in the front o' the others, suddenly and without warnin' there came a crack that would have made your heart stand still, a fearsome sound that was like the crack o' doom, that cut the cheering like it had been severed.

God knows there's been many a story about breakin' ice and drookit skaters, but this was different as hell from heaven.

With these very eyes I saw it, and the memory still gars me shudder. The ice broke, and Geordie Lang went through it like a stane. The ane minute he was skimming like a bird—the next he was gane through a jaggy hole, out of which the black water slathered like cankered bluid. The others coming behind swerved away like things demented. Geordie alone went doun.

It all happened in a second before ye could draw breath. A gasp, then a groan, went up the crowd; then a fearsome shout of horror. Weir's red face whitened like a clout.

"God Almighty!" cried Colquhoun, and he flung his gun ahint him, and started racing up the ice. Many a one was frichted, and there was a great rush to the shore, but some of us followed the keeper.

Oh, it was a dreadful, dreadful business. When we reached the spot there wasna a sign of Geordie, and when we tried to draw near the broken edge, a crackin' started that would have daunted the stoutest heart. Out they rushed from the village with ropes and a ladder, but not a sign of Geordie could we see. Then Callum, that had been in the race, tore off his skates. He had kenned Geordie well, and now he was frantic-like with grief.

"I'll get him," he shouts. "I'll get him!"

Well, they tied a rope around Callum, and after he had skimmed along the ladder, into that icy water he went. 'Twas the bravest thing I've ever seen. Once he went doun, then twice, then once again. And the third time he came up—his face pale, his teeth chatterin' in his heid, his hair sleekit ower his brow, and he had Geordie in his arms.

Ye never heard such a shout as was lifted then. But that was the pity o't, for 'twas no use at all. Geordie was dead. We tried a' things when we got him to the bank, every mortal thing, for an hour on end, but 'twas all useless. Gae'n doun he must have bashed his head upon the ice, but, whatever the cause, there he lay, cold and lifeless on the loch shore.

Oh, it was a weary business, and there was a terrible to-do. One said one thing, and one said another. A great outcry arose against Colquhoun, who had been made responsible for the arrangements and had said that the course was fit. Distracted, the keeper was, and he kept swearing to me he had been twice to Ardmurren that very mornin'. Ay, and so he had. But he'd never ta'en thought to go round the island and come back by the middle. That's where the ice was thinnest ye see; and the heat of the sun had just finished it.

Well, what was done was done, and that was all about it, and it was neither time nor place for casting hard words about. And as Provost I had my say. I silenced them all, and the upshot was that poor Geordie's body was put on a farm wagon, and covered with due reverence. Then with Weir's gig in front, off we started on the drive back to Levenford.

God! When ye think on how we came spankin' out in the sunshine, that goin' back was weary, weary wark. Never a single word passed between the Bailie and myself the whole road back. Ye see there was Martha to be thought of now; ay, and the telling of her. Not that I feared her grief. No. I'm an auld man now, and can speak plain. I feared the black bitterness of her tongue.

Well, when we drew near to Levenford, the sky had clouded over and a fine smir of rain had come on. Ye may well guess I had little relish for my task, and when we turned into Church Street my eye louped when I saw the parish minister walking slowly along the pavement. It was just that hour of the Saturday when he went to Martha's and quick as look at him I cried out to him to stop.

The minister was a small spectacled man, with a stoop; a man fond of the book-learning, but a good man he was for all that, ay, both in the pulpit and out of it. He wasna one to flinch, and when he saw 'twas his duty to go to Martha, then he put his teeth together, and marched with me to the shop.

Well, I make no pretence of bein' what I'm not. I was fair shaken with what I had seen upon the loch, and I had no stomach for muckle more. When the minister and myself went into that shop my heart was thump, thumping against my ribs like a hammer.

Martha was there right enough; standing ahint her counter, waiting for the son that had disobeyed her. Ye could see from the look in her eye that she was ready to chastise him—not with whips but with scorpions. Ay, and before we could speak, she let out at us. Seeing us together she jaloused in her wrang-headed fashion that we had come to plead for Geordie.

"It's no use, minister," she cries out, "there's no use your comin' to ask me to let him off. He maun dree his own weird."

A kind of shiver went through me as I heard her.

"Martha, Martha, woman," says the minister in a quiet voice, "ye must forgive your son."

"Not till he goes on his bended knees," she rasps out; "not till he begs my forgiveness." Her eyes glowered at him. But the minister didna flinch.

"I charge you, Martha Lang, to forgive your son," says he again; "and do it now or you may regret it all your born days."

A twisted look drew ower Martha's face, and she flung out, "Not till I've punished him for what he's done."

"Punish him you will not," says the minister in a sorrowful voice. "That's all bye with now."

Then he told her what had happened.

There was a sort of twitching came into Martha's cheek, but she shouted: "I dinna believe ye. It's a lee ye're telling me to frighten me and get him off. I'll punish him."

The words were no sooner out of her mouth than the door opened. The men had come up with the wagon, and what with the crowd that had gathered outside and the rain and all things, they had thought fit to fetch in what they had brought without delay.

As they came in, staggerin' a wee, for he was a heavy weight and the step was difficult, I stood stricken like. I couldna take my eyes off Martha. In a second of time she had seen all. Her face went like stane, her eyes were like wounds in the strange whiteness of it, and her look was like a woman possessed. She didna stir. No! Even as they went past her into the kitchen, she stood rigid, glowering at the wall as though she struggled with her own breathing. They were trying to get poor Geordie up to the bedroom, but they couldna manage him decently up the ladder. Then suddenly she opened her lips in speech.

"Put him there," she calls out in a loud voice, pointing to the sofa in the kitchen.

They put him down as she had bid.

"Now leave me by my lane," she cries out in a voice that would have daunted ye. "Leave me by my lane."

God! I was glad to get out of the place I'll warrant. The minister was the last to leave the shop. He stood for a long time looking at her, raised his arm, then dropped it, made as though to speak, but was silent, and at long last came out into the rain.

None that saw that Hogmanay in Levenford forgot it to their dying day. Folks walked in the streets as though they were in the kirk, and spoke in whispers. Ay, when they passed the shop in Church Street they didna dare to speak at all.

We were poor company in the Club on that night. As ye ken, it's aye been the custom for the members to see in the New Year in richt royal fashion, like we're doin' this nicht; but for once that custom lapsed. And 'twas the same in the toun. When the clock struck the twal', beating out the old, beatin' in the new, not a sound was heard. No bells, no horns, no singing at the Cross—just a deathly quiet. And when the last stroke faded awa' we put on our ulsters and went home.

It was wet and dreary and dark now. Ay, it was a thaw richt enough; and as we splashed home through the street ye could hear the drip, drip of water from the eaves, and the rain trickling as it ran doun the window-panes like tears.

Four or five of us there were, all goin' the same road, and as we passed the corner of Dobbie's Loan we saw a thin slant of light gashed out into the darkness. It wasna a bricht, warm light that might come from a blithe and tidy house, but 'twas pale and dim, and because we kenned it came from Martha's kitchen 'twas a'most fearsome.

John Grierson was with us, a man that wasna easy fleyed, and something of a scoffer to the bargain. Scandalous if ye like, but nothing would do but he must go to the window, and take a keek at what was goin' on inside. And so, muckle against our judgement, we followed him doun the Loan, and looked into that uncanny window.

Well, what we saw ye never could believe, but it's gospel truth for a' that. The room was full of shadows, but by the thin light of the candle we saw Martha Lang walking up and doun like a woman demented. Ay, it was her, though by ordinar' never would I have kenned her. She had a shrunken shilpit look about her as if she had fallen into herself, and her hair had turned to the colour of driven snow. She was wringing her hands like she was wrastlin' with something, and all the time moaning out Geordie's name.

The Book was lying open on the kitchen table and once or twice she made as though to pick it up to read. But she couldna. No, she couldna.

"Geordie! Geordie!" she went on crying out aloud. Then all of a sudden she turned and flung herself down on her knees by the low couch. She put one arm around her dead son's neck, so that his head twisted and fell ower on her own flat breast like a bairn's, and with her other hand she started fondling his cauld stiff face and smoothing back his plastered hair.

The face of the corpse, streakit in that candle's light, looked up at her with a ghastly grin that would have turned ye with horror. And Martha, Black Martha mind ye, began rocking herself back and forrit on her knees, distracted by her grief.

"Geordie! Geordie!" she cries out in a desperate voice, "I never kenned I loved ye till the now, but I did, my son, I did." On and on she went.

Not one of us moved hand or foot. Rooted to the ground we stood in fear and sorrow. Through the drip, drip of the rain came that strange and moving sound, which I will never to my dying day forget. Ay, 'twas the fearsome sound of Martha's sobbing.

Fred Urquhart

ALICKY'S WATCH

Alexander's watch stopped on the morning of his mother's funeral. The watch had belonged to his grandfather and had been given to Alexander on his seventh birthday two years before. It had a large tarnished metal case and he could scarcely see the face through the smoky celluloid front, but Alexander treasured it. He carried it everywhere, and whenever anybody mentioned the time Alexander would take out the watch, look at it, shake his head with the senile seriousness of some old man he had seen, and say: "Ay, man, but is that the time already?"

And now the watch had stopped. The lesser tragedy assumed proportions which had not been implicit in the greater one. His mother's death seemed far away now because it had been followed by such a period of hustle and bustle: for the past three days the tiny house had been crowded with people coming and going. There had been visits from the undertakers, visits to the drapers for mourning-bands and black neckties. There had been an unwonted silence with muttered "sshs" whenever he or James spoke too loudly. And there had been continual genteel bickerings between his two grandmothers, each of them determined to uphold the dignity of death in the house, but each of them equally determined to have her own way in the arrangements for the funeral.

The funeral was a mere incident after all that had gone before. The stopping of the watch was the real tragedy. At two o'clock when the cars arrived, Alexander still had not got over it. He kept his hand in his pocket, fingering it all through the short service conducted in the parlour while slitherings and muffled knocks signified that the coffin was being carried out to the hearse. And he was still clutching it with a small, sweaty hand when he took his seat in the first car between his father and his Uncle Jimmy.

His mother was to be buried at her birthplace, a small mining village sixteen miles out from Edinburgh. His father and his maternal grandmother, Granny Peebles, had had a lot of argument about this. His father had wanted his mother to be cremated, but Granny Peebles had said: "But we have the ground, Sandy! We have the ground all ready waiting at Bethniebrig. It would be a pity not to use it. There's plenty of room on top of her father for poor Alice. And there'll still be enough room left for me—God help me!—when I'm ready to follow them."

"But the expense, Mrs. Peebles, the expense," his father had said. "It'll cost a lot to take a funeral all that distance, for mind you we'll have to have a lot o' carriages, there's such a crowd o' us."

"It winna be ony mair expensive than payin' for cremation," Granny Peebles had retorted. "I dinna hold wi' this cremation, onywye, it's ungodly. And besides the ground's there waiting."

The argument had gone back and forth, but in the end Mrs. Peebles had won. Though it was still rankling in his father's mind when he took his seat in the front mourning-car. "It's a long way, Jimmy," he said to his brother. "It's a long way to take the poor lass. She'd ha'e been better, I'm thinkin', to have gone up to Warriston Crematorium."

"Ay, but Mrs. Peebles had her mind made up aboot that," Uncle Jimmy said. "She's a tartar, Mrs. Peebles, when it comes to layin' doon the law."

Although Alexander was so preoccupied with his stopped watch he wondered, as he had so often wondered in the past, why his father and his Uncle Jimmy called her Mrs. Peebles when they called Granny Matheson "Mother". But he did not dare ask.

" 'We have the ground at Bethniebrig, Sandy,' " mimicked Uncle Jimmy. " 'And if we have the ground we must use it. There'll still be room left for me when my time comes.' The auld limmer, I notice there was no word aboot there bein' room for you when *your* time comes, m'man!"

Alexander's father did not answer. He sat musing in his new-found dignity of widowerhood; his back was already bowed with the responsibility of being father and mother to two small boys. He was only thirty-one.

All the way to Bethniebrig Cemetery Alexander kept his hand in his pocket, clasping the watch. During the burial service, where he was conscious of being watched and afterwards when both he and James were wept over and kissed by many strange women, he did not dare touch his treasure. But on the return journey he took the watch from his pocket and sat with it on his knee. His father was safely in the first car with Mr. Ogilvie, the minister, and his mother's uncles, Andrew and Pat. Alexander knew that neither his Uncle Jimmy nor his Uncle Jimmy's chum, Ernie, would mind if he sat with the watch in his hand.

"Is it terrible bad broken, Alicky?" asked James, who was sitting between Ernie and his mother's cousin, Arthur.

"Ay," Alexander said.

"Never mind, laddie, ye can aye get a new watch, but ye cannie get a new——"

Ernie's observation ended with a yelp of pain. Uncle Jimmy grinned and said: "Sorry, I didnie notice your leg was in my way!"

The cars were going quicker now than they had gone on the way to the cemetery. Alicky did not look out of the windows; he tinkered with his watch, winding and rewinding it, holding it up to his ear to see if there was any effect.

"Will it never go again, Alicky?" James said.

"Here, you leave Alicky alone and watch the rabbits," Ernie said, pulling James on his knee. "My God, look at them! All thae white tails bobbin' aboot! Wish I had a rifle here, I'd soon take a pot-shot at them."

"Wish we had a pack o' cards," said Auntie Liz's young man, Matthew. "We could have a fine wee game o' Solo."

"I've got my pack in my pocket," Ernie said, raking for them. "What aboot it, lads?"

"Well——" Uncle Jimmy looked at Cousin Arthur; then he shook his head. "No, I dinnie think this is either the time or the place."

"Whatever you say, pal!" Ernie gave all his attention to James, shooting imaginary rabbits, crooking his finger and making popping sounds with his tongue against the roof of his mouth.

The tram-lines appeared, then the huge villas at Newington. The funeral cars had to slow down when Clerk Street and the busier thoroughfare started. James pressed his nose against the window to gaze at the New Victoria which had enormous posters billing a "mammoth Western spectacle".

"Jings, but I'd like to go to that," he said. "Wouldn't you, Alicky?"

But Alicky did not look out at the rearing horses and the Red Indians in full chase. He put his watch to his ear and shook it violently for the fiftieth time.

"I doubt it's no good, lad," Uncle Jimmy said. "It's a gey auld watch, ye ken. It's seen its day and generation."

The blinds were up when they got back, and the table was laid for high tea. Granny Matheson and Granny Peebles were buzzing around, carrying plates of cakes and tea-pots. Auntie Liz took the men's coats and hats and piled them on the bed in the back bedroom. Alicky noticed that the front room where the coffin had been was still shut. There was a constrained air about everybody as they stood about in the parlour. They rubbed their hands and spoke about the weather. It was only when Granny Matheson cried: "Sit in now and get your tea," that they began to return to normal.

"Will you sit here, Mr. Ogilvie, beside me?" she said. "Uncle Andrew, you'll sit there beside Liz, and Uncle Pat over there."

"Sandy, you'll sit here beside me," Granny Peebles called

170

from the other end of the table. "And Uncle George'll sit next to Cousin Peggy, and Arthur, you can sit——"

"Arthur's to sit beside Ernie," Granny Matheson cut in. "Now, I think that's us all settled, so will you pour the tea at your end, m'dear?"

"I think we'd better wait for Mr. Ogilvie," Granny Peebles said stiffly. And she inclined her head towards the minister, smoothing the black silk of her bosom genteelly.

Alicky and James had been relegated to a small table, which they were glad was nearer to their Granny Matheson's end of the large table. They bowed their heads with everyone else when Mr. Ogilvie started to pray, but after the first few solemn seconds Alicky allowed himself to keek from under his eyelashes at the dainties on the sideboard. He was sidling his hand into his pocket to feel his watch when Tiddler, the cat, sprang on to the sideboard and nosed a large plate of boiled ham. Alicky squirmed in horror, wondering whether it would be politic to draw attention to the cat and risk being called "a wickèd ungodly wee boy for not payin' attention to what the minister's sayin' about yer puir mammy," or whether it would be better to ignore it. But Mr. Ogilvie saved the situation. He stopped in the middle of a sentence and said calmly in his non-praying voice: "Mrs. Peebles, I see that the cat's up at the boiled ham. Hadn't we better do something about it?"

After tea the minister left, whisky and some bottles of beer were produced for the men, and port wine for the ladies. The company thawed even more. Large, jovial Uncle Pat, whose red face was streaming with sweat, unbuttoned his waistcoat, saying: "I canna help it, Georgina, if I dinna loosen my westkit I'll burst the buttons. Ye shouldna gi'e fowk sae much to eat!"

"I'm glad you tucked in and enjoyed yourself," Granny Peebles said, nodding her head regally.

"Mr. Ogilvie's a nice man," Granny Matheson said, taking a cigarette from Uncle Jimmy. "But he kind o' cramps yer style, doesn't he? I mean it's no' like havin' one o' yer own in the room. Ye've aye got to be on yer p's and q's wi' him, mindin' he's a minister."

"Ye havenie tellt us who was all at the cemetery," she said, blowing a vast cloud of smoke in the air and wafting it off with a plump arm. "Was there a lot o' Bethniebrig folk there?"

"Ay, there was a good puckle," Uncle Pat said. "I saw auld Alec Whitten and young Tam Forbes and——"

"Oh, ay, they fair turned out in force," Uncle Jimmy said.

"And why shouldn't they?" Granny Peebles said. "After all, our family's had connections with Bethniebrig for generations. I'm glad they didnie forget to pay their respects to puir Alice." And she dabbed her eyes with a small handkerchief, which had never been shaken out of the fold.

"I must say it's a damned cauld draughty cemetery yon," Uncle Andrew said. "I was right glad when Mr. Ogilvie stopped haverin' and we got down to business. I was thinkin' I'd likely catch my death o' cauld if he yapped on much longer."

"Uncle Pat near got his death o' cauld, too," Uncle Jimmy grinned. "Didn't ye, auld yin?"

"Ay, ay, lad, I near did that!" Uncle Pat guffawed. "I laid my tile hat ahint a gravestone at the beginnin' of the service and when it was ower I didna know where it was. Faith, we had a job findin' it."

"Ay, we had a right search!" Uncle Jimmy said.

"It's a pity headstones havenie knobs on them for hats," Auntie Liz said.

"Really, Lizzie Matheson!" cried Granny Peebles.

Auntie Liz and the younger women began to clear the table, but Alexander noticed that Auntie Liz did not go so often to the scullery as the others. She stood with dirty plates in her hands, listening to the men who had gathered around the fire. Uncle Pat had his feet up on the fender, his large thighs spread wide apart. "It's a while since we were all gathered together like this," he remarked, finishing his whisky and placing the glass with an ostentatious clatter on

172

the mantelpiece. "I think the last time was puir Willie's funeral two years syne."

"Ay, it's a funny thing but it's aye funerals we seem to meet at," Uncle Andrew said.

"Well, well, there's nothin' sae bad that hasna got some guid in it," Uncle Pat said. "Yes, Sandy lad, I'll take another wee nippie, thank ye!" And he watched his nephew with a benign expression as another dram was poured for him. "Well, here's your guid health again, Georgina! I'm needin' this, I can tell ye, for it was a cauld journey doon this mornin' frae Aberdeen, and it was a damned sight caulder standin' in that cemetery."

Alexander squeezed his way behind the sofa into the corner beside the whatnot. Looking to see that he was unnoticed, he drew the watch cautiously from his pocket and tinkered with it. As the room filled with tobacco smoke the talk and laughter got louder.

"Who was yon wi' the long brown moth-eaten coat?" Uncle Jimmy said. "He came up and shook hands wi' me after the service. I didnie ken him from Adam, but I said howdye-do. God, if he doesnie drink he should take doon his sign!"

"Och, thon cauld wind would make anybody's nose red," Matthew said.

"Ay, and who was yon hard case in the green bowler?" Ernie said.

"Ach, there was dozens there in bowlers," Uncle Jimmy said.

"Ah, but this was a *green* bowler!"

Uncle Jimmy guffawed. "That reminds me o' the bar about the old lady and the minister. Have ye heard it?"

Alexander prised open the case of the watch, then he took a pin from a small box on the whatnot and inserted it delicately into the works. There was loud laughter, and Ernie shouted above the others: "Ay, but have ye heard the one about——?"

"What are ye doin', Alicky?" James whispered, leaning over the back of the sofa.

"Shuttup," Alexander said in a low voice, bending over the watch and poking gently at the tiny wheels.

"I dinnie see why women can't go to funerals, too," Auntie Liz said. "You men ha'e all the fun."

"Lizzie Matheson!" Granny Peebles cried. "What a like thing to say! I thought ye were going to help your mother wash the dishes?"

It was going! Alicky could hardly believe his eyes. The small wheels were turning—turning slowly, but they were turning. He held the watch to his ear, and a slow smile of pleasure came over his face.

"What are you doing there behind the sofa?"

Alexander and James jumped guiltily. "I've got my watch to go!" Alicky cried to his father. "Listen!"

"Alexander Matheson, have you nothing better to do than tinker wi' an auld watch?" Granny Peebles said. "I'm surprised at ye," she said as she swept out.

Abashed, Alicky huddled down behind the sofa. James climbed over and sat beside him. They listened to the men telling stories and laughing, but when the room darkened and the voices got even louder the two little boys yawned. They whispered together. "Go on, you ask him," James pleaded. "You're the auldest!"

James went on whispering. Beer bottles were emptied, the laughter and the family reminiscences got wilder. And presently, plucking up courage, Alexander went to his father and said: "Can James and I go to the pictures?"

There was a short silence.

"Alexander Matheson," his father cried. "Alexander Matheson, you should be ashamed o' yersel' sayin' that and your puir mother no' cauld in her grave."

"Och, let the kids go, Sandy," Uncle Jimmy said. "It's no' much fun for them here."

"We're no' here for fun," Alexander's father said, but his voice trailed away indecisively.

"You go and put the case to your granny, lad, and see what she says," Uncle Jimmy said. He watched the two boys go to the door, then looking round to see that Mrs. Peebles was still out of the room, he said: "Your Granny Matheson."

Five minutes later, after a small lecture, Granny Matheson gave them the entrance money to the cinema. "Now remember two things," she said, showing them out. "Don't run, and be sure and keep your bonnets on."

"Okay," Alicky said.

They walked sedately to the end of the street. Alicky could feel the watch ticking feebly in his pocket, and his fingers caressed the metal case. When they got to the corner they looked round, then they whipped off their bonnets, stuffed them in their pockets, and ran as quickly as they could to the cinema.

Ronald Macdonald Douglas

A WOMAN OF THE ROADS

His name was Drummond, and he was a good-looking
gentlemanly sort of chiel, of between thirty and thirty-five,
with crisp hair and a well-cropped bit of a moustache: and that
was about all anyone in the neighbourhood knew of him.

He had come to the district from God-knows-where three
years ago come Lammas.

The little place that he had rented is called Drochit, from
the old broken bridge that spans the burn below; and the
name of it, like lots of other names about the Borders, just
goes to prove that the Gaelic was once the language of all
Scotland—in the Lowlands as well as in the Highlands.

Drochit stands back no more than fifty yards from the
main road that runs south from Edinburgh to Carter Bar on
the English border. It is about a mile out of the village, and is,
maybe, three miles from Ancrum—and that, surely, is another
good Gaelic name.

Drochit had stood empty for a long time before Drummond
took it; and now that he is away it looks like standing empty
for ever.

It is a poor bit of a place: an old stone-built cottage with a
grey slate roof, and a couple of small windows. There is, maybe, an acre of ground with it, and two or three tumbledown
outbuildings, and that is all.

Drummond kept a cow—though God knows what he did
with the milk—and a couple of pigs, and there may have been
a dozen draggle-tailed hens wandering about. It was easily
seen that the man didn't know what he was doing, and that

he was not used to the life. The carter who had brought his things from the station at St. Boswells when first he came, said that the man had some grand stuff—what there was of it: book-cases, and a fine oak table, and good-looking chairs and a bed; and boxes, heavy with books, and trunks that were plastered with foreign labels. The man was a mystery; and he turned out to be, to the neighbours, an impudent devil, too; but after a while he had the sense to clear out.

He lived alone; or, at least, he lived alone for the first two years or so—and that is where the impudence came in—for suddenly, less than a week after the big storm of last year, a woman had been seen about the place—a big, fine-looking woman all right, but a brazen bizzem. And she stayed with him until they left the place together, and no one knows where they went, or where they are.

She came down into the village shop one day, as large as life, to buy a few things; and gave out that she was Mistress Drummond, and that she was living up at Drochit.

The impudence of it was overpowering; for she had been into that very shop, on the night of the storm, begging; and after that, with the threepence she got from Auld Lucky Oliver, she had sat in Craw's inn across the way, with half a pint of beer in front of her, from half-past seven until nine o'clock when Geordie had turned her out. The rain had been coming down in sheets, and a wind had been blowing enough to knock you off your feet; but what could Geordie do?—nine o'clock was nine o'clock, and the law was the law; and, after all, it was easy seen that she was just a woman of the roads, a kind of tinker-body, and used to the weather and that sort of thing. But Geordie is a kindly enough callant, and he had given her bread and cheese, and a sixpence, and had shown her the road to take.

And there she was, a few days after, living at Drochit, and having the cheek to say she was the man's wife. Of course, living there, she couldn't do anything else, for everybody knows well enough that there is only one room in the cottage, that is kitchen and bedroom and everything else.

177

It was easy seen what had happened: she had left Geordie Craw's inn at nine o'clock, and had taken the Edinburgh road. She must have seen Drummond's light as she came near Drochit, and had gone up to beg, and the man had taken her in. No doubt the callant had been lonesome enough, and she had been glad of a shelter—a woman like that would think nothing of going to a strange man for the sake of a bed on a night like that. But Drummond should have put her on the road again, early the next morning before anyone got to know. Then it might not have been so bad; but to go on stopping there, and to come down among decent respectable folk with a cock and bull yarn like that, was just plain shamelessness; and he was as much to blame as she was.

How they came to arrange things, that first night or exactly what happened, no one ever knew, of course, but everyone could guess. And she was a fine-looking woman all right. . . .

But here is the truth, and this was the way of it:

It was blowing a gale outside, and the rain that had poured incessantly all the day was blashin' against the window panes, threatening almost to smash them in. But inside the cottage of Drochit everything was cosy enough. A great fire, of coals and green-wood, was roaring and leaping up the chimney, throwing its heat and its flickering light into every corner and cranny of the one big room.

The huge iron kettle, hanging on its cleek above the flames, began to boil and spit. Jim Drummond swung it to one side, and pushed the big pan that was full of water nearer to the fire. From under the bed he dragged a long tin bath.

A boiling tub, with mustard in it, was the thing he needed after the soaking he had got earlier on when he had gone to see to the hens and the two pigs. The milk his cow had given stood in a white enamelled pail over by one of the two windows. He was going to have a pint of it, hot, before he got into bed, with a stiffening of whisky in it; the rest of it would go to the pigs next day, after Judy had had her share. Judy lay rolled up on the rug before the fire.

178

"A hell of a night, Judy," he said, "and God help any poor devil that's out in it."

The dog blinked and wagged her tail; she didn't care, for she was all right.

"Come on, then, shift out of that." He pushed the dog aside as he pulled the tin bath up before the fire. The dog jumped into a chair.

The man found towels and soap.

He began to undress, before pouring out the water from the kettle and the pan. He had reached the stage of pushing his braces from his shoulders, when the dog stiffened, and jumped down. Her ears were cocked, and her tail stood out. Then she growled, and went sniffing at the door.

The man looked round, and listened. Over the noise of the storm he thought he heard the sounds of knocking. The dog leapt back and barked.

"Who the devil can that be?" the man muttered, half to himself, and half to the dog that still continued to bark and to growl.

"Be quiet!" he commanded, and then, loudly, through the door, he called: "Who's there?"

A voice seemed to answer, but the man could hear little for the dog and the noise of the rain and the wind.

He turned the big key in the lock and shot back the bolt. The door was flung back out of his grasp by the wind, and a blash of rain swept in.

A woman stood on the step—a woman soaked to the skin, and beaten down by the force of the wind. She raised her face and blinked in the light, the water pouring down from the brim of her hat, her black hair blowing in wet masses about her eyes.

"Good God!" Drummond glared at the pitiful sight standing before him, framed in the doorway.

"Here, come in." He slammed the door to, and bolted it again against the storm. The woman stood still, just inside the door.

"Come on, up to the fire. Good heavens!"

He slung the bath away, and dragged an armchair forward. The dog, quietened by her master's attitude, crept to the woman's side to lick her cold, limp hand.

Drummond brought a tumbler, half-filled with whisky. He filled it up with boiling water. He handed the glass to the woman.

"Here, scoff that!" he commanded, and took from her the sodden hat she had removed.

She sipped a little of the whisky and water, and then gave him back the tumbler; but he forced it on her again, and made her drink more than half of it.

A cloud of steam began to rise from her drenched garments. The man told her to take them off. She refused; but, as they argued, he could see it was not modesty that held her back: there was something else. At last, she made a move, after he had told her that she could not sit in wet clothes all night; or, that if she did, she would put him to the trouble and expense of having her buried.

She looked at him, with the dumb pleading of an animal in her eyes; then she turned away. It was good to be inside, away from the wind and the rain; it was good to sit by a fire; it was good to be ordered about by a man. She felt better and stronger already.

"All right," she said suddenly, and rose. He did not make the hypocritical pretence of turning away.

She smiled at him—a queer twisted little smile that had nothing wanton in it.

She began to unbutton the wretchedly thin and soaking jacket, that she had kept fastened to the throat. At the second button, he saw she had nothing on beneath. She continued to unfasten the coat; then, slowly, she took it off. She had nothing on above her skirt: from the waist upwards she was naked, and her skin glistened with the rain that had beaten through the poor material.

She turned her head aside.

"That was why," she whispered.

He gave her a towel, and she dried the upper part of her

180

body. After that, she stood still, but the man said nothing. She fingered the waist-band of her skirt.

"Shall I? Must I?" she asked, pitifully.

He knew what she meant. He pointed to the steam still rising, and insisted:

"Of course. You must."

She slipped a hook from its eye, and ripped at the placket: the skirt, heavy with water, fell about her feet. She had nothing else on but her draggled stockings and her broken shoes.

Then suddenly, she dropped back into the chair. She bent forward, her face sunk in her hands, and she was crying.

The man patted her shoulder. Not knowing what to say, he placed the towel over her knees, but she made no movement, although her legs were as wet as her body had been.

He dragged out the bath again, and filled it from the kettle and the pan; then he cooled it down with cold water taken from a bucket. He emptied a mustard tin into the bath, and stirred the water with his hand.

"Come on," he pleaded, but the woman still cried softly into her cupped hands.

The man looked down on her, and then dropped on his knees. He took the towel and rubbed her thighs. She moved to allow him to do so, leaning back, but still covering her eyes.

Gently, he rolled down, and removed, her torn and muddied stockings. Her feet, that must once have been beautiful, were bruised and cut and red. A little trickle of blood ran from a long scratch on her instep.

He lifted her feet, pushed the bath closer, and placed her feet in the water. He bathed her legs; and when that was done, he rose, and lifted her bodily from the chair and lowered her, huddled up, into the bath. She laughed at that through her tears. He bathed her back, holding huge spongefuls of water up to her shapely shoulders, letting the hot water trickle down.

Then he told her to stand up, and helped her to rise. She stood in the bath, her body steaming in the heat of the fire as

181

her clothing had done. He dried her, warming the towels before the fire, and she permitted his ministrations gladly.

He removed the cushion her body had soiled and damped, putting another in its place on the chair. He made her sit down, her feet still in the water; then he lifted her feet, one by one, and dried them gently, and with care for their bruises and their cuts. He rose, and lifted the bath away.

She thanked him for all he had done, but he merely grunted, and she wondered if he were angry. She felt like a little child; and, childlike, was half-afraid. Until he came back, and, smiling at her, offered her his pyjamas. She refused to take them, saying that she had been trouble enough, and that he would need them for himself. She told him that she was beautifully warm, and, that as he had seen her, was still looking at her, had even bathed her and dried her, it didn't matter much.

He dropped the pyjamas beside her, without further argument, and moved away to prepare the supper. He filled a pan with milk. As he came back to put it on the fire, she was still naked, and stroking the dog.

"What's her name?" she asked.

He told her; and then set about laying the table.

When he had finished, and had taken the milk from the fire, he told her again to put on the pyjamas. Telling her that she would need them to sleep in, anyway.

At that, she raised her eyes, and asked where he would sleep, and how. He told her, in the armchair and in his clothes. When she remonstrated, and said that she could not put him out to that extent, and that she could not rob him of his bed, and that that would never do, he demanded of her almost brutally:

"Well then, where are you going to sleep?"

She told him, unhesitatingly: "With you. If you will let me. You're not afraid, are you?" she asked.

He laughed, and threw the pyjamas at her.

"Put them on," he said. "I have a clean soft shirt that'll do for me."

Recognizing the folly of arguing further, and knowing, too, that really she would be glad of the covering, she slipped the jacket on, and then into the trousers she put her long, fine limbs.

"They fit"—she tried to laugh—"I'm not much smaller than you."

He brought her a brush and a comb, and handed her a mirror. She smiled her thanks.

"I even believe I've some shaving-powder—talcum—somewhere," he said, and went rooting in a drawer.

He brought the powder, and with it a piece of cotton wool, explaining that that was the best he could do in that direction.

She thought it all too wonderful—everything, and said so. She sighed, and he looked at her, but said nothing. She was wondering what might be the outcome of it all, and what would happen in the morning.

After supper, through which they scarcely spoke, he motioned to the bed.

"You must be tired?" he suggested.

She told him no, although she had tramped nearly fifteen miles that day, having slept out on the Cheviots the night before.

She went over to the bed. He had turned the covers down.

"Which side shall I lie?" she asked quietly, and half-shyly.

"Wherever you like. Please yourself."

She crawled over to the far side.

He gave the dog some scraps and some milk; and then, standing by the fire, he undressed. From the bed she watched him, even as he had watched her.

A few minutes later he lay down beside the woman. He kept a space between them; and lay on his back, watching the firelight as it flickered on the raftered roof. Outside, the storm still raged.

They lay still, for a long time. Then she moved, and, accidentally, her feet touched his. Suddenly he felt her hand groping for his own. He clutched at it, and turned towards her, to see tears glistening in her eyes; and all in a moment, she flung herself close to him, and she was sobbing as though her heart would break; and he, too, was near to tears, and his arms were about her—holding her as though he would never let her go.

And through her sobs she was moaning: "God! O God!"

And he was whispering to her, brokenly; and in his emotion, out came Scottish accents and Scottish idiom, and Gaelic words from his northern youth:

"*A Mhàiri a ghràidh, mo chridhe! Tha mo chridhe làn!* Oh, Mairi, woman, my wife, what for did ye ever go from me? And where have you been?"

184

Margaret Hamilton

JENNY STAIRY'S HAT

Neighbours had often seen the bowler hat as they stood at the door, waiting for Jenny to bring a morsel of sugar or marge, to be paid back out of next week's rations. Jenny kept herself to herself, and never would ask you in, though her house must be tidy enough, old maid that she was, with never a man or bairn coming in to mess things.

"I see you've your young man in, Jenny," they said, winking at the hat hanging up in the lobby.

On the way downstairs they would laugh at the idea of Jenny Stairy with a man—her in that old coat that fitted where it touched her because she had got it second-hand from a customer. Somebody had once said the coat came out of the Ark and Jenny came with it—as the female ostrich.

There was no doubt in anyone's mind that the hat had belonged to one of Jenny's brothers and she kept it to scare off burglars.

But Jenny, owning nothing of value, was not afraid of thieves, and the hat, ancient and curly-brimmed, would have deceived no one.

The hat belonged to a time when Jenny was not a stairy, but young Jenny McFadyen, selling pipeclay and pails to other people from behind the ironmonger's counter. It was not a shop where lads had much reason to come in for chaff, but somehow they found their way there.

"I'll cairry up ma mither's paraffin, Jenny."

"Whaur's your bottle?"

"Ach, I'll hae to come back wi' it the morn."

Then, her slenderness had not turned to gauntness, and her hair, now so thin and scraped, was a soft light crown above her face. It was a peaked, inscrutable face, with brown eyes which made men try to follow her at night if they caught a glimpse of her in the gaslight of the street. And, with it all, she was a douce-looking creature whom you could take home to your mother and be sure of a welcome for her as your intended.

But none of the young men who came about the shop was ever allowed to take Jenny home, or even walk out with her. They were too much like her own brothers—and besides there was Peter Abercromby.

Peter worked in a lawyer's office. He had spoken to Jenny at the corner one night, asked her the way to somewhere in such a refined voice that she answered. While he was seeing her home, she discovered that he lived with his mother only a few blocks away.

Every Saturday night after that he was waiting for her when the shop closed. Minnie Walker from the draper's next door used to tease half-jealously if Jenny and she came out together.

"My, some folks is fair gettin' up in the world—I'll need to tell the chaps they've nae chance wi' their bunnets an' dungarees!" she would cry a shade too loudly, so that Jenny, going forward to take Peter's arm in his navy-blue suit, would be certain he had heard.

But he never gave any sign. Precisely he raised his bowler hat and said, "Good evening, Jenny. What's your news?"

There was never any. At least, she couldn't tell him what old McNair the ironmonger had said yesterday to the woman who was buying a chamber-pot, or how the other night, washing the window, she had been so afraid that . . .

So she always said, "Oh, nothing much, Peter. What's *your* news?"

He would set off primly on an account of how something had gone missing in the office and he, Peter, had miraculously been able to find it.

Then the inevitable: "My mother's been not so well."

Jenny had never seen his mother, but she came to know her as a woman always at death's door, but never quite being pulled through. Peter was her only child, and Jenny sometimes wondered how she would get on, looking after his mother, when, if. . . . Or would theirs be one of those courtships which went on for years, waiting for the man's mother to die?

Because of his bowler hat and navy suit, Jenny could never be sure of anything. Walking with him through the streets, she would feel sick with waiting for the moment when he judged it dark enough to put his arm round her.

Sometimes she edged him towards a doorway, but he steered firmly away, talking all the time.

"I was reading in the papers. About this Irish home rule . . ."

When he talked of what he read in the papers, his mouth became a peashooter, sending out the words in self-righteous little bursts. It was a firm thin mouth that could kiss rather well, except that he took it away too soon.

In winter Jenny took him home for his supper. The McFadyens lived on the top flat, in a room and kitchen—Tom and Jim and Jenny and their father and mother. With them all in the kitchen it was a crush for supper, because Tom and Jim were big loud men, and Peter used to turn pale and a little shrewish, sitting with his tea in his hand.

Once they almost came to blows over Irish home rule, because Jim and Tom had Irish mates in the shipyard where they worked and they wouldn't believe what Peter had read in the papers.

"A lot of ignoramuses!" Peter was saying, with angry foam on his lips.

"What did you say, mister?" Jim got to his feet, putting down his cup.

From the other side Tom lumbered over, and Peter, smallish at the best of times, looked like a midge between two bulls.

"Peter—your tea's out!" Jenny plunged in at the more dangerous side, which was Jim's, and by questions about milk and sugar, to which she knew the answers, created a diversion long enough to save the peace.

She got her mother to "speak to" Tom and Jim, and they began to go out on Saturday nights. Jim had a girl called Isa Bain, and Tom could always find pals at a street corner.

"Is Lord Muck awa'?" they would ask, coming in on pretended tip-toe. "Can a chap get into his ain hoose?"

With Jim and Tom out, Peter talked away happily. Jenny, gripped by a merciless longing for the few minutes when she would have Peter to herself, saying goodnight on the stair, had less than usual to say. Her mother ignored Peter, as she did everyone, because she was too tired to notice. But her father would listen, smiling now and then with a strange sweetness behind his moustache. His smile was a sign of weakness, but you loved him for it—or Jenny did.

"Ach Faither, you're hopeless!" was the worst you could ever say to him, and sometimes only the fact that he was there made life in the cramped flat seem worth while.

"We'll need to get you out of all this," Peter murmured one night on the stairhead.

"Him and his *all this*!" thought Jenny, too indignant to feel exalted by this near proposal.

Then he kissed her and she forgot everything except the hope that he would kiss her again. But he never did, and tonight as usual he withdrew his arm and pattered down the long stairs. She listened to hear the last of his rubber soles on the two front steps of the close.

Jenny did most of the housework because her mother was often in bed. She did not suffer from "nerves" as Peter's mother did. Her body had been distorted at the birth of Jim, her second child; she had gone on to have a third and fourth, who died, and a fifth, Jenny, who miraculously lived.

Jenny minded none of the work except the windows. Sometimes, if Jim were out, she could get Tom to wash them. But, if both brothers were in, they would sit, one on each side of the fire, with their feet on the hob, and Jenny would grit her teeth as she sat or stood on the window-sills, not daring to look down, yet doing it in case she would forget how high she was.

She enjoyed washing down the stairs, moving down the long flight on her knees, with her pail and clayey water. When she was almost finished she liked to look up and see the top steps already dry and clean, except for the footmark which was certain to have been left by a Docherty child, slithering up to the house next door.

Sometimes her father would come up, unsteady because he had been drinking. Jenny, hearing his first dragging steps in the close, would leave her pail and go running to help him.

"You're a good lass, Jenny," he always insisted all the way up.

Neighbours, though they heard, thought little about it, for old McFadyen was a painter—a trade that gave you a thirst if anything did. But they wondered what his daughter felt about it, her that was supposed to be making such a good match for herself.

Jenny was used to it as part of her father, the weakness that made her love him. Cleaning the stair lavatory after he had been sick, she would grow angry and resolve to give him a tongueing, but when she came in and saw the bowed man, looking so miserable, with the thin streaks of hair across his head, it would all boil down to "Ach Faither, you're hopeless!"

Peter Abercromby was a teetotaller and Jenny respected him for it. But she sometimes wondered whether a dram wouldn't make him more—well . . .

Peter's mother died at last. Jenny saw the notice in the paper and knew that this, more than any kissing on the stair, would bring matters to a head.

He did not come to meet her that Saturday. It was not to be wondered at, since it was the day after the funeral. All through the following week, by an effort of will, she kept herself away from his house. It was not her "place" to go unless he asked her, but she had sent a letter of sympathy with an offer to "perform any service whatsoever within my power to assist you in bearing this grievous burden of sorrow which has descended upon you (and yours)"—copying it word for word from a book in case she would make mistakes.

On Friday night he came to see her. She was dusting in the room and it was Jim who went to the door.

"Here's Lord Muck!" he called loudly, but Jenny, her fingers plucking feverishly at her apron strings as she rushed to bring Peter in, was not at all bothered.

They sat on the sofa, inches apart. Peter was nervous and played with his hat, suspended awkwardly between his navy-blue knees. She ought to have taken it from him, she . . .

"Thank you for your letter, Jenny."

"Your mother, did she . . .?"

He told her about it. The sudden pain, the doctor, the ambulance. The operation but it was too late. Appendicitis. To think it should have carried her off after the years of suffering she had had with other things.

There seemed to be nothing more to say. Of course he would not have had time to read the papers since. . . . But he was beginning as usual:

"I was reading in the papers. About an Archduke who's been murdered. It may mean war for France. But it would be foolish for this country to . . ."

He went on in normal peashooter fashion. She could hear Jim's and Tom's voices raised angrily, then the slam of the kitchen door. The two of them slept in the parlour and they had an early rise in the morning. If only Peter would hurry.

She knew what he had come for. It was not very decent so soon after his mother's death, but what was a man to do with a two-room-and-kitchen house and no woman to clean and look after him?

At last he was saying: "Jenny, we've . . . ep . . . been going steady . . . ep . . . for two years now. I was wondering . . ."

Jenny waited. Surely tonight he would kiss her twice,

surely now she would be free of the doubt that made her afraid to open her mouth in case an uncouth word would shatter everything between them.

"So, Jenny, I thought maybe . . ."

Jim and Tom burst in without knocking.

"Coortin's feenished fur the nicht, mister!"

"Awa' hame to your bed an' we'll get to oors!"

Jim caught him under the oxters and Tom seized his feet.

His voice beat punily against their muscular strength. Jenny caught at his arm as it clutched the air.

"Jim an' Tom . . . pit him doon . . . are ye no' ashamed o' yoursel's . . . pit him doon!"

Tom dropped his feet for an instant to open the outside door but Peter could not get his balance in time and he was lifted again and dumped on the mat outside.

"Oh, Peter, you'll need to mind they're rough craters—no' like you. They didny mean ony hairm . . ."

Peter picked himself up, dusted his trousers and mopped his mouth for a high-pitched parting shot:

"You'll hear from my solicitors!"

Afterwards they found his hat on the parlour floor and they hung it in the lobby in case he would come back for it.

Jenny told Minnie Walker about it. She had to tell someone, for it got worse with bottling up. This was Monday, and Peter hadn't shown up on the Saturday and there had been a long dead Sunday between.

Minnie was sympathetic. She was a squat, dark girl, and, although her mother owned the draper's shop where she worked, it didn't seem likely that she would ever get a husband.

"Thae men!" she said vehemently. "Oh my God, Jenny, is it no' terrible whit they can dae to ye?"

Then the cut meant as comfort:

"Ach, ye're weel rid o' him if he doesny think enough o' ye to come back."

That was what her mother said, it was what any decent girl ought to feel especially if she had plenty of boys eager to take Peter's place. But Jenny felt only part of it: he hadn't cared enough to come back.

The next Saturday, before shop closing time, she thought she saw him outside, pacing on the pavement as he always did. She hung back, afraid yet eager to go out. When at last she did, it was as if the blow had fallen all over again on a place already tender. The pavement was wet and empty. Even Minnie had closed her door early and was gone. Jenny walked home alone in the rain.

Things happened in the next few weeks. War began. Jim, having got Isa Bain into trouble, married her. Tom joined the H.L.I. and was sent to England.

Jenny lived through it, a little remote, none too hearty at Isa's wedding, but outwardly almost the same Jenny, steeling herself to wash the windows, and choking off the lads who came into the ironmonger's. Once she went for a walk with a boy in new khaki, but he was so shyly passionate and so like Tom that she ran away from him.

She took to washing the stairs on Saturday nights, and would pause, wringing her cloth, every time a rubber-soled foot fell on the close. Only when a downstairs door had banged or the inevitable Docherty child had slipped up past her, did she begin again, wiping in skilful semi-circles.

When she had finished each step, and before it was dry, she would take her pipeclay and at each side trace a row of loops, like a child's first attempt at writing. Mrs. Docherty across the landing had no time for such fancywork, and every time Jenny's turn came round she had to trace her whirligigs afresh. But in the mornings she liked to see them gleaming, white against the grey stone, like a promise of something the day never brought.

Jim came up one night, alone, the stairs being too much for Isa with her time so near. He lifted Peter Abercromby's hat from its peg in the lobby and birled it into the kitchen.

"Ye needny be keepin' that ony mair."

"How?"

"He can get yin oot o' stock. He's marryin' Minnie Walker next week."

It must be true enough, because Isa's mother lived next door to the Walkers.

Jenny went to wash the stair. It was not her turn, but the stair was the only place where she could be alone.

Savagely she slapped her cloth back and forward. Minnie Walker with her "You're well rid of him . . ." She remembered the night when she had seen Peter outside and Minnie had been away so early . . . probably chaffing him as she locked the door, talking of Jenny and saying, "You're well rid of *her*," till he believed it and went with Minnie.

Minnie need never be unsure of Peter, because of her mother's money.

Far below in the close, feet were stumbling up the first few steps. Neighbours heard, and knew it was Willie McFadyen again, with a drop over much. But they listened in vain for Jenny coming down to help him.

He crept up, making a long slow job of each step. He stopped behind Jenny, but her cloth moved ruthlessly on.

"*Fule!*" she muttered tensely, thinking of that dirty job, tonight of all nights.

But he shuffled on past the lavatory and into the house.

When she went up there was no sign of him in the kitchen. She emptied her pail and, after a gurgle of water in the sink waste came Jim's voice saying to his mother: "It's no' oor war—Tom wasny needin' to fash himsel'."

Then the banging on the door . . . somebody screaming . . . "Mrs. McFadyen . . . your man's fell ower the windy!"

He was lying at the edge of the pavement with the empty pail a few yards from him and water trickling down the gutter.

"It was the pail I seen first," said Mrs. McLean, one stair up. "An' then the puir man cam' efter it . . ."

Other neighbours were muttering something about "a dirty shame, letting a drunk man wash a windy."

They put a cushion under his head, and Jenny's mother was weeping stormily. She had been tired and silent for so long that it was a wonder to discover she could weep.

Jenny's tears gushed suddenly as they lifted him and his arms fell helplessly. He had done this for her because she had been angry and he loved her.

"Aye, it was the pail I seen first," Mrs. McLean was beginning for more of the neighbours.

"Could he no' have minded," thought Jenny, lashing against her sobs, "*I washed it masel' last nicht!*"

Jenny came home one day and found her mother selling Peter Abercromby's hat to a rag woman at the door. Angrily, Jenny hung it up and sent the woman away.

"We're takin' nothin' frae him, d'ye hear?"

Her mother shrugged. "Whaur's the money to come frae?"

There was good money in munition work, but the hours were long when you had housework to do as well.

So one evening, after she had finished at the ironmonger's, Jenny made her way to a part of the town where there were clean red tenements, occupied mainly by professional and business men with their families. She chose a close at random and climbed the first stair. Her feet longed to run back down the stair and all the way home. But she went on and chapped at a stained glass door.

"Were you wantin' anybody to wash the stairs?"

The woman came out . . . a full-bosomed personage, chewing the last bite of her tea, so that you could not read the expression on her face. Jenny shrank, but held her head up.

"D'you mean it, my girl?"

"Y-yes."

"Oh, thank *goodness*! I was beginning to think I'd have to wash them myself."

It was easy. The whole stair dropped like a plum into her lap, at threepence per landing, twice a week. Soon she had the close on either side as well. Charwomen had gone to munitions, and she could have had more work if she had been able to do it.

At first she pretended that people passing would think she was washing her own stair. She always said "Good evening," and gentlemen especially were profuse in their apologies for marking her steps.

One evening a little boy came calling, "Jenny Stairy, Jenny Stairy!"

She turned as if to ward off a blow. But he was a nice little boy, whose daddy was fighting in France, and he only wanted to know why the stair dried white after she had made it black with her wet cloth.

Soon afterwards Jenny gave up her work in the shop, and became a full-time stairy. Her mother had taken a shock which left her paralysed down one side, and Jenny could not be away from her for more than a few hours at a time.

Jenny Stairy became a familiar figure in her own street and in the district where she worked—a skinny creature with her hair pulled back, because she had no time for frizzing, and hands and feet made ungainly by the chilblains which were a result of washing stairs and closes in all weathers.

She had a routine rather than a life: getting up in the morning, attending to her mother, going to work, coming back to attend to her mother, going to work, coming back. Sometimes people wanted her to clean house for them, but she would not do it in case she would not please them or they would ask her to wash windows. She stuck to her routine, day in, day out, for years.

Once at New Year she put whirligigs on a close, but the lady asked her not to do it again, it made the place look so common. On Jenny's own stair the whorls still gleamed in the morning, like symbols of hope not dead.

There was a man called Ibbets, whom she saw every Tuesday and Friday. He was a foreman carpenter who had strayed into that quarter because of war wages and the scarcity of houses, and there had been quite a sensation at the time, because the "tone" of the place was supposed to be lowered.

But as tenants the Ibbets were peaceful enough, and it was not long before a neighbour was handing Jenny the pail and pipeclay for Mrs. Ibbets, who was said to be "not too well", with a significant tap of the forehead.

Because he lived so far from his work, John Ibbets was in for his dinner and out again in the short time it took Jenny to wash the stair.

"It's indigestion you'll get," she said one day, moving aside for him the second time. "You should carry a piece."

"Ach no, I come hame for the pleasure o' seein' you."

She coloured at that, and the next time she was silent, letting him pass. But he caught her waist with his arm, and she saw that his smile was sweet, as her father's had been.

He was tall, too, like her father, with thinning hair and restless eyes. She found herself thinking about him often, as she had not done with a man, Kemp, who sometimes spoke to her when she was working.

He said he remembered her from the old days in the ironmonger's.

"Ach, come on, ye mind me fine," he said persuasively, standing in her way, so that she had almost to wash over his square-toed boots.

She thought it likely enough, although she did not remember him. He was exactly the type that had come about the shop—broad and clumsy like her brother Tom, now married since the war, and living in the Midlands.

Kemp was doing well for himself in the building line. He was a widower and he wanted Jenny to come and clean for him.

"No . . . I couldna." That was all she would answer, and by and by his sister came to keep house for him.

But every Tuesday and Friday Jenny watched for John Ibbets, twice in a quarter of an hour. Always as he passed he put his hand on her and called some pleasantry to which she replied as he raced up or down the stair.

One evening on her way from work she met him, and he

turned back with her. He did not seem to read the papers, or, if he did, he did not tell her what was in them. Neither of them talked very much, but when they reached the close he came inside and kissed her.

It was a melting experience, and he left his mouth where it was till she took her own away. She would have done anything for him.

"Jenny," he said, his arms still round her, "Jenny, would you come and clean for us whiles?"

She had to go at night when he was there, because his wife hated women and might do her an injury. It was only once a week, and Jenny arranged for Isa, Jim's wife, to look in and make sure her mother was all right. In return, Jenny kept the children for a night to let Jim and Isa go out.

It was a queer exchange—a night at the cinema for two hours' scrubbing under the eye of a woman who never relaxed. Mrs. Ibbets had once been pretty in a dark way, but now she was a wizened creature, with an air of knowing something more terrible than anybody else could imagine. Her husband stroked her shoulders and talked to her continually.

"Ach, Martha, she canny get me when you're here. Nobody can get me . . . d'ye no' ken that, ye daft lassie?"

She would giggle, with a distortion of her face like lightning tearing a small stubborn rock.

Once Jenny asked John Ibbets as he passed up the stair: "What made her like that?"

He could not stop to answer, for his wife watched at the window, and was always waiting for him behind the door.

On his way down he muttered: "Once away our holidays . . . a girl . . . there was no harm in it, but she caught us . . . she tried to do hersel' in."

Jenny knew it was a lie. At least she knew there was more. His mouth was weak like her father's and he did not drink. A woman would always be tortured by doubts if she were fool enough to love him. Unless he were tied to another woman whom he could not love because she was wrong in the mind.

Twenty-five years later the Abercromby drapery stores (three branches) had sold out at a big price to a combine firm. Jenny was still washing stairs.

Her mother had died, and she might have taken a job, but she made no change in her life except that she cleaned at the Ibbets' twice a week instead of once. She took no other cleaning, although Kemp had asked her again and again.

The depression years had hit John Ibbets hard, but he gave Jenny more money than he need have done for two nights' cleaning. She put some of it in the bank, because she thought she might need it if ever . . .

But Mrs. Ibbets lived on. People said sympathetically, "Why doesn't he put her in a home?" But Jenny thought he ought to let her be.

Since the war began again, John Ibbets had been making good money, but he was a tired man whose voice had dwindled from constantly talking to his wife.

On the twenty-fifth anniversary of the night when he had first kissed her in the close, Jenny finished her scrubbing and left the Ibbets' as usual. He rushed after her, banging the door behind him.

He was sixty-five and she was over fifty, a gaunt woman whom neighbours had compared with an ostrich. But they walked home, and up the long stairs to her house, and were happy together.

The next day she went out with a firm step; the chalky curls on the stair were bright, and she thought she did not need their comfort any more.

She went to start her work, but as she passed the Ibbets' close there was a crowd gathered round. The district had "gone down" since the days when it was full of teachers and businessmen. The wives of tradesmen and minor clerks were Jenny's employers now, and a few of them stood in a knot about the close.

"It was wee Jean says to me, *'Mammy, what's the funny smell? . . .'*"

Mrs. Ibbets. Mr. Ibbets had gone out and left her. Poor

man, he'd paid for it now. He came in . . . they must have gone to bed.

She'd got up, turned on the gas, put her head in the oven. He must have been dead beat, he never wakened. The policeman could hardly go in, it was so thick.

"Jenny . . . you're not to take it like that. Aye, it's a shock . . . an' you've lost a good job . . . but there's plenty more. She's better away, poor soul, an' he . . ."

"It was wee Jean says to me, *'Mammy, what's the funny smell? . . .'*"

She had been alone in her own house for a long time. It must have been evening when she heard feet come up the stair. Heavy feet, but dulled with rubber soles. Then a thumping at the door.

She went at last. He had been turning away, but he came back. It was Kemp, the widower.

"Jenny . . . they're away now . . . you'll be needin' work . . . if there's nobody else before me . . . would you come an' clean for me?"

He was pathetic, knowing he should not have come so soon, but not knowing how else to make sure of her.

Jenny had always been quiet about things. Her brothers had cheated her out of marriage with a man who loved her less than his dignity. She had been left alone to bear the burden of her mother's helplessness. She had been indirectly to blame for the death of the two men she had loved. And now a man was asking something from her.

Gently she closed her door against him.

But a neighbour, coming up the stair half an hour later, saw something black whirling past her and out through the close. Before she could reach it, the missile had rolled away under the wheels of a lorry in the street. She recognized it, crushed as it was. It was Jenny Stairy's bowler hat.

Edward Scouller

MURDOCH'S BULL

Indeed you wouldn't be far wrong if you said that Murdoch
loved that bull. On a winter's night he would come into its
stall and speak to it like it was a Christian, quietening it when
the glare of his lamp in its red eyes made the brute stamp and
rattle its chain. In the Gaelic he would talk to it, you know,
calling it the silliest names that nobody uses except to a baby
or maybe to a girl. And he would catch one of those great
spreading horns of its and pull the shaggy hair that hung
down over its eyes and rub his big, three-fingered hand up
and down its forehead. The beast would snort and stare at him
till it saw that this was just Murdoch that wouldn't do it any
harm. Then he would stoop his head and the two of them, the
savage bull and the half-witted lad, would rub their brows
together.

Of course, there was no harm in Murdoch, no harm whatever. It was just the queer bit that was in all the Portmor
MacLachlans. There was his old grandmother now, Giorsal
Pharuig, her that reared Murdoch after his mother went off
to the mainland—and Dear knows where she is now, but the
father was killed before ever Murdoch was born. Giorsal was
queer too: she would never leave that dirty old black house of
hers down Portmor, and the new laird building the grand
house for her in Glasard with a slated roof and water pipes in
the sink and all. She was no companion for a growing boy,
but who else was there to do anything for him? Everybody
has their own troubles to look after.

The bull belonged to old Giorsal. And what she wanted

with a brute like that and her with only six cows and a farm no bigger than a croft was what everybody in the island often wondered. Maybe it was just because Murdoch made such a work with it. He was just twelve when the bull was born, and he helped Niall Dubh and Calum with the calving: he was a knowledgeable lad with cattle even if they'd never managed to get a word of schooling into him. By the time the bull was four years old there wasn't his like in Mara, no nor in all the Hebrides. He stood fifteen hands high and must have weighed anything up to fourteen hundred pounds. Yellow he was, and with those huge horns of his and the broad chest and the short legs he was a perfect picture. But what use was he to Giorsal? He was just going to waste on a small place like Portmor, or indeed on the island of Mara at all. And then he got so wild too. You daren't come within half a mile of the MacLachlan's place without making sure of where he was. There was no use of keeping near a dyke either, for he'd leap dyke or gate like a dog rounding up sheep.

Well, when old Giorsal died—rest her soul!—Murdoch came to the Grants at Killoran. And the bull came with him. Of course, it was good of the Grants to take the orphan boy in, but he was worth his keep anywhere. He couldn't be trusted with a message, but he could do a man's work and more in the fields, and at night when he wasn't on the hills with that bull he'd sit in the barn playing on his mouth-organ. A lovely player he was too, and quick to pick up a tune.

In the long run folk began to complain about Murdoch's bull. It wasn't so bad for us that knew about it and that knew the likeliest roads to keep clear of it when we were near Killoran. But poor old Rory Mor that had to cross the Grants' land to get from the shore to his house was in terror of his life of the brute. Twice it chased him on his way home from the lobsters. It would have been laughable if it hadn't been a shame to see the old man so frightened. There was once it went after him and he just got into his hen-house and no more. The bull couldn't get through the door for its horns, but it stood roaring and foaming and throwing up the turfs with its

feet and the sparks nearly flying out of its eyeballs. Seumas
Grant and two of the men tried to drive it back with hayforks,
but it turned on them and scattered them too. In the end it
was poor silly Murdoch they had to send for. He was only
fifteen at the time. They kept shouting at him to be careful,
but he just walked right up to the bull and caught it by the
horns and turned it round and walked away with it.

But that wasn't the funny bit of the story. Murdoch
wouldn't ever talk to Rory after that, because, he said, Rory
must have been annoying the poor bull. The Grants tried to
bring him round to let it be sold, for they were people that
never liked to bother or be bothered by anybody. But Murdoch, that was namely through the island for his gentleness
and good temper, he flew into such a rage that they thought
he'd take a fit. He swore he'd kill anybody that laid a finger
on his bull to sell it.

Of course it got more and more vicious as it grew older.
But the more people talked against the beast the more Murdoch doted on it. Poor lad, he was so proud of being the only
one on the island that could manage this bull. It made him
twice as fond of it to know that it made folk respect him that
more often laughed at him. You would even see him walking
along beside it with his arm across its neck and him gabbling
away to it more than he ever talked to the folks at the farm.
Of course nobody talked much to poor Murdoch at any time.
He was a quiet, decent, biddable lad; but he had such a ganching tongue that it wasn't easy to know what he was saying,
and it wasn't often worth knowing anyhow.

At last there was a terrible to-do about the bull. It chased
some of the summer visitors from the hotel and tossed one of
them into the loch. The laird happened to be in Mara at the
time, and the visitors and the hotel folk complained to him. So
on the Sunday he set out himself to see the Grants and Murdoch. The Grants were away into Scalasaig to church, and
Murdoch was out in the fields as usual with his bull when the
laird arrived.

He came on the pair of them there, and you would have

thought the animal knew what he was come about. The bull was as quiet and gentle as an old collie. He even let the stranger stroke his nose. And Murdoch in his ganching, mixed-up way telling the laird all the time there was no harm in the bull, only folk wouldn't let it alone. So in the long run the laird said he could keep it for a while if he'd watch it better when strangers were about.

Poor Murdoch was so glad to get keeping his bull that he couldn't get a word out of him for the ganch-ganching and stuttering. So the laird bid him good-bye and turned to walk back to the road. He hadn't gone twenty steps when the bull down with its head, up with its tail and went after him with a noise like thunder. Before Murdoch could even shout to it to stop, it had its head under the laird and flung him into the middle of a whin bush. It was a mercy he wasn't killed. But Murdoch got hold of the bull and quietened it while the laird struggled up and got on to the road.

There was only one thing for it after that: the bull had to be either killed or sold. They got a buyer for it quick enough, a man over in Oban that was buying for an Australian. The night the bull went away, half the island of Mara was along to see what pranks it would play on the road. Everyone swore it would kill someone before they got it out on the ferry-boat to the *Dunara*. It was the middle of the night when they brought it from Killoran, but at every door you could see women and children peering out; the men were all helping with the bull. They had put a ring in its nose with a rope to it, and they had tied one hind foot to a fore one. Every man had a thick stick, and two or three had forks. There were four or five dogs. It was a queer sight to see the whole of them jogging along in the dark, their lanterns bobbing up and down, and all of them keeping one eye on the bull and one on the side of the road.

And there was the famous bull in the middle of them walking along as tame and quiet as a kitten. Maybe it was dazed with all the lights and the crowd, or maybe it was wondering where it was going. Or maybe it knew it was finished with its tantrums in Mara. You can never tell what a bull's thinking, or whether it's thinking at all. It walked on the ferry as if it had been doing nothing else all its life, and didn't even struggle much when they put the belly-straps on it and slung it on to the steamer.

They could hardly get Murdoch off the *Dunara*. He cried, and he cried, just like the big senseless baby he was, and wanted to take the bull back ashore with him. However, they got him away at last, and he went off the ferry and up the road roaring and weeping. Of course folk said he'd soon forget about the bull, because he was just like a baby in everything but his size and strength, and babies soon forget.

But Murdoch didn't seem to forget. He wouldn't speak to anybody. He just went prowling about the barn and the byre and the hills at all hours of the day and night, and wouldn't play on his mouth-organ, not even to please Mrs. Grant that had always been able to understand him and work with him.

Then one night he didn't come to the kitchen for his porridge at supper-time, and in the morning they got his body all battered and broken in the water below the cliffs at Kilchattan. Maybe he fell over: he was only a silly lad after all.

Robert MacLellan

THE MENNANS

The drinkin watter at Linmill had come at ae time frae a wal
on the green fornent the front door. The auld stane troch was
there yet, big eneuch for playin in, but the pump was lyin
amang the rubbish in a corner o the cairt shed, and the hole it
had come oot o was filled up wi stanes. The wal had gaen dry,
it seems, juist efter I was born, and in my day the watter for
the hoose was cairrit up frae the bottom orchard by Daft
Sanny, twa pails at a time.

The wal in the bottom orchard was juist inside the Linmill
hedge. There were twa trochs there, big round airn anes sunk
into the grun, and the ane faurer frae the spoot had a troot in
it to keep the watter clean. Through the hedge, tae, in Tam
Baxter's grun, there was anither troch, and it was fou o
mennans, for Tam was a great fisher and needit them for bait.

I gaed doun to the wal to play whiles, but I didna bother
muckle wi oor ain troot. It was aye Tam's mennans I gaed for.
I didna try to catch them, I was ower feart for that, but whan
I had creepit through the hedge by the hole aside the honeysuckle I lay on my belly watchin them, wi my lugs weill
cockit for the bark o Tam's dug.

I was fell fond o catching mennans, but seldom got the
chance. I wasna alloued doun to Clyde withoot my grandfaither, for I had to be liftit twa-three times on the wey ower
the bank, and in the simmer he was aye gey thrang in the
fields, gafferin the warkers. Sae when I wantit badly but
couldna gang I just gaed through the hedge and had a look
in Tam's troch. It helpit me to think o the mennans in Clyde,

for they aw had the same wey o soumin, gowpin at the mou and gogglin their big dowei een.

For a lang while I had the notion than Tam foun his mennans for himsell, but ae day whan I was on my wey back to the hoose efter takin a finger-length o thick black doun the field to my grandfaither I met a big laddie frae Kirkfieldbank wi a can in his haund.

"Whaur are ye gaun wi the can?"

"To the Falls."

"What's in it?"

"Mennans."

"Let me see."

The can was fou.

"What are ye takin them to the Falls for?"

"To sell them to Tam Baxter."

"Will Tam buy them?"

"He buys them for the fishin."

"What daes he pey ye?"

"A penny a dizzen."

"Hoo mony hae ye?"

"Twenty-fower."

"That'll be tippence."

"Ay."

I could haurdly believe it. I thocht o aw the mennans I had catchit and gien to the cats. I could hae bocht the haill o Martha Baxter's shop wi the siller I had lost.

Aw I could dae noo was mak a clean stert. The cats could want efter this.

At lowsin time that day I was waitin for my grandfaither at the Linmill road-end. It was airly in my simmer holiday, afore the strawberries were ripe, and he was warkin wi juist a wheen o the weemen frae roun aboot, weedin the beds. I heard him blawin his birrel and kent he wadna be lang, for he was in the field neist to the wal yett, and that was juist ower the road.

The weemen cam through the yett first, some haudin their backs, for it was sair wark bending aw day, and ithers rowin up their glaurie aprons. They skailed this wey and that, and syne cam my grandfaither, wi the weeders in ae hand and his knee-pads in the tither. I cam oot frae the hedge and gaed forrit to meet him.

"Whan will ye tak me to Clyde again, grandfaither?"

"What's gotten ye noo?"

"I want doun to Clyde to catch mennans."

"Ay ay, nae doobt, but it's time for yer tea, and syne ye'll hae to gang to yer bed."

"Ay, but can I no gang the morn?"

"We'll see what yer grannie says."

"But she aye says na."

"What's pat it into yer heid to catch mennans?"

"I like catchin mennans."

"Ay, ay, nae doobt."

"Grandfaither?"

"Ay?"

"Tam Baxter peys a penny a dizzen for mennans."

"Wha telt ye that?"

"A laddie frae Kirkfieldbank."

"Weill, weill."

"Daes he?"

"I daursay."

"It wad be grand to hae some mennans to sell him."

"Ay, weill, we'll see. I'll be weedin aside Clyde the morn."

"Will ye lift me doun ower the bank, then?"

"Mebbe. I'll ask yer grannie."

He didna ask her at tea-time, and I was beginnin to think he had forgotten, but when he cairret me ower to my bed he gied me a wink o his guid ee, the tither was blin, and I jaloused he hadna.

Shair eneuch, whan he had feenished his denner the neist day, and I had forgotten aboot the mennans athegither, for the baker had come in the mornin and gien me a wee curran loaf, he gaed to the scullery and cam back we ane o the milk cans.

"Hae ye a gless jaur ye could gie the bairn?"

My grannie soundit crabbit, but it was juist her wey.

"Ye'll fin ane in the bunker."

He took me to the scullery and foun the gless jaur.

"Come on," he said.

My grannie cried frae the kitchen.

"Dinna let him faw in, noo, or ye needna come back."

We gaed oot into the closs withoot peyin ony heed.

On yer wey doun to Clyde ye took the same road as ye did to the wal, and as faur as the wal the grun was weill trampit, but faurer doun there was haurdly mair to let ye ken the wey than the space atween the grosset busses and the hedge, and there the grun was aw thistles and stickie willie. He cairrit me ower that bit, to save my bare legs, and we hadna gaen faur whan the rummle of Stanebyres Linn grew sae lood that we could haurdly hear oorsells. Not that I wantit to say ocht, for near the soun of the watter I was aye awed, and I was thinkin o the mennans soumin into my jaur.

We cam to the fute o the brae and turnt to the richt, alang the bank abune the watter, and were sune oot o the orchard aside the strawberry beds. The weemen were waitin to stert the weedin, sittin on the gress aneth the hazels, maist o them wi their coats kiltit up and their cutties gaun.

I didna like to hae to staun fornent the weemen. They couldna haud their silly tongues aboot my bonnie reid hair, and ane o them wad be shair to try to lift me, and as my grannie said they had a smell like tinkers, aye warkin in the clartie wat cley. My grandfaither saw them stertit at ance, though, and syne turnt to tak me doun to Clyde.

The wey ower the bank was gey kittle to tak, wi the rocks aw wat moss, and I grippit my grandfaither ticht, but he gat me to the bottom wi nae mair harm nor the stang o a nettle to my left fute. He rubbit the stang wi the leaf o a docken, and tied a string to the neck o my jaur, and efter tellin me no to gang near the Lowp gaed awa back up to his wark.

An awesome laneliness cam ower me as sune as he had turnt his back. It wasna juist the rummle o the Linn frae faurer doun the watter; it was the black hole aneth the bank at my back whaur the otters bade, and the fearsome wey the watter gaed through the Lowp. The front o the hole was hung ower wi creepers, and ye couldna be shair that the otters werena sittin ben ahint them, waiting to sneak oot whan ye werena lookin and put their shairp teeth in to yer legs. The Lowp was waur. It was doun a wee frae the otter hole, across a muckle rock, whaur the haill braid watter o Clyde, sae gentle faurer up, shot through aneth twa straucht black banks like shinie daurk-green gless; and the space atween the banks was sae nerra that a man could lowp across. It wasna an easy lowp, faur abune the pouer o a laddie, yet ye foun yersell staunin starin at it, fair itchin to hae a try. A halflin frae Nemphlar had tried it ance, in a spate whan the rocks were aw spume, and he had landit short and tummelt in backwards, and they say it was nae mair nor a meenit afore his daith-skrech was heard frae Stanebyres Linn itsell, risin abune the thunner o the spate like a stab o lichtnin.

The sun was oot, though, and I tried no to heed, and trith to tell gin it hadna been sae eerie it wad hae been lichtsome there, for in aw the rock cracks whaur yirth had gethert there were hare-bells growin, sae dentie and wan, and back and forrit on the mossie stanes that stude abune the watter gaed wee willie waggies, bobbin up and doun wi their tails gaun a dinger, and whiles haein a dook to tak the stour aff their feathers.

I didna gie them mair nor a look, for I had come to catch mennans, and as I grippit my can and jaur and gaed forrit ower the rock to the whirlies I could feel my hairt thumpin like to burst through my breist. It was aye the same whan I was eager, and it didna help.

The whirlies were roun holes in the rock aside the neck o the Lowp, worn wi the swirl o the watter whan it rase in spate and fludit its haill coorse frae bank to bank; but whan Clyde was doun on a simmer day they were dry aw roun, wi juist a pickle watter comin haufwey up them, clear eneuch to let ye see the colours o aw the bonnie chuckies at the fute. Noo there was ae whirlie wi a shalla end, and a runnel that cam in frae Clyde itself, and on a hot day, gin aw was quait, the mennans slippit ben, about twenty at a time, to lie abune the warm chuckies and gowp in the sun. That was the whirlie for me, for gin ye bade quait eneuch till the mennans were aw weill ben, and laid yer jaur in the runnel wi its mou peyntin to them, and syne stude up and gied them a fricht, they turnt and gaed pell mell into it.

I laid doun my can and creepit forrit, and shair eneuch the mennans were there, but I couldna hae been cannie eneuch, for the meenit I gaed to lay my jaur in the runnel they shot richt past and left the whirlie toom. It was a peety, but it didna maitter. I kent that gin I waitit they wad syne come back.

The awkward thing was that if ye sat whaur ye could see the runnel the mennans could see yersell, sae I had to sit well back and juist jalouse whan they micht steer again. I made up my mind no to move ower sune.

Wi haein nocht to dae I fell into a dwam, and thocht o this thing and that, but maistly o the siller Tam Baxter peyed for the mennans. Syne my banes gat sair, sittin on the hard rock, and I moved a wee to ease mysell a bit. On the turn roun my ee spied the otter hole, and I could hae sworn I saw the creepers movin. I began to feel gey feart, and my thochts took panic, and it wasna lang afore I was thinkin of the halflin that fell in the Lowp, though I had tried gey hard no to.

I lookit up the bank to see if my grandfaither was watchin, and shair eneuch there he was, staunin lookin doun on me to see that I was aw richt. I felt hairtent then, and pat my finger to my mou to keep him frae cryin oot to me, for I kent that gin he did he wad ask me hoo mony mennans I had catchit, and I didna want to hae to tell him nane.

Kennin he was there I grew eager to show him what a clever laddie I was, and I kent I had gien the mennans rowth of time to win back ben the whirlie, sae aw at ance I lowpit forrit and laid my jaur in the runnel, but I was sae hastie that I laid it wrang wey roun. It didna maitter, though, for the mennans were ben, dizzens o them, and they couldna win oot. Quick as a thocht I turnt the jaur roun and geid a lood skelloch. They shot this wey and that, and syne for my jaur, and whan I saw that some o them were into it I poued hard on my string.

I was ower eager, for the jaur gaed richt ower my heid and broke on the rock at my back, and the mennans I had catchit flip-flappit for the watter as hard as they could gang. I grabbit my can and gaed efter them, but they were gey ill to haud, and by the time I had twa o them safe the ithers were back into Clyde.

I stude up. I was richt on the edge o the Lowp.

I couldna tak my een off the glessie daurk-green watter, and I kent the whirlie was somewhaur ahint me, sae I didna daur step backwards. I juist stude still wi my breist burstin, and my wame turnin heid ower heels, till I gey nearly dwamt awa.

I didna, though. I gaed doun on my knees, aye wi my can grippit ticht, and had a wee keek roun. The whirlie was ahint me, but faurer up the rock than I had thocht. I creepit weill past it and lookit up the bank.

My grandfaither wasna there. He hadna been watchin efter aw.

I ran to the bank fute and cried oot, but wi the rummle o the watter he didna hear me, and I stertit to greet. I grat gey sair for a lang while, and syne tried to sclim up the bank, but I slippit and tummelt my can.

It hadna ae bash, but the mennans were gaen. I gied my een a rub wi my guernsey sleeve and stertit to look for them. In the end I spied them, bedirten aw ower and hauf deid. I mindit then that I hadna filled my can wi watter.

Whan they were soumin again they syne cam roun, though ane o them lay for a while wi its belly up, and I thocht it wad dee. Whan it didna I was hairtent again, and began to wish I could catch anither ten.

I had nae gless jaur.

I foun a wee hole in the rock and pat the mennans in, and syne gaed to the whirlie. It was toom, for I hadna keepit quait, but I tried my can in the runnel and foun a bit it wad fit. I wasna dune yet.

I tied my string to the can haunle and sat doun to wait again.

I had a waur job this time to keep mysell in haund, tryin no to think o the horrid end I wad hae come to gin I had fawn ower the edge o the Lowp, but I maun hae managed gey weill, for I didna seem to hae been sittin for a meenit whan my grandfaither's birrel gaed.

It was time to gang hame. I could haurdly believe it.

I gaed forrit to meet him as he cam doun the bank.

"Hoo mony mennans hae ye catchit?"

"Juist twa. I broke my jaur."

"Dear me. Whaur's the can?"

"It's ower by the runnel. I hae tied my string to the haunle."

"And whaur are yer twa mennans?"

"In a wee hole."

"Quait, then, and we'll hae ae mair try. It's time to gang hame."

He sat doun and cut himsell a braidth o thick black, and whan his pipe was gaun and the reek risin oot o it I gat richt back into fettle. I sat as still as daith, wishin his pipe had been cleaner, for it gied a gey gurgle at ilka puff, and I was feart it wad frichten the mennans. But I didna daur say ocht.

Aw at once, without warnin, he lowpit for the runnel wi the can. I lowpit tae.

The can was useless. The mennans saw it and gaed back ben the whirlie. They juist wadna try to win oot.

"Fin a stane," said my grandfaither.

I ran to the fute o the bank and foun a stane.

"Staun ower the whirlie and pitch it in hard."

I lat flee wi aw my strength. The stane hit the watter wi a plunk. The mennans scattert and shot for the runnel. My grandfaither liftit the can.

Whan my braith cam back I gaed ower beside him.

"Hoo mony hae we gotten?"

He was doun on his hunkers wi his heid ower the can.

"I canna coont. They winna bide still."

My hairt gied a lowp. There wad shairly be a dizzen this time. But I was wrang.

"Eicht," he said.

I had a look myself. I coontit them three times. There were eicht and nae mair.

"Come on, then. Fin the ither twa and we'll win awa hame."

I was fair dumfounert.

"But I hae juist ten, grandfaither. I need anither twa still."

"Na, na, we're late. Yer grannie'll be thinkin ye're drount."

"But I need a dizzen."

"What dae ye want a dizzen for?"

"For Tam Baxter's penny."

"Dinna fash aboot Tam Baxter. I'll gie ye a penny mysell."

"But I want to mak my ain penny."

"Na na."

"They'll juist be wastit."

"We'll gie them to the cats. Whaur did ye put the first twa?"

I took him ower to the wee hole. They were still there. He pat them in the can wi the ithers and made for the bank.

"I'll tak the mennans up first."

He gaed awa up and left me. Whan he cam doun again I had stertit to greet.

"Come on, son. I'll gie ye tippence."

But it didna comfort me. I had wantit sae hard to mak a penny o my ain, and I juist needit twa mennans mair. It was past tholin.

Whan we cam to the wal I was begrutten aw ower. He stude for a while.

"Haud on, son. Ye'll hae yer dizzen yet."

He took the tinnie that hung frae the wal spoot. It was there for the drouthie warkers.

"We'll put the mennans in this."

He had a gey job, for it didna leave them muckle watter, but he managed.

"Bide here and haud on to it. Keep ae haund ower the tap or they'll lowp oot."

He left me wi the tinnie and took the can through the hedge. I jaloused at ance what he was efter, and my hairt stertit to thump again, but there was nae bark frae Tam's dug. It maun hae been tied at his back door.

My grandfaither cam back.

"Here ye are, then. Put thae anes back."

I lookit in the can. There were twa in it. I toomed in the ithers.

"That's yer dizzen noo. Ye can tak them to Tam the morn."

I kent I couldna face Tam the morn.

"Daes he no coont his mennans, grandfaither?"

"Na na, he has ower mony for that."

"But it's stealin."

"Dinna fash aboot that. Tam's laddies whiles guddle oor troot."

It was the trith, and they didna aye put it back, but still I kent I couldna face him.

We cam to the wal yett.

"Grandfaither?"

"Aye?"

"I think we'll juist gie them to the cats efter aw."

"What wey that?"

"I'm feart. I couldna face Tam Baxter."

"Nonsense."

"I couldna, grandfaither."

"He'll ken naething."

"He micht fin oot."

"Deil the fear."

We cam to the closs mou.

"Grandfaither?"

"What is it?"

"Juist let me gie them to the cats."

"Aw richt, then. Please yersell."

George Friel

THOUGHTLESS

When their mother died, Plottel's father and uncles, wondering how much they would get, gathered again in the house where they fought together as boys. Their only sister, who after her marriage stayed next door to the old woman and daily attended her, acted as hostess, and the six brothers questioned her furtively, but she told them all she had no idea how much money there was. So six heads were busy working out what the accumulated dividends from the Co-operative Society should come to, and trying to guess the value of the insurance policies. The five brothers who had visited their mother about a dozen times in twenty years became fidgety to think how easily their sister could cheat them, and when the family riot which always arose when they met under one roof was ended by their departing separately, each in a fury at the selfishness of the others, the hostess was left alone with her eldest brother. He was a tramway inspector, and the spinsters of the parish thought him the "nicest" of the Plottels—which was high praise, for the Plottels were locally considered a fine old family.

What he and his sister said when they were alone cannot now be known, but the other Plottels made a guess. Each told his suspicions to his wife, boasting of his acuteness in having them, only to find her jeer at him that for all he thought himself so smart he had marched out in a rage and left those two twisters to plot alone together. To decry the cleverness of a Plottel male is a dangerous thing, and the indiscreet wife provoked a tirade of insults from the husband she mocked, followed by an aloof silence which allowed him to keep the money righteously to himself when it came, since he wasn't on speaking terms with her.

The complaint of the poorer Plottels—and in spite of their parochial reputation the Plottels were mainly a paupered crew—was that those who most needed the money got the least. It was declared among them, when they spoke to each other in the kinship of feeling cheated, that the tramway inspector, who had no children, had got fifty pounds and the sister forty-five. But Plottel's uncle round the corner, with ten children and a wife who had so burdened him with debt that he had long ago become tired of debt-collectors accosting him at the gate every pay-day and given up his work to live on the charity of the parish, got five pounds, which lasted him less than a week.

Plottel's father was given eleven pounds, and went into a theatrical temper at the insignificance of it, although his total earnings were a pound a week from insurance canvassing which he did in default of those revue-tours regularly promised but never given him. He almost spoke to his wife again, until he remembered he was treating her with silent contempt, and so he was left with only the four walls and his frightened family to rage at. For a moment he made to tear the notes and throw them in the fire, just to show what he thought of his brother and sister and their filthy money. But he crumpled them instead and pitched them across to a corner of the dresser, and then when nobody was looking he hid them inside a small tin box on the mantelpiece.

After he bought himself boots and an overcoat and a new suit, he had about half the money left; and since he gave her none of it, his wife went to the hiding place and took a little every week. She saw everything he did, even when she seemed deliberately not looking at him, and she was so well used to his subterfuges that she unscrupulously explored his pockets and all the places he hid his money when he had any. Then, when he was out, teaching the children to scorn him, she laughed with them at his vanity making him assert he kept them all in the lap of luxury and didn't get enough attention and respect.

When he saw the money dwindle, Mr. Plottel took it out of the tin box and kept it in a purse which he carried always with him and put under his pillow at night. In a short time the purse too was empty, and he threw it into a drawer of rubbish.

The youngest child was later given the tin box to play with, and opening and shutting it in the pleasure of digital operations he thrust scraps of paper into it, pulling them out to shove them in again. "I've got money," he said as his father stood near him shaving in the kitchen. "You used to have money in here, didn't you?"

Mr. Plottel, sneezing with the lather he always managed to brush up into his nostrils, turned and gaped at the child, and understood that not only his wife but the whole family had known where he first hid the money. "You've said it," he said, spitting in the sink. "Used to have. But the man who could keep money in this house . . ."

"You made a damned good effort to keep it," said Mrs. Plottel, stoking the fire with damp potato peelings. "You made sure you gave none away."

"It went just the same," said Mr. Plottel. "As soon as my back was turned."

"It went on your back, you mean," said Mrs. Plottel. "On your own back, the same as always."

"You'll be telling me next that you got nothing," said Mr. Plottel.

"I had to take what I got," said Mrs. Plottel. "And God knows that wasn't much."

"It's a millionaire you should have married," said Mr. Plottel.

"And that wouldn't have been you," retorted his wife.

"Oh, would it not?" cried Mr. Plottel, as if he were wronged in not being rated a millionaire.

The child stopped playing and stared with uncertain fear at his parents, recognizing in his mother's tone and in the shout of his father's rhetorical question the setting to their frequent quarrels. Open-mouthed and shaking he moved away from his father and sidled into a corner behind his mother.

"Well, I don't think so somehow," said Mrs. Plottel. "God knows you never had much. But what you do get, goes on yourself. Every time. The rest of us can want. Maybe you expect me to keep this house and your family on nothing."

"I bought what I needed," shouted Mr. Plottel, fiercely lathering his chin with a straggle-haired brush. "I've got to look after myself. I get damn little attention from you. You're too damned lazy. And bloody stupid as well. It wouldn't matter how much you got. A bloody spendthrift, that's all you are."

"It's kind of hard to be a spendthrift when you don't get any money to spend," said Mrs. Plottel, fondling the head of the child come timidly clutching at her side. "As soon as you do get a little money, off you go and put it on your back. Number one comes first with you all the time."

"I've got to look smart in my business," said Mr. Plottel, stirring his brush in the shaving mug, straightening with pride as he mentioned his business, the word alone sufficient stimulus for him again in a daydream to see himself triumphant in a glorious limelight destiny.

"And what is your business?" asked Mrs. Plottel.

Having no precise answer ready, and hearing her begin, in the advantage of his silence, to retail the history of their married life and assert he hadn't given her a proper wage for ten years, Mr. Plottel, his chin bearded with still unrazored lather, threw half a loaf at her offending calm in an oathful fury, and the child began to cry.

With his legacy spent, he was again reduced to the little he earned by insurance canvassing, selling household goods on commission round the doors, and tracing debt-defaulters for moneylenders. Although it was now many years since he last appeared on the stage, he still talked as if he were only briefly and accidentally, through the conspiracy of freemasons, out of that theatrical work which was his proper and splendid career, a career far from being over as his wife slightingly declared, but just about to begin. When he was unexpectedly offered a place in a small touring company, he left the moneylender to find someone else to trace his defaulters, and practising old speeches, changing his voice to make his monologue sound a dialogue, he happily packed his bags. But he came back in a fortnight, ranting that he was an artiste, not an errand-boy or a stage-carpenter as well, and so Mrs. Plottel understood that once again his talent has been misused if not indeed unrecognized.

Back in the city to canvass for anything from insurance policies to fancy pencils, Mr. Plottel—who said he was the best canvasser in Glasgow, and implied he was the more to be admired therein since he also insisted canvassing wasn't his proper line—found his commission so small that he couldn't afford to give his wife anything. Mrs. Plottel then pawned the overmantel, sold the furniture article by article, and spied through the keyhole when she heard the ragwife come up the stair to see if it were coppers or crockery were being given in exchange for old garments and woollen rags. If it were crockery, she did not answer the ragwife's knock, but kept her precious bundle till the woman with coppers came.

So began one of the longest and worst periods of the family's poverty, while the mother gathered her children like chicks around her, leaving her husband to go on alone in the silence he had begun, serving without a word to him such meals as could be put together, and without a word Mr. Plottel would hungrily watch her and sit down immediately at the place set for him. He always ate alone, partly because he made so much noise with his defective false teeth that the sensitive children, who didn't like his company anyway, preferred to wait in their hunger rather than appease it at once by sitting down beside him, and partly because he was always so impatient to eat that a single meal had to be hastily prepared to satisfy him first.

But the children, because of their intelligence, were popular with the spinsters who taught them in the parish school, and noticing their increasing bootless shabbiness and malnutrition the spinsters gossiped among themselves. Soon, after mass or benediction or some Catholic social evening, they gossiped to their married friends, even hinting to the tramway inspector's plump and benevolent wife, whose childless comfort made them the more sympathetic for the many ill-clad and ill-fed nephews and nieces to whom they felt, for all they admired her parochial energy, she did not attend with the interest and generosity proper to a relative and a churchworker. Then in the week before Christmas Plottel himself, with the crust of a slice of bread fried in margarine in his hand, opened the door to a rhythmical knocking and saw on the landing a grocer's boy with a large basket, covered with sacking, at his feet.

"Plottel's?" said the grocer's boy.

Plottel bit the crust and stared with wondering hunger at the basket.

"Is this Plottel's?" repeated the grocer's boy impatiently.

Plottel nodded to the small nameplate, easily overlooked beside the door. "Can't you read?" he asked, and looked again and more hungrily at the crammed-seeming basket. Mrs. Plottel came forward in slow curiosity from the kitchen to see what was going on. When she saw the basket she gaped.

"Plottel's order," said the grocer's boy, touching his cap to her.

Mrs. Plottel looked from the basket to him, and looked down at the basket again. "Bring it in," she said suddenly jerking her head to motion him and looking like a penniless gambler determined to take the risk of palming a card. With obvious effort the boy raised the basket and entered. Plottel and his wife followed him into the kitchen, questioning each other with their eyes in speechless amazement. When the basket was emptied Mrs. Plottel gave the boy all the money she had, fourpence received that afternoon for rags.

Jabbering in loud excitement the children clustered round the unusually packed table, struggling against the attempts of their elder sister, a grave religious-minded girl of twelve, to force her way to the front, and grabbing at the bags and parcels to tear them open in impatient exploration.

"Mother," said the timid jostled girl, "you shouldn't have taken it. It must be a mistake."

"Well, it's their mistake," said Mrs. Plottel, who had long decided scrupulous honesty was too expensive for her to practise. "And anybody who can afford all that can afford to lose it, too."

Leaning against the dresser she watched her family complete a rapid survey of the contents of the basket.

"Ach, this is only sugar!" "Look, currant bun!" "What's this?"

"Rice," said the eldest girl, working her elbow like a piston.

"Pooh, margarine!"

"Butter," corrected the girl, almost right at the front, and pulling the fingers of one hand nervously now with those of the other in her conflict between a fear wherein she foresaw her mother in jail for stealing and her excitement at seeing so many provisions. "Don't you know butter when you see it?"

"Ach, it's all the same," said her brothers.

"It's not all the same!" cried the girl, her morbid worry conquered by her desire to show she knew something about groceries.

"Eggs!" "Cheese!" "Ugh, this is only lentils!" "Biscuits!" "Gingerbread!" "Pickles!" "That's only bread!" "Tch, oatmeal!" "Oh, look, a tin of pineapples!" "Tea, tea, more tea!" "Apple jelly, strawberry jam, cocoa, grapenuts!" "Ugh, haricot beans! I thought it was something!" "Ham!"

"That's not ham, it's bacon," shouted the nervous girl in immediate pleasure, wholly happy now she could show off her superior knowledge.

The floor was littered with the discarded wrappings of provisions.

"There's no milk," said Mrs. Plottel coming forward to see exactly what there was, and trying to calculate how much the lot had cost. "They might have thought of putting in a tin of condensed milk."

"But mother," said the eldest girl, worried again in her fading excitement, "how do you know it's for us? You shouldn't have taken it. You don't know who it might have been for."

"It's ours now," said Mrs. Plottel grimly.

"But mother," repeated the girl, nervously pulling her fingers again.

"Mother your granny," said Mrs. Plottel, marshalling the goods into a semblance of order.

The next day the eldest girl was given by the nun in charge of the school a sealed letter to take home to her mother. The letter asked them all to pray for the donor of a basket of provisions they should have received.

"What's a donor?" asked Mrs. Plottel, holding the letter as if it had an infection on it.

"A lady," said the girl gravely. "It's an Italian word."

"I wonder who it is," muttered Mrs. Plottel. "My God, if it's that big fat lump. . . . Ach, what does it matter! Even if it is, she can afford it."

But the workings of parochial charity were not finished. A few evenings later, when Mr. Plottel had gone out as usual to a music-hall where he would be admitted for nothing on showing his card, and Mrs. Plottel sat half asleep before a fire stoked with dross and refuse, there was a solemn knock at the door. The children stopped quarrelling and Mrs. Plottel jolted to a scared wakefulness. It was their custom, caused by the troublesome visits of factor's clerks and debt-collectors, never to open the door unless the person knocking was insistent and plainly determined to get an answer. So everyone sat perfectly still and quiet in order not to give the would-be visitor the unnecessary encouragement of hearing people within the house. The solemn knock came again, deepening their hush, and realizing that so late in the evening it could hardly be anyone come to demand money owing, Mrs. Plottel rose with experienced noiselessness and tried to spy through the keyhole. Then, after waiting till the knock was repeated to make it seem that the third one was the first to her hearing, she turned back to the kitchen and coughed there, making a long-practised rustle as if she were coming along the lobby, and turned again to open the door. Two tall, bowlered men in black overcoats darkened the threshold.

"Mrs. Plottel?" said one, and each raised his bowler half-an-inch.

Mrs. Plottel nodded, too startled to speak, and stood blocking the entrance.

"We're from the Saint Vincent de Paul Society," said the one who had already spoken, and his partner bowed supportingly.

"Oh, come in!" said Mrs. Plottel, assuming the graciousness of a lady. Her respect for the Church making her immediately courteous even to the lay emissaries of a charitable organization connected with it, she was willing to let them enter that kitchen from which, because of its untidy and usually unclean poverty, all callers were normally excluded. The dark representatives of benevolence went clumsily past her as she gestured them, each taking off his hat and nervously smoothing his hair with a large gloved hand. Too embarrassed to go any further when they saw the littered confusion of the penniless kitchen, they stuck shyly at the doorway to it.

"We were told," said the one who was evidently to be the spokesman of the mission, "I mean, we were advised, er, we were recommended. . . ."

"Yes?" said Mrs. Plottel, holding her head high, standing facing them again with her back to the kitchen, and with one hand behind her signalling the children to be quiet, although they were too interested in awe to move.

"I mean, we've come to see you," plunged the speaker. His silent partner nodded approval of the statement. Mrs. Plottel almost retorted "So I see," but checked her natural sarcasm and bowed.

"You see, we were told you were—you were—you were

having a hard time of it just now," hurried the spokesman, running the fingers of one hand round the crown of his bowler held against his chest. "We were asked to see if you could be helped—I mean, if we could help you. I mean. . . ."

"Yes?" said Mrs. Plottel encouragingly.

"Your husband isn't working?" he fired suddenly, toning the statement for a question.

"No," said Mrs. Plottel, who since she got nothing out of it refused to call her husband's irregular canvassing working, although Mr. Plottel himself thought it very hard work. "I've been all over Partick, Whiteinch, Govan, Plantation and Kinning Park the day," he would say in the evening. "Up and down stairs, up and down stairs. And no bloody thanks for it."

"You'll find it hard to feed and clothe your family?" said the spokesman slowly, as if confronted with data from which inferences must be made with great caution.

"Occasionally," said Mrs. Plottel gently.

"Does he drink?" darted the speaker, nervously fingering the doorjamb.

"Oh, no," said Mrs. Plottel, drawing out the vowels.

"You see, we have to ask that, you know, just to make sure," mumbled the speaker, embarrassedly apologetic. "Well, you know, there's no use helping people, trying to help people, if the man would just drink it."

"No," said Mrs. Plottel.

"He's all right to you—'n' to the children?"

"Oh, well, yes," answered Mrs. Pottel not quite surely.

"He's all right really? Just, he's not working, is that it?" asked the spokesman with a strange hopefulness, as if reluctant to hear Mr. Plottel had any definite and constant failings.

"That's it," Mrs. Plottel, never an argumentative woman, agreed readily. "He was all right when he had a job. It's all because he'd never stick in one. The stage, the stage, all the time. And of course that work never lasts. It's no use unless you're at the very top. Where he never was near. And now he can't get a proper job. Men won't give him a job just for him to leave when the fancy takes him."

"I see," said the spokesman. "You're quite sure he doesn't drink?"

"Oh, no; he never touches it. It's just he won't stick in one job. Throws them away for a month with a revue or something like that. The head man in the insurance said it was a great pity the stage had got into his blood. He could have had his own office today, he said, if he had only been content to stay in the business. Oh, but that was years ago!"

"Except for that he's not bad?" said the spokesman.

"Oh well, no," said Mrs. Plottel, beginning to tire of the questioning which seemed unprofitable to her. "He's all right when he's working. Just, he's a wee bit—well, a wee bit selfish. . . . Thoughtless, really. That's all," she hurried, having found the word. "He's just thoughtless."

"Hm," grunted the hitherto silent partner in the mission. Mrs. Plottel stared at the two men, waiting the next move, and they stared at the floor, one fingering his bowler, the other caressing the jamb of the doorway. Then the one who had done all the talking slowly brought out a wallet from his inside pocket, and gave Mrs. Plottel two pound notes from it. Mumbling words she was too excited to hear, he turned from her, putting on his hat, and in rapid embarrassment, like a soldier caught out of step and hurrying to create the semblance of coincidence, his partner imitating him. When she had shown them out, Mrs. Plottel staggered back into the kitchen laughing merrily, and banging the door behind her she leaned against it, waving the notes. The children, already mobilized, jumped quarrellingly round her to snatch the notes as she flourished them teasingly just above their hands.

"How much did you get?" they cried. "Oh, mother, get us fish and chips!"

"What's the time?" said Mrs. Plottel. She lifted her coat from the couch, her hat from the floor, and looked for her shoes while the boys cried: "I'll go!" "I'll go!" "I'll go!" "I'll go!"

"It's all right," she said, easing her shoes from where they were jammed under the fender. "I know what I want myself."

She came back with the fish and chips they wanted, and two bottles of Guinness for herself. When Mr. Plottel came in, the bottles were empty and hidden and the wrappings of the fish and chips burned. But none of them had remembered to put away the salt cellar, and the eldest girl, who with a fiction-bred fastidiousness had used a fork for her chips, had left it lying beside her plate. With the sharpness of experience Mr. Plottel stared at the salt and the fork, and looked round the room like a policeman. The next morning he spoke in a friendly tone to his wife, and told her his boots were needing mending.

"Will I just send them down?" he asked pleasantly, clearing the breakfast table for her.

Mrs. Plottel looked round at him, bewildered at the calm assurance of his implication that she could afford it, and many bitter charges confusedly phrased themselves in her head. Then turning away, in tired impartiality resignedly she said, "Oh, I suppose you might as well."

"I don't understand it," she said to her family in the evening when as usual Mr. Plottel went out to a music-hall. "He seems to smell money. Asks me can he send his boots down. Asks me, if you please! Meaning I pay. My money's for him, but his is for himself. Oh, he's great! But I wish I knew how he got to know!"

Continuing his friendly tone, Mr. Plottel said he needed a new shirt. When she bought him one and paid for the repair of his boots, and gave the grocer something on account that her credit might get a fresh lease, Mrs. Plottel had two half-crowns left. Looking at the coins unfamiliarly located in her purse, she muttered: "They shouldn't have given me so much. What the hell use to me is their charity once in a blue moon? And you're all still needing boots. However, the old boy's provided for. I suppose that's all that matters."

John Buchan

THE OUTGOING OF THE TIDE[1]

Men come from distant parts to admire the tides of Solloway, which race in at flood and retreat at ebb with a greater
speed than a horse can follow. But nowhere are there queerer
waters than in our own parish of Caulds at the place called the
Sker Bay, where between two horns of land a shallow estuary
receives the stream of the Sker. I never daunder by its shores,
and see the waters hurrying like messengers from the great
deep, without solemn thoughts and a memory of Scripture
words on the terror of the sea. The vast Atlantic may be fear-
ful in its wrath, but with us it is no clean open rage, but the
deceit of the creature, the unholy ways of quicksands when the
waters are gone, and their stealthy return like a thief in the
night-watches. But in the times of which I write there were
more awful fears than any from the violence of nature. It was
before the day of my ministry in Caulds, for then I was a bit
callant in short clothes in my native parish of Lesmahagow;
but the worthy Doctor Chrystal, who had charge of spiritual
things, has told me often of the power of Satan and his emissaries in that lonely place. It was the day of warlocks and
apparitions, now happily driven out by the zeal of the General
Assembly. Witches pursued their wanchancy calling, bairns
were spirited away, young lassies selled their souls to the evil
one, and the Accuser of the Brethren in the shape of a black
tyke was seen about cottage-doors in the gloaming. Many

---

[1] From the unpublished Remains of the Reverend John Dennistoun, sometime minister of the Gospel in the parish of Caulds, and author of *Satan's
Artifices against the Elect.*

and earnest were the prayers of good Doctor Chrystal, but the evil thing, in spite of his wrestling, grew and flourished in his midst. The parish stank of idolatry, abominable rites were practised in secret, and in all the bounds there was no one had a more evil name for this black traffic than one Alison Sempill, who bode at the Skerburnfoot.

The cottage stood nigh the burn in a little garden with lilyoaks and grosart-bushes lining the pathway. The Sker ran by in a linn among hollins, and the noise of its waters was ever about the place. The highroad on the other side was frequented by few, for a nearer-hand way to the west had been made through the Lowe Moss. Sometimes a herd from the hills would pass by with sheep, sometimes a tinkler or a wandering merchant, and once in a long while the laird of Heriotside on his grey horse riding to Gledsmuir. And they who passed would see Alison hirpling in her garden, speaking to herself like the illwife she was, or sitting on a cutty-stool by the doorside with her eyes on other than mortal sights. Where she came from no man could tell. There were some said she was no woman, but a ghost haunting some mortal tenement. Others would threep she was gentrice, come of a persecuting family in the west, that had been ruined in the Revolution wars. She never seemed to want for siller; the house was as bright as a new preen, the yaird better delved than the manse garden; and there was routh of fowls and doos about the small steading, forby a wheen sheep and milk-kye in the fields. No man ever saw Alison at any market in the countryside, and yet the Skerburnfoot was plenished yearly in all proper order. One man only worked on the place, a doited lad who had long been a charge to the parish, and who had not the sense to fear danger or the wit to understand it, Upon all others the sight of Alison, were it but for a moment. cast a cold grue, not to be remembered without terror. It seems she was not ordinarily ill-faured, as men use the word. She was maybe sixty years in age, small and trig, with her grey hair folded neatly under her mutch. But the sight of her eyes was not a thing to forget. John Dodds said they were the een of a deer with the devil ahint them, and indeed they would so appal an onlooker that a sudden unreasoning terror came into his heart, while his feet would impel him to flight. Once John, being overtaken in drink on the roadside by the cottage, and dreaming that he was burning in hell, woke and saw the old wife hobbling towards him. Thereupon he fled soberly to the hills, and from that day became a quiet-living humbleminded Christian. She moved about the country like a wraith, gathering herbs in dark loanings, lingering in kirkyairds, and casting a blight on innocent bairns. Once Robert Smillie found her in a ruinous kirk on the Lang Muir where of old the idolatrous rites of Rome were practised. It was a hot day, and in the quiet place the flies buzzed in crowds, and he noted that she sat clothed in them as with a garment, yet suffering no discomfort. Then he, having mind of Beelzebub, the god of flies, fled without a halt homewards; but, falling in the Coo's Loan, broke two ribs and a collar-bone, the whilk misfortune was much blessed to his soul. And there were darker tales in the countryside, of weans stolen, of lassies misguided, of innocent beasts cruelly tortured, and in one and all there came in the name of the wife of the Skerburnfoot. It was noted by them that kenned best that her cantrips were at their worst when the tides in the Sker Bay ebbed between the hours of twelve and one. At this season of the night the tides of mortality run lowest, and when the outgoing of those unco waters fell in with the setting of the current of life, then indeed was the hour for unholy revels. While honest men slept in their beds, the auld rudas carlines took their pleasure. That there is a delight in sin no man denies, but to most it is but a broken glint in the pauses of their conscience. But what must be the hellish joy of those lost beings who have forsworn God and trysted with the Prince of Darkness, it is not for a Christian to say. Certain it is that it must be great, though their master waits at the end of the road to claim the wizened things they call their souls. Serious men, notably Gidden Scott in the Back of the Hill and Simon Wauch in the sheiling of Chasehope, have seen Alison wandering on the wet sands, dancing to no earthly music, while the heavens, they said, were full of lights and sounds which betokened the presence of the prince of the powers of the air. It was a season of heart-searching for God's saints in Caulds, and the dispensation was blessed to not a few.

It will seem strange that in all this time the presbytery was idle, and no effort was made to rid the place of so fell an influence. But there was a reason, and the reason, as in most like cases, was a lassie. Forby Alison there lived at the Sker-burnfoot a young maid, Ailie Sempill, who by all accounts was as good and bonnie as the other was evil. She passed for a daughter of Alison's, whether born in wedlock or not I cannot tell; but there were some said she was no kin to the auld witch-wife, but some bairn spirited away from honest parents. She was young and blithe, with a face like an April morning and a voice in her that put the laverocks to shame. When she sang in the kirk folk have told me that they had a foretaste of the music of the New Jerusalem, and when she came in by the village of Caulds old men stottered to their doors to look at her. Moreover, from her earliest days the bairn had some glimmerings of grace. Though no minister would visit the Skerburnfoot, or if he went, departed quicker than he came, the girl Ailie attended regular at the catechizing at the Mains of Sker. It may be that Alison thought she would be a better offering for the devil if she were given the chance of forswear-ing God, or it may be that she was so occupied in her own dark business that she had no care of the bairn. Meanwhile the lass grew up in the nurture and admonition of the Lord. I have heard Doctor Chrystal say that he never had a com-municant more full of the things of the Spirit. From the day when she first declared her wish to come forward to the hour when she broke bread at the table, she walked like one in a dream. The lads of the parish might cast admiring eyes on her bright cheeks and yellow hair as she sat in her white gown in the kirk, but well they knew she was not for them. To be the bride of Christ was the thought that filled her heart; and when at the fencing of the tables Doctor Chrystal preached from

Matthew nine and fifteen, "Can the children of the bride-chamber mourn, as long as the bridegroom is with them?" it was remarked by sundry that Ailie's face was liker the countenance of an angel than of a mortal lass.

It is with the day of her first communion that this narrative of mine begins. As she walked home after the morning table she communed in secret and her heart sang within her. She had mind of God's mercies in the past, how He had kept her feet from the snares of evildoers which had been spread around her youth. She had been told unholy charms like the seven south streams and the nine rowan berries, and it was noted when she went first to the catechizing that she prayed "Our Father which wert in heaven," the prayer which the ill-wife Alison had taught her, meaning by it Lucifer who had been in heaven and had been cast out therefrom. But when she had come to years of discretion she had freely chosen the better part, and evil had ever been repelled from her soul like Gled water from the stones of Gled brig. Now she was in a rapture of holy content. The drucken bell—for the ungodly fashion lingered in Caulds—was ringing in her ears as she left the village, but to her it was but a kirk-bell and a goodly sound. As she went through the woods where the primroses and whitethorn were blossoming, the place seemed as the land of Elam, wherein there were twelve wells and three-score and ten palm trees. And then, as it might be, another thought came into her head, for it is ordained that frail mortality cannot long continue in holy joy. In the kirk she had been only the bride of Christ; but as she came through the wood, with the birds lilting and the winds of the world blowing, she had mind of another lover. For this lass, though so cold to men, had not escaped the common fate. It seemed that the young Heriotside, riding by one day, stopped to speir something or other, and got a glisk of Ailie's face, which caught his fancy. He passed the road again many times, and then he would meet her in the gloaming or of a morning in the field as she went to fetch the kye. "Blue are the hills that are far away" is an owercome in the countryside, and while at first on his side

it may have been but a young man's fancy, to her he was like
the god Apollo descending from the skies. He was good to
look on, brawly dressed, and with a tongue in his head that
would have willed the bird from the tree. Moreover, he was
of gentle kin, and she was a poor lass biding in a cot-house
with an ill-reputed mother. It seems that in time the young
man, who had begun the affair with no good intentions, fell
honestly in love, while she went singing about the doors as
innocent as a bairn, thinking of him when her thoughts were
not on higher things. So it came about that long ere Ailie
reached home it was on young Heriotside that her mind
dwelt, and it was the love of him that made her eyes glow
and her cheeks redden.

Now it chanced that at that very hour her master had been
with Alison, and the pair of them were preparing a deadly pit.
Let no man say that the devil is not a cruel tyrant. He may
give his folk some scrapings of unhallowed pleasure; but he
will exact tithes, yea of anise and cummin, in return, and there
is aye the reckoning to pay at the hinder end. It seems that
now he was driving Alison hard. She had been remiss of late,
fewer souls sent to hell, less zeal in quenching the Spirit, and
above all the crowning offence that her bairn had communi-
cated in Christ's kirk. She had waited overlong, and now it
was like that Ailie would escape her toils. I have no skill of
fancy to tell of that dark collogue, but the upshot was that
Alison swore by her lost soul and the pride of sin to bring the
lass into thrall to her master. The fiend had bare departed
when Ailie came over the threshold to find the auld carline
glunching by the fire.

It was plain she was in the worst of tempers. She flyted on
the lass till the poor thing's cheek paled. "There you gang,"
she cried, "troking wi' thae wearifu' Pharisees o' Caulds,
whae daurna darken your mither's door. A bonnie dutiful
child, quotha! Wumman, hae ye nae pride?—no even the
mense o' a tinkler-lass?" And then she changed her voice, and
would be as soft as honey. "My puir wee Ailie! was I thrawn
till ye? Never mind, my bonnie. You and me are a' that's left,

232

and we maunna be ill to ither." And then the two had their dinner, and all the while the auld wife was crooning over the lass. "We maun 'gree weel," she says, "for we're like to be our lee-lane for the rest o' our days. They tell me Heriotside is seeking Joan o' the Croft, and they're sune to be cried in Gledsmuir kirk."

It was the first the lass had heard of it, and you may fancy she was struck dumb. And so with one thing and another the auld witch raised the fiends of jealousy in that innocent heart. She would cry out that Heriotside was an ill-doing wastrel, and had no business to come and flatter honest lasses. And then she would speak of his gentle birth and his leddy mother, and say it was indeed presumption to hope that so great a gentleman could mean all that he said. Before long Ailie was silent and white, while her mother rimed on about men and their ways. And then she could thole it no longer, but must go out and walk by the burn to cool her hot brow and calm her thoughts, while the witch indoors laughed to herself at her devices.

For days Ailie had an absent eye and a sad face, and it so fell out that in all that time young Heriotside, who had scarce missed a day, was laid up with a broken arm and never came near her. So in a week's time she was beginning to hearken to her mother when she spoke of incantations and charms for restoring love. She kenned it was sin; but though not seven days syne she had sat at the Lord's table, so strong is love in a young heart that she was on the very brink of it. But the grace of God was stronger than her weak will. She would have none of her mother's runes and philters, though her soul cried out for them. Always when she was most disposed to listen some merciful power stayed her consent. Alison grew thrawner as the hours passed. She kenned of Heriotside's broken arm, and she feared that any day he might recover and put her stratagems to shame. And then it seems that she collogued with her master and heard word of a subtler device. For it was approaching that uncanny time of year, the festival of Beltane, when the auld pagans were wont to sacrifice to their god Baal. In this season warlocks and carlines have a special dispensation to do evil, and Alison waited on its coming with graceless joy. As it happened, the tides in the Sker Bay ebbed at this time between the hours of twelve and one, and, as I have said, this was the hour above all others when the powers of darkness were most potent. Would the lass but consent to go abroad in the unhallowed place at this awful season and hour of the night, she was as firmly handfasted to the devil as if she had signed a bond with her own blood. For then, it seemed, the forces of good fled far away, the world for one hour was given over to its ancient prince, and the man or woman who willingly sought the spot was his bond-servant for ever. There are deadly sins from which God's people may recover. A man may even communicate unworthily, and yet, so be it he sin not against the Holy Ghost, he may find forgiveness. But it seems that for this Beltane sin there could be no pardon, and I can testify from my own knowledge that they who once committed it became lost souls from that day. James Deuchar, once a promising professor, fell thus out of sinful bravery and died blaspheming; and of Kate Mallison, who went the same road, no man can tell. Here, indeed, was the witch-wife's chance, and she was the more keen, for her master had warned her that this was her last. Either Ailie's soul would be his, or her auld wrinkled body and black heart would be flung from this pleasant world to their apportioned place.

Some days later it happened that young Heriotside was stepping home over the Lang Muir about ten at night—it being his first jaunt from home since his arm had mended. He had been to the supper of the Forest Club at the Cross Keys in Gledsmuir, a clamjamfry of wild young blades who passed the wine and played at cartes once a fortnight. It seems he had drunk well, so that the world ran round about and he was in the best of tempers. The moon came down and bowed to him, and he took off his hat to it. For every step he travelled miles, so that in a little he was beyond Scotland altogether and pacing the Arabian desert. He thought he was the Pope of Rome, so he held out his foot to be kissed, and rolled twenty yards to the bottom of a small brae. Syne he was the King of France, and fought hard with a whin-bush till he had banged it to pieces. After that nothing would content him but he must be a bogle, for he found his head dunting on the stars and his legs were knocking the hills together. He thought of the mischief he was doing to the auld earth, and sat down and cried at his wickedness. Then he went on, and maybe the steep road to the Moss Rig helped him, for he began to get soberer and ken his whereabouts.

On a sudden he was aware of a man linking along at his side. He cried, "A fine night," and the man replied. Syne, being merry from his cups, he tried to slap him on the back. The next he kenned he was rolling on the grass, for his hand had gone clean through the body and found nothing but air.

His head was so thick with wine that he found nothing droll in this. "Faith, friend," he says, "that was a nasty fall for a fellow that has supped weel. Where might your road be gaun to?"

"To the World's End," said the man; "but I stop at the Skerburnfoot."

"Bide the night at Heriotside," says he. "It's a thought out of your way, but it's a comfortable bit."

"There's mair comfort at the Skerburnfoot," said the dark man.

Now the mention of the Skerburnfoot brought back to him only the thought of Ailie and not of the witch-wife, her mother. So he jaloused no ill, for at the best he was slow in the uptake.

The two of them went on together for a while, Heriotside's fool head filled with the thought of the lass. Then the dark man broke silence. "Ye're thinkin' o' the maid Ailie Sempill," says he.

"How ken ye that?" asked Heriotside.

"It is my business to read the herts o' men," said the other.

"And who may ye be?" said Heriotside, growing eerie.

"Just an auld packman," said he—"nae name ye wad ken, but kin to mony gentle houses."

"And what about Ailie, you that ken sae muckle?" asked the young man.

"Naething," was the answer—"naething that concerns you, for ye'll never get the lass."

"By God, and I will!" says Heriotside, for he was a profane swearer.

"That's the wrong name to seek her in, anyway," said the man.

At this the young laird struck a great blow at him with his stick, but found nothing to resist him but the hill-wind.

When they had gone on a bit the dark man spoke again. "The lassie is thirled to holy things," says he. "She has nae care for flesh and blood, only for devout contemplation."

"She loves me," says Heriotside.

"Not you," says the other, "but a shadow in your stead."

At this the young man's heart began to tremble, for it seemed that there was truth in what his companion said. and he was ower drunk to think gravely.

"I kenna whatna man ye are," he says, "but ye have the skill of lassies' hearts. Tell me truly, is there no way to win her to common love?"

"One way there is," said the man, "and for our friendship's sake I will tell it you. If ye can ever tryst wi' her on Beltane's Eve on the Sker sands, at the green link o' the burn where the sands begin, on the ebb o' the tide when the midnight is bye but afore cock-crow, she'll be yours, body and soul, for this world and for ever."

And then it appeared to the young man that he was walking his lone up the grass walk of Heriotside with the house close by him. He thought no more of the stranger he had met, but the words stuck in his heart.

It seems that about this very time Alison was telling the same tale to poor Ailie. She cast up to her every idle gossip she could think of. "It's Joan o' the Croft," was aye her owercome, and she would threep that they were to be cried in kirk on the first Sabbath of June. And then she would rime on about the black cruelty of it, and cry down curses on the lover, so that her daughter's heart grew cauld with fear. It is terrible to think of the power of the world even in a redeemed soul. Here was a maid who had drunk of the well of grace and tasted of God's mercies, and yet there were moments when she was ready to renounce her hope. At those awful seasons God seemed far off and the world very nigh, and to sell her soul for love looked a fair bargain. At other times she would resist the devil and comfort herself with prayer; but aye when she woke there was the sore heart, and when she went to sleep there were the weary eyes. There was no comfort in the goodliness of spring or the bright sunshine weather, and she who had been wont to go about the doors lightfoot and blithe was now as dowie as a widow woman.

And then one afternoon in the hinder end of April came young Heriotside riding to the Skerburnfoot. His arm was healed, he had got him a fine new suit of green, and his horse was a mettle beast that well set off his figure. Ailie was stand-ing by the doorstep as he came down the road, and her heart stood still with joy. But a second thought gave her anguish. This man, so gallant and braw, would never be for her; doubtless the fine suit and the capering horse were for Joan of the Croft's pleasure. And he in turn, when he remarked her wan cheek and dowie eyes, had mind of what the dark man said on the muir, and saw in her a maid sworn to no mortal love. Yet the passion for her had grown fiercer than ever, and he swore to himself that he would win her back from her phantasies. She, one may believe, was ready enough to listen. As she walked with him by the Sker water his words were like music to her ears, and Alison within-doors laughed to herself and saw her devices prosper.

He spoke to her of love and his own heart, and the girl hearkened gladly. Syne he rebuked her coldness and cast scorn upon her piety, and so far was she beguiled that she had no answer. Then from one thing and another he spoke of some true token of their love. He said he was jealous, and

R

craved something to ease his care. "It's but a small thing I ask," says he; "but it will make me a happy man, and nothing ever shall come atween us. Tryst wi' me for Beltane's Eve on the Sker sands, at the green link o' the burn where the sands begin, on the ebb o' the tide when midnight is bye but afore cock-crow. For," said he, "that was our forebears' tryst for true lovers, and wherefore no for you and me?"

The lassie had grace given her to refuse, but with a woeful heart, and Heriotside rode off in black discontent, leaving poor Ailie to sigh her lone. He came back the next day and the next, but aye he got the same answer. A season of great doubt fell upon her soul. She had no clearness in her hope, nor any sense of God's promises. The Scriptures were an idle tale to her, prayer brought her no refreshment, and she was convicted in her conscience of the unpardonable sin. Had she been less full of pride she would have taken her troubles to good Doctor Chrystal and got comfort; but her grief made her silent and timorous, and she found no help anywhere. Her mother was ever at her side, seeking with coaxings and evil advice to drive her to the irrevocable step. And all the while there was her love for the man riving in her bosom and giving her no ease by night or day. She believed she had driven him away and repented her denial. Only her pride held her back from going to Heriotside and seeking him herself. She watched the road hourly for a sight of his face, and when the darkness came she would sit in a corner brooding over her sorrows.

At last he came, speiring the old question. He sought the same tryst, but now he had a further tale. It seemed he was eager to get her away from the Skerburnside and auld Alison. His aunt, the Lady Balcrynie, would receive her gladly at his request till the day of their marriage. Let her but tryst with him at the hour and place he named, and he would carry her straight to Balcrynie, where she would be safe and happy. He named that hour, he said, to escape men's observation for the sake of her own good name. He named that place, for it was near her dwelling, and on the road between Balcrynie and

Heriotside, which fords the Sker Burn. The temptation was more than mortal heart could resist. She gave him the promise he sought, stifling the voice of conscience; and as she clung to his neck it seemed to her that heaven was a poor thing compared with a man's love.

Three days remained till Beltane's Eve, and throughout the time it was noted that Heriotside behaved like one possessed. It may be that his conscience pricked him, or that he had a glimpse of his sin and its coming punishment. Certain it is that, if he had been daft before, he now ran wild in his pranks, and an evil report of him was in every mouth. He drank deep at the Cross Keys, and fought two battles with young lads that angered him. One he let off with a touch in the shoulder, the other goes lame to this day from a wound he got in the groin. There was a word of the procurator-fiscal taking note of his doings, and troth, if they had continued long he must have fled the country. For a wager he rode his horse down the Dow Craig, wherefore the name of the place is the Horseman's Craig to this day. He laid a hundred guineas with the laird of Slipperfield that he would drive four horses through the Slipperfield loch, and in the prank he had his bit chariot dung to pieces and a good mare killed. And all men observed that his eyes were wild and his face grey and thin, and that his hand would twitch as he held the glass, like one with the palsy.

The eve of Beltane was lown and hot in the low country, with fire hanging in the clouds and thunder grumbling about the heavens. It seems that up in the hills it had been an awesome deluge of rain, but on the coast it was still dry and lowering. It is a long road from Heriotside to the Skerburnfoot. First you go down the Heriot Water, and syne over the Lang Muir to the edge of Mucklewham. When you pass the steadings of Mirehope and Cockmalane you turn to the right and ford the Mire Burn. That brings you on to the turnpike road, which you will ride till it bends inland, while you keep on straight over the Whinny Knowes to the Sker Bay. There, if you are in luck, you will find the tide out and the place

239

fordable dryshod for a man on a horse. But if the tide runs, you will do well to sit down on the sands and content yourself till it turn, or it will be the solans and scarts of the Solloway that will be seeing the next of you. On this Beltane's Eve the young man, after supping with some wild young blades, bade his horse be saddled about ten o'clock. The company were eager to ken his errand, but he waved them back. "Bide here," he says, "and birl the wine till I return. This is a ploy of my own on which no man follows me." And there was that in his face as he spoke which chilled the wildest, and left them well content to keep to the good claret and the soft seat and let the daft laird go his own ways.

Well and on, he rode down the bridlepath in the wood, along the top of the Heriot glen, and as he rode he was aware of a great noise beneath him. It was not wind, for there was none, and it was not the sound of thunder, and aye as he speired at himself what it was it grew louder till he came to a break in the trees. And then he saw the cause, for Heriot was coming down in a furious flood, sixty yards wide, tearing at the roots of the aiks, and flinging red waves against the dry-stone dykes. It was a sight and sound to solemnize a man's mind, deep calling unto deep, the great waters of the hills running to meet with the great waters of the sea. But Heriot-side recked nothing of it, for his heart had but one thought and the eye of his fancy one figure. Never had he been so filled with love of the lass, and yet it was not happiness but a deadly secret fear.

As he came to the Lang Muir it was geyan dark, though there was a moon somewhere behind the clouds. It was little he could see of the road, and ere long he had tried many moss-pools and sloughs, as his braw new coat bare witness. Aye in front of him was the great hill of Mucklewham, where the road turned down by the Mire. The noise of the Heriot had not long fallen behind him ere another began, the same eerie sound of burns crying to ither in the darkness. It seemed that the whole earth was overrun with waters. Every little runnel in the bog was astir, and yet the land around him was as dry as flax, and no drop of rain had fallen. As he rode on the din grew louder, and as he came over the top of Mirehope he kenned by the mighty rushing noise that something uncommon was happening with the Mire Burn. The light from Mirehope sheiling twinkled on his left, and had the man not been dozened with his fancies he might have observed that the steading was deserted and men were crying below in the fields. But he rode on, thinking of but one thing, till he came to the cot-house of Cockmalane, which is nigh the fords of the Mire.

John Dodds, the herd who bode in the place, was standing at the door, and he looked to see who was on the road so late.

"Stop," says he, "stop, Laird Heriotside. I kenna what your errand is, but it is to no holy purpose that ye're out on Beltane Eve. D'ye no hear the warning o' the waters?"

And then in the still night came the sound of Mire like the clash of armies.

"I must win over the ford," says the laird quietly, thinking of another thing.

"Ford!" cried John in scorn. "There'll be nae ford for you the nicht unless it be the ford o' the River Jordan. The burns are up, and bigger than man ever saw them. It'll be a Beltane's Eve that a' folk will remember. They tell me that Gled valley is like a loch, and that there's an awesome folk drooned in the hills. Gin ye were ower the Mire, what about crossin' the Caulds and the Sker?" says he, for he jaloused he was going to Gledsmuir.

And then it seemed that that word brought the laird to his senses. He looked the airt the rain was coming from, and he saw it was the airt the Sker flowed. In a second, he has told me, the works of the devil were revealed to him. He saw himself a tool in Satan's hands, he saw his tryst a device for the destruction of the body, as it was assuredly meant for the destruction of the soul, and there came on his mind the picture of an innocent lass borne down by the waters with no place for repentance. His heart grew cold in his breast. He had but one thought, a sinful and reckless one—to get to her side, that the two might go together to their account. He heard the roar of the Mire as in a dream, and when John Dodds laid hands on his bridle he felled him to the earth. And the next seen of it was the laird riding the floods like a man possessed.

The horse was the grey stallion he aye rode, the very beast he had ridden for many a wager with the wild lads of the Cross Keys. No man but himself durst back it, and it had lamed many a hostler lad and broke two necks in its day. But it seemed it had the mettle for any flood, and took the Mire with little spurring. The herds on the hillside looked to see man and steed swept into eternity; but though the red waves were breaking about his shoulders and he was swept far down, he aye held on for the shore. The next thing the watchers saw was the laird struggling up the far bank, and casting his coat from him, so that he rode in his sark. And then he set off like wildfire across the muir towards the turn-pike road. Two men saw him on the road and have recorded their experience. One was a gangrel, by name M'Nab, who was travelling from Gledsmuir to Allerkirk with a heavy pack on his back and a bowed head. He heard a sound like wind afore him, and, looking up, saw coming down the road a grey horse stretched out to a wild gallop and a man on its back with a face like a soul in torment. He kenned not whether it was the devil or mortal, but flung himself on the roadside, and lay like a corp for an hour or more till the rain aroused him. The other was one Sim Doolittle, the fish-hawker from Allerfoot, jogging home in his fish-cart from Gledsmuir fair. He had drunk more than was fit for him, and he was singing some light song, when he saw approaching, as he said, the pale horse mentioned in the Revelations, with Death seated as the rider. Thoughts of his sins came on him like a thunder-clap, fear loosened his knees, he leaped from the cart to the road, and from the road to the back of a dyke. Thence he flew to the hills, and was found the next morning far up among the Mire Craigs, while his horse and cart were gotten on the Aller sands, the horse lamed and the cart without the wheels.

At the tollhouse the road turns inland to Gledsmuir, and he

who goes to Sker Bay must leave it and cross the wild land called the Whinny Knowes, a place rough with bracken and foxes' holes and old stone cairns. The tollman, John Gilzean, was opening his window to get a breath of air in the lown night when he heard and saw the approaching horse. He kenned the beast for Heriotside's, and, being a friend of the laird's, he ran down in all haste to open the yett, wondering to himself about the laird's errand on this night. A voice came down the road to him bidding him hurry; but John's old fingers were slow with the keys, and so it happened that the horse had to stop, and John had time to look up at the gash and woful face.

"Where away the nicht sae late, laird?" says John.

"I go to save a soul from hell," was the answer.

And then it seems that through the open door there came the chapping of a clock.

"Whatna hour is that?" asks Heriotside.

"Midnicht," says John, trembling, for he did not like the look of things.

There was no answer but a groan, and horse and man went racing down the dark hollows of the Whinny Knowes.

How he escaped a broken neck in that dreadful place no human being will ever tell. The sweat, he has told me, stood in cold drops upon his forehead; he scarcely was aware of the saddle in which he sat; and his eyes were stelled in his head, so that he saw nothing but the sky ayont him. The night was growing colder, and there was a small sharp wind stirring from the east. But, hot or cold, it was all one to him, who was already cold as death. He heard not the sound of the sea nor the peesweeps startled by his horse, for the sound that ran in his ears was the roaring Sker Water and a girl's cry. The thought kept goading him, and he spurred the grey till the creature was madder than himself. It leaped the hole which they call the Devil's Mull as I would step over a thistle, and the next he kenned he was on the edge of the Sker Bay.

It lay before him white and ghastly, with mist blowing in wafts across it and a slow swaying of the tides. It was the

better part of a mile wide, but save for some fathoms in the
middle where the Sker current ran, it was no deeper even at
flood than a horse's fetlocks. It looks eerie at bright midday
when the sun is shining and whaups are crying among the sea-
weeds; but think what it was on that awesome night with the
powers of darkness brooding over it like a cloud. The rider's
heart quailed for a moment in natural fear. He stepped his
beast a few feet in, still staring afore him like a daft man. And
then something in the sound or the feel of the waters made
him look down, and he perceived that the ebb had begun
and the tide was flowing out to sea.

He kenned that all was lost, and the knowledge drove him
to stark despair. His sins came in his face like birds of night,
and his heart shrank like a pea. He knew himself for a lost
soul, and all that he loved in the world was out in the tides.
There, at any rate, he could go too, and give back that gift of
life he had so blackly misused. He cried small and soft like a
bairn, and drove the grey out into the waters. And aye as he
spurred it the foam should have been flying as high as his
head; but in that uncanny hour there was no foam, only the
waves running sleek like oil. It was not long ere he had come
to the Sker channel, where the red moss-waters were roaring
to the sea, an ill place to ford in midsummer heat, and certain
death, as folks reputed it, in the smallest spate. The grey was
swimming, but it seemed the Lord had other purposes for
him than death, for neither man nor horse could drown. He
tried to leave the saddle, but he could not; he flung the bridle
from him, but the grey held on, as if some strong hand were
guiding. He cried out upon the devil to help his own, he
renounced his Maker and his God; but whatever his punishment, he was not to be drowned. And then he was silent, for
something was coming down the tide.

It came down as quiet as a sleeping bairn, straight for him
as he sat with his horse breasting the waters, and as it came
the moon crept out of a cloud and he saw a glint of yellow hair.
And then his madness died away and he was himself again, a
weary and stricken man. He hung down over the tides and

caught the body in his arms and then let the grey make for the shallows. He cared no more for the devil and all his myrmidons, for he kenned brawly he was damned. It seemed to him that his soul had gone from him and he was as toom as a hazel-shell. His breath rattled in his throat, the tears were dried up in his head, his body had lost its strength, and yet he clung to the drowned maid as to a hope of salvation. And then he noted something at which he marvelled dumbly. Her hair was drookit back from her clay-cold brow, her eyes were shut, but in her face there was the peace of a child. It seemed even that her lips were smiling. Here, certes, was no lost soul, but one who had gone joyfully to meet her Lord. It may be that in that dark hour at the burn-foot, before the spate caught her, she had been given grace to resist her adversary and flung herself upon God's mercy.

And it would seem that it had been granted, for when he came to the Skerburnfoot there in the corner sat the weird-wife Alison, dead as a stone and shrivelled like a heather-birn.

For days Heriotside wandered the country or sat in his own house with vacant eye and trembling hands. Conviction of sin held him like a vice: he saw the lassie's death laid at his door, her face haunted him by day and night, and the word of the Lord dirled in his ears telling of wrath and punishment. The greatness of his anguish wore him to a shadow, and at last he was stretched on his bed and like to perish. In his extremity worthy Doctor Chrystal went to him unasked and strove to comfort him. Long, long the good man wrestled, but it seemed as if his ministrations were to be of no avail. The fever left his body, and he rose to stotter about the doors; but he was still in his torments, and the mercy-seat was far from him. At last in the back-end of the year came Mungo Muirhead to Caulds to the autumn communion, and nothing would serve him but he must try his hand at this storm-tossed soul. He spoke with power and unction, and a blessing came with his words, the black cloud lifted and showed a glimpse of grace, and in a little the man had some assurance of salvation. He became a pillar of Christ's Kirk, prompt to check abominations, notably the sin of witchcraft, foremost in good works; but with it all a humble man, who walked contritely till his death. When I came first to Caulds I sought to prevail upon him to accept the eldership, but he aye put me by, and when I heard his tale I saw that he had done wisely. I mind him well as he sat in his chair or daundered through Caulds, a kind word for every one and sage counsel in time of distress, but withal a severe man to himself and a crucifier of the body. It seems that this severity weakened his frame, for three years syne come Martinmas he was taken ill with a fever, and after a week's sickness he went to his account, where I trust he is accepted.

ACKNOWLEDGMENTS

Acknowledgments are due to the following for permission to reprint these stories:

Messrs. Jonathan Cape Ltd. and the author for the story "Kind Kitty" by Eric Linklater; Messrs. J. M. Dent & Sons Ltd. for the story "Something Different" by Orgill Mackenzie from *Poems and Stories*; Messrs. Jonathan Cape Ltd., Messrs. William Maclellan and the author for the story "A Wee Nip" by Edward Gaitens from *Growing Up*; Serif Books Ltd. and the author for the story "Checkmate" by Moray McLaren from *A Dinner with the Dead*; *The Scots Magazine* and the author for the story "In the Family" by Naomi Mitchison; *The Scottish Daily Express* and the author for the story "The Kitten" by Alexander Reid; Messrs. Faber & Faber Ltd. and the author for the story "The Tax-Gatherer" by Neil M. Gunn from *The White Hour*; the Scottish *Outlook* and the author for the story "The Hallowe'en Party" by Winifred Duke; the Scottish *Outlook* and the author for the story "The Big Wheel" by Ruthven Todd; Messrs. Gerald Duckworth & Co. for the story "Beattock for Moffat" by R. B. Cunninghame-Graham from *Scottish Stories*; the B.B.C., *New World Writing* and the author for the story "Flowers" by Robin Jenkins; Messrs Jarrolds for the story "Smeddum" by Lewis Grassic Gibbon from *Scottish Scene*; Messrs. Methuen & Co. Ltd. and the author for the story "The Head" by Dorothy Haynes from *Thou Shalt Not Suffer a Witch*; the B.B.C. and the author for the story "The Disinherited" by J. F. Hendry; Messrs. Methuen & Co. Ltd. and the author for the story "Alicky's Watch" by Fred Urquhart from *The Last Sister*; Messrs. William Maclellan and the author for the story "Jenny Stairy's Hat" by Margaret Hamilton from *No Scottish*

Acknowledgments

Twilight; *The Modern Scot* and the author for the story "Murdoch's Bull" by Edward Scouller; Mr. John Murray and *The New Alliance* for the story "The Mennans" by Robert MacLellan; *The Adelphi* and the author for the story "Thoughtless" by George Friel; Messrs. William Blackwood and Sons for the story "The Outgoing of the Tide" by John Buchan from *The Watcher on the Threshold*.